HUGUETTE

BOOKS BY THE AUTHOR

Murder in the Marais
Murder in Belleville
Murder in the Sentier
Murder in the Bastille
Murder in Clichy
Murder in Montmartre
Murder on the Ile Saint-Louis
Murder in the Rue de Paradis
Murder in the Latin Quarter
Murder in the Palais Royal
Murder in Passy
Murder at the Lanterne Rouge
Murder Below Montparnasse
Murder in Pigalle
Murder on the Champ de Mars
Murder on the Quai
Murder in Saint-Germain
Murder on the Left Bank
Murder in Bel-Air
Murder at the Porte de Versailles
Murder at la Villette

Three Hours in Paris
Night Flight to Paris

Huguette

CARA BLACK

Published in the United States by
Soho Press, Inc.
227 W 17th Street
New York, NY 10011
www.sohopress.com

Copyright © 2025 by Cara Black

All rights reserved.

Library of Congress Cataloging-in-Publication Data
Names: Black, Cara, 1951- author
Title: Huguette / Cara Black.
Description: New York, NY : Soho Crime, 2025.
Identifiers: LCCN 2025021641

ISBN 978-1-64129-449-2
eISBN 978-1-64129-450-8

Subjects: LCGFT: Fiction | Novels
Classification: LCC PS3552.L297 H84 2025 | DDC 813/.54--dc23/eng/20250523
LC record available at https://lccn.loc.gov/2025021641

Map: © Loren Ward
Map illusration: iStock

Interior design by Janine Agro, Soho Press, Inc.

Printed in the United States of America

10 9 8 7 6 5 4 3 2 1

EU Responsible Person (for authorities only)
eucomply OÜ
Pärnu mnt 139b-14
11317 Tallinn, Estonia
hello@eucompliancepartner.com
www.eucompliancepartner.com

In memory of Dora "Denise" Damensztein.

For the real Huguette and the ghosts

"But people cannot choose their time; they are caught in it, and it can break over them with all the violence of a tidal wave."
>   —**Countess Ingeborg Kálnoky with Ilona Herisko,**
>   ***The Guest House***

"Victory finds a hundred fathers but defeat is an orphan."
>   —**Count Galeazzo Ciano,**
>   **Benito Mussolini's foreign minister**

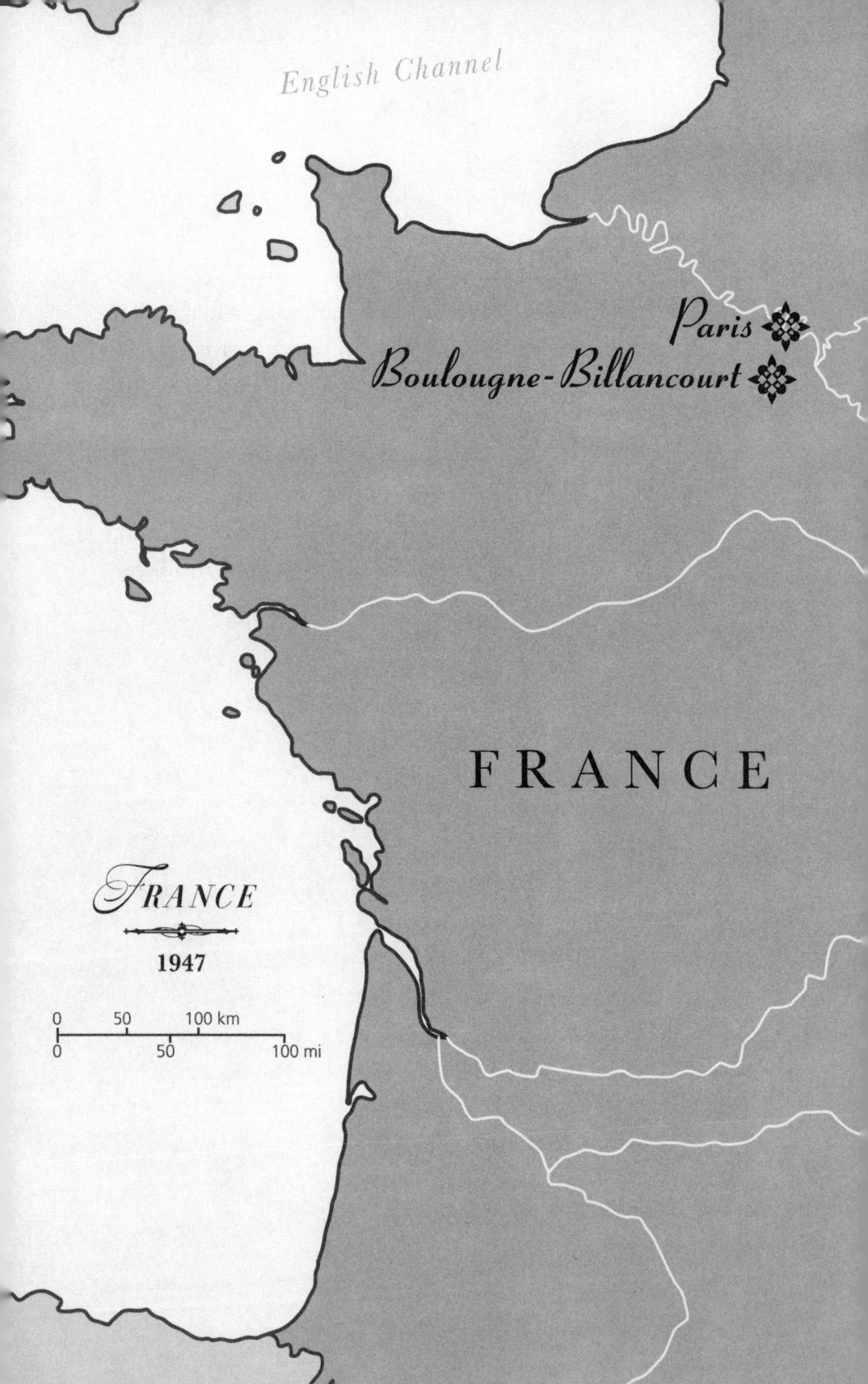

Frankfurt

GERMANY

Rhine

Seine

Lyon

Rhône

Cannes

Sea

Early December 1947

Étoile Office, Lyon

—

At her office window, Huguette hardly saw the mist hugging the sluggish Rhône or dawn slashing copper on the horizon. After a moment of staring at awakening Lyon, a city that felt more like *home* now than she'd ever thought possible, she turned back to her desk and leaned down to unlock the safe. Rubbing her knuckles, she looked at the stacks of cash within.

Money carried a weight she would have welcomed when she'd been hungry. Now she had more than she thought possible. Too much.

She closed the safe. Touched the medal of Saint Christopher on her neck. And got to work.

Soon she heard a discreet knock and Simone Delambry, her assistant, entered, pushing a rolling cart with a coffee carafe and cups on top, money bags on the tray below.

"*Bonjour*, Mademoiselle Lise. Here's the weekend's takings."

Huguette—known to those she worked with as Lise de Jouvenal—smiled. "*Merci*, Simone."

Every Monday, she and Simone sorted the receipts from the ticket offices and cinema concessions and confirmed amounts in the account books. Their morning was fueled by good coffee from the café downstairs, one of four Huguette owned.

As profits climbed, the surplus soared, and figures swirled in her head—what to buy next? A building or two—or three—was on her agenda.

Simone, a war widow who spoke little, was the sharpest person Huguette had met in a long time. She had been an indispensable part of Huguette's business since her first week in Lyon, when Simone had helped negotiate a union contract with the cinema's employees. Huguette, frankly, had needed all the help she could get.

She looked over her shoulder every day. Wary the past would catch up with her. And every day she had to prove she could do this.

Would she ever not be afraid? She wondered if she'd have to hide like a burrowing animal all her life. Late at night, she sometimes felt like giving up, unsure of what to do to shake the demons of her past off once and for all. But in the meantime, what she *could* do was work with good people like Simone by her side.

DOWNSTAIRS IN THE *BOUCHON*, WHAT the Lyonnais called a bistro, chalked on the slate menu board was *turnips, chestnut terrine, rutabaga.* Always rutabagas. Skipping lunch, Huguette ordered a coffee. She didn't want to know how the chef procured ingredients to prepare pike quenelles with lobster sauce for *special* patrons. Postwar outages continued, but thanks to their refurbished generator, the wall sconces didn't flicker and dim. The Germans' bullet holes, filled and sanded, hardly showed on the stone facade.

She lifted up a silver-plated knife from the place setting to check her roots in its thin reflection. Time for another dye job. She tilted the blade to adjust her glasses, which were fake, and this time in the knife's reflection she caught a face staring through the window. A face from her past.

Claude Leduc.

Emotions flipped and her insides churned as he opened the door to the *bouchon* and entered, approaching her table. Words choked in her throat.

She'd dreaded being found out. Hoped this day never came.

But who was she fooling?

She'd been so careful, but it wasn't enough. He'd betrayed her and she'd run. Without a trace, she'd thought. How had he found her? Where could she go to get away? Why did she want to feel the warmth of his arms again?

He reached out to her with something in his hand, and she stiffened, gripping the butter knife—but he was holding out a pocket-sized red booklet. A bilingual map of Paris. "I thought you might need an updated one."

Why would she need that? She didn't know what to say.

Had he been tipped off? Led a squad to Lyon? Would he finally turn her in?

Frantic, she looked around for any eyes on them but saw only passersby, busy and intent. She could make a run for it.

"No one knows I'm here," he said, as if he'd read her thoughts. "This is between us. I've got two questions, that's all. Then I'm gone."

Ridiculous to run, she thought, and she resigned herself to whatever fate he'd brought with him from Paris.

"Not here."

SHE SHOULDERED HER EMERGENCY KIT: cash; a faux ID issued in 1947 for a Madeleine Colbert, occupation: seamstress, with her left and right thumbprints and touched-up photo; a brown wool jacket with tortoiseshell buttons bought from a rag seller; a cloche-style hat to cover her hair; a stub of carmine lipstick; a thimble; a spool of thread; and an open-ended train ticket to

Marseille, all of which fit into hidden custom compartments in her market bag.

Twenty minutes later, she joined Claude on a hillside bench overlooking *vieux* Lyon's Renaissance buildings, the terracotta rooftops, the medieval streets sloping under the Fourvière hill, to the lapping current of the Saône below and across the wide Place Bellecour to the Rhône. The rivers threading Lyon made her homesick for the Seine, the first thing she'd seen every morning out her window for seventeen years.

From under his newspaper, a Lyon daily, Claude produced a small tin tray bearing two demitasses with steaming thick espresso.

How had he managed that?

"My fault you missed your coffee," he said. "Luckily the café owner, a romantic, obliged and let me bring you this. I said we needed *privacy*."

He smiled and jerked his chin to the café quayside with a broad terrace.

"First question: sugar or not?"

Caught off guard, she smiled. "*Non, merci.*" While grateful for the thought, she saw this gesture for what it was—a technique to disarm people. She sipped. Delicious. It should have been; she owned the roastery.

"Maybe not up to Parisian standards, but the Lyonnais are masters of cuisine."

Or so they thought.

His voice sounded light but she heard an undertone, and it made her restless. "What do you want, Claude Leduc?"

"To enjoy coffee with you."

She scoffed. Did he still think she was a naïve little girl? After everything they'd been through? "Don't tell me this is a social call."

"I'm not a *flic* anymore. I'm a *detective privé* now. Clients pay me to investigate. My field's missing persons."

"Who paid you to find me?"

Hesitating, he looked away.

She set down the small demitasse. "Of course, you're not honest with me. You'll lie again."

"I never lied to you." But he hesitated again, a pained look on his face. A face she'd once thought open, sincere, caring.

"I'm leaving," she said.

"Just give me a minute. Please."

"*One* minute." She glanced at her watch. Pigeons fluttered down the path and pecked at crumbs scattered by an old man.

He steepled his hands, matching fingertip to fingertip. She noticed his bruised thumbnail. His shoulders broad under a well-worn corduroy jacket and his hair curled over his collar. Those deep-seeing eyes.

"Will you do me a favor?"

She wanted to hit him.

"There's going to be a trial in Paris in two months. Honoré Gisors, the *notaire*, is the defendant."

Her fingers gripped the demitasse.

"Your testimony's needed—"

She interrupted. "But it's been, what, two years?"

Two long years, she could see in his eyes.

"Homicide cases remain open until they're solved. Justice can finally be done."

Justice?

"Too late for that." She sipped her coffee and tasted nothing but fear.

"The past never goes away."

She'd like to forget. If only the phantoms would let her.

"But you betrayed me."

"Think what you want," said Claude. "Alain sold me out, too. His actions made it clear I had to leave the force."

She'd wondered about Alain. But did it really change anything? "You took my money."

Claude pulled an envelope from his inner jacket pocket. "Here's my portion returned."

Her jaw dropped. She set down the demitasse.

"When I found out what happened, you'd disappeared." He grinned. "I did use it to start my detective agency. Now business is booming, and I can repay you. You know, after the war, finding people is in hot demand. My new *métier*."

"You must be good."

"I found you."

His warm hands were holding hers. She felt the magnetic pull.

"But I would have found you anyway."

Then he was pulling her close. Kissing her. And she responded, folding into him, until his grip tightened and she remembered herself.

"*Non.*" She pulled back. "How dare you ask me? I'm not that person anymore."

Claude took her chin to look deep into her eyes. "Testify, then you can disappear again. For good this time."

Why couldn't this just go away? *Leave me alone*, she wanted to scream. In her limited experience, men did nothing but take.

But Claude had helped her when he hadn't needed to. And now, he'd asked her for something—the others never asked.

She pulled away from his hand, staring out at the river instead.

Claude stood. She didn't want him to go. A wistfulness emanated from him. He said, "It's your chance to right a wrong, Huguette. To bring your father's murderer to justice."

At what cost?

April 1945 • Two and a Half Years Earlier

Maison de la Maternité
The Forest at the Outskirts of Sceaux

—

In the chill slate gray afternoon, seventeen-year-old Huguette heard an owl hooting from the old tiled roof eaves.

"Trust me, that's a sign," said Lena.

Huguette waddled through the courtyard's snow, clutching her belly. Her breath came out in puffy clouds. "What does it mean?"

"My grandmother said when an owl hoots, it means a girl."

Huguette took Lena's arm and they crossed the courtyard, watching out for black ice.

This had been the coldest winter Huguette could remember, and even in April it wasn't over. Everyone complained as they shivered in the former sixteenth-century Cistercian abbey, their maternity home, surrounded by the forest. At least she and Lena could warm up in the steaming laundry where they worked.

Despite France's Libération, the war dragged on as the Allies pressed to Berlin. Coal was scarce. The maternity home's food consisted of moldy root vegetables, thistle soup, and turnips when they were lucky.

The baby kicked—the little bastard. She cradled her stomach, wishing all this was over. That her ankles weren't swollen.

That she wasn't so big she couldn't bend down and tie her own bootlaces. That it was out and gone.

She'd tried to find a back-alley abortion and get rid of this thing. But that cost money she hadn't had.

And her conscience hadn't let her.

The deep snowdrifts made it impossible to tramp to Mass in her condition. To once again ask forgiveness for her sins. Sins so grievous she couldn't even tell them in the confessional.

At the laundry entrance, she smiled at Lena.

"Happy birthday, Lena."

"You remembered?"

She slipped a hair clip into Lena's chapped palm—aquamarine enamel, one of a pair.

"*Merci.*" Surprised, Lena kissed Huguette on both cheeks. "How did you know I love aquamarine? It's my favorite color."

Huguette half smiled. "I love the color, too—that's why my mother gave me this."

Lena gasped. "*Mais non*, Huguette! If this was your mother's, I can't accept this."

"Gifts are for sharing, my *maman* said. She sent me a pair so now we both have one. Let's clip it to your braid."

On Huguette's birthday last year, *maman* had sent her the clips, and Papa and Luc had found a black market gâteau meringue. An aching despair clawed just above where the baby kicked as Huguette snapped the hair clip in place. All three were gone. It felt like more than a lifetime ago. When Lena smiled at her, she tried to hide how her eyes had misted over.

They entered the laundry by the hot pressing machines and headed to the laundry tubs. The old stone walls breathed a grimness contrasting with the homey smell of Marseille green laundry soap and humid warmth. Both girls took their stations and reached for linens to start washing. Huguette's back preemptively ached as she considered the workday ahead. Still, she was grateful for what she had, and those who had helped her thus far; before coming to this maternity home, she'd stayed at a convent in Paris, where the nuns had sheltered her until she couldn't hide her pregnancy anymore.

On a late November evening, Sister Agnés had put her on the train bound for Sceaux. In her bag were stale bread and cheese and twenty francs. Sister Agnés said arrangements were in place for the baby's adoption.

The maternity home was a workhouse. The girls labored in the laundry until their time approached, then they switched to sewing. Still, better than having to go out in her condition and being accused of sleeping with the enemy. At Libération, she'd seen pregnant women paraded through the streets, hair forcibly shorn, signs reading "*Boche* baby" hanging from their necks.

The little thing kicked again. Would its hair be blond, its eyes blue? A dead ringer for the man who'd impregnated her?

She hated its father, wished him dead.

On dark gray evenings under the worn feather duvet, she'd hear her mother's voice:

Make a plan, prepare for any eventuality, survive.

Oh, Huguette had plans. There was the IOU from the Italian deserter, Enzo. He owed her papa money; she'd find him and collect. Then she could find a job accounting for a café—she'd always liked numbers. Thoughts like these got her through the pain of her daily existence.

She'd get a new start.

Something warm trickled down her legs. *Zut*, the tub had overflown again. But *non*, it was from inside her.

Lena rang the shift bell. The clanging reverberated, calling everyone to stop work.

"What's happening?" Huguette gasped.

"You're having a baby, that's what."

PANIC-STRICKEN, SHE FOUND HERSELF IN the birthing room, her legs spread open. The midwife, a short round-faced woman, rushed in and took over from the attendant, whose bony arms were sliding sheets under Huguette. The midwife unbuttoned Huguette's soapy smock and felt her stomach, checked her.

She was sweating. Screaming with every contraction.

"It's breech. I need assistance. Call the doctor," said the midwife.

The attendant made the sign of the cross. "He's back in the village."

She heard them whispering: *snowdrifts . . . impossible in time . . . only seventeen . . .*

"You'll have to help. Ever assisted on a breech birth before?"

"Never," said the attendant.

"Always a first time."

"What's the matter?" Huguette cried out from the wave of pain.

The midwife got close to Huguette's face. "The baby's turned around. For me to get your baby out, I've got to turn the head back."

"You mean . . . there's something wrong . . . ?"

Suddenly she didn't want it to die.

"You must cooperate . . . You can't push, no matter how much it hurts."

Huguette nodded. Sweat beaded her brow.

The midwife spread out sheets on the tiled floor, helped Huguette down to get on all fours. "Don't push," the midwife reminded.

The waves of pain intensified. Huguette struggled not to push.

"Give her gas," said the midwife. "I need her relaxed."

The attendant hemmed and hawed. "It's expensive."

"Do it."

A rubber mouthpiece clapped over her mouth. She was breathing and breathing, trying not to strain.

"I'm trying to turn the baby around," the midwife said.

The pain was knifelike. Huguette was panting like a horse.

"Good job," said the midwife.

She endured a cramping pain for what felt like forever.

"*Now* push."

Her insides were ripping.

"Again. Little breaths."

Tearing her open. Crying into the rubber. Begging it to be over.

"Big push. One more."

She squeezed her eyes shut and screamed as it tore her apart.

A slithering sound, a snap of scissors. A little whinny of a baby's cry. Relief and exhaustion filled her.

"A boy."

"Let her hold him," said the midwife.

"It won't be for long," said the attendant.

Then she was righted, propped with pillows on the floor. A blood-smeared little bundle was thrust in her arms. A baby boy.

"I'm going to sew up some tears," the midwife said. "You'll feel some pinching."

A pink mushroom nose, blond fuzz of hair.

"Oww."

The baby startled, flapping his tiny arms like wings.

She gritted her teeth at the pain, calmed him in her arms.

He leaned into her warmth, his mouth sucking, and she fell in love. He was hers.

THE SNOWSTORM RAGED ALL NIGHT. Tore down power lines. Without heat for the nursery, the newborns were kept with their mothers—not a standard procedure. Huguette cocooned the baby to keep him warm and helped him breastfeed as the midwife taught her. They both slept on and off in a milky daze.

She wanted to hate this little pink face, the fist that opened and clutched her finger. Despise him. Yet he didn't look like *him*, the man who was emblazoned in her memory forever. She'd never forget the Catholic cross hanging around his neck—the hypocrite. Out of a violent act had come such a sweet innocent creature.

She thought she would resent this little thing—so helpless, so needy. But she couldn't. No one had wanted or needed her for a long time.

She would not give him a name—she would stop herself from calling him anything but *baby*. They were only going to take him away.

The countryside lay tufted with billows of pristine white snow—everything ground to a halt. All adoptions, they were informed, were held up by the weather. Huguette healed her stitches in the mothers' ward and recovered her strength. Slept with the baby in her arms. Fed the hungry thing, his tiny eyelashes quivering and his mushroom nose crinkling, until he was sated.

Almost four weeks later in May, the sun finally broke out to melt the snow. Icicles dripped from the eaves and became puddles.

"See the sunbeams dancing." Huguette pointed out the light to her cooing baby. She'd unraveled her wool mittens and used the wool to clumsily knit him a tiny vest. Now she wrapped him in it, set him cozy in his bassinet, and went to bathe using the large nearby sink under the window while the hot water lasted. Once she was clean, her curly hair brushed and braided, she felt human.

Huguette checked her baby sleeping in the bassinet. Breathing and rosy cheeked. Then fell asleep herself in bed. In her dream her mother drifted, smiling, surrounded by butterflies. *"One door closes and another opens. You'll do the right thing for the baby."*

She woke with a start. Her arms were empty, cold. And no baby in the bassinet, only his tiny vest. Sensing something wrong, she pulled on her boots, took his vest, and crossed the puddles of melted snow in the courtyard to the office.

Madame Silot, *la directrice*, motioned her in. Her eyes were a flintlike gray. Hard. Huguette smelled wine on her breath. "Hello, Huguette," Madame Silot said. "I'm glad you're here so we can discuss your future."

Her future? Huguette shook her head, confused. "Future? Where's my baby?" she asked.

"*Ah*, his new parents came. Very nice people."

"New parents?"

"Your baby went to a good home. An excellent family."

Ice cracked Huguette's insides. "I didn't say goodbye."

"We don't recommend it, Huguette," Madame Silot said. She indicated the chair opposite her desk. "Please, sit."

Huguette's full breasts tugged at her dress. She wanted to feed her baby. "I'm full of milk . . ."

"You're lucky. Some girls can't nurse. Their milk dries up," Madame Silot said, her smile hollow. She snapped her fingers. "Just like that. But you'll work as a wet nurse. Good pay. Then you can transition back to full-time in the laundry. What do you say?"

Huguette couldn't hear a single word she was saying. "Where did my baby go?"

"Huguette, you signed a release form. The parents are well-off, upright citizens who will offer your baby a good life."

Had she signed a release? Maybe at the convent? "I don't remember . . ."

"The nuns assisted in finding a wonderful family who wanted your child. A very special child, *non*? So few are willing to adopt a German baby. Believe me, you're lucky."

How had the *directrice* known? Huguette had told the nuns the father was an altar boy. Only her friend Marina knew the real father's identity, and not even she knew his name.

Huguette's horror must have shown on her face, because Madame Silot smirked. "Think I couldn't tell? I can count. And with that blond hair! But the nuns vouched that you'd had a Catholic baby."

Huguette didn't know whether to thank her or spit on her. Grasping for more answers, she looked around the office and saw a folder marked ORPHELINAT on the desk.

The director noticed her gaze. "Most of the babies born here go to the orphanage. You didn't want that for him, did you?"

Huguette didn't want any of this.

Madame Silot's elbow slipped off the edge of the table, none too steady. "Go nurse the newborns. By your return I'll have the paperwork ready."

For relief, Huguette nursed a newborn boy in the nursery. Scrawny and fussy, he wiggled nonstop. His suck hurt. No sweet milky scent emanated from him.

She was still so confused. How could they have just taken her baby like that? Wasn't there anything else Madame Silot could tell her?

Once she'd finished her shift at the nursery, she crossed the slushy courtyard again. Green sprouts poked out of the wet earth. Spring knocked on winter's door.

She found the director's office door ajar. Before she could knock, she heard Madame Silot speaking. Wary and knowing she shouldn't interrupt, she waited, hearing a boring phone conversation to do with supplies of bleach and detergent. The phone clunked back onto the receiver, but just as she was about to knock and go in, the phone trilled and Madame Silot answered. Probably another long conversation. Impatient, Huguette wanted to know more about her baby, what this future Madame Silot talked about was.

"Yes, that's right," she was saying. "A baby boy. The family made a contribution to the church as usual, sister, and none the wiser about the parentage, as we agreed. Of course, the receipt . . ."

Huguette went still. It almost sounded like she was speaking about Huguette's baby—but what did she mean by *contribution*? But there were lots of babies born here. Huguette crept closer to hear better.

The director hung up and dialed a number. Her voice lowered when she said, "Listen, the mother could be a problem . . . just signed the adoption papers today. *Non*, that's not the price we agreed on. My commission for boys is higher. *Oui* . . . in an hour."

Huguette's jaw had dropped. If this meant what she thought it did—

But then there was another click as Madame Silot hung up, and the sound of her shoes on the floor. Huguette quickly melted into the next doorway as the director made her unsteady way down the corridor to the nursery.

She wanted to know where her baby had gone. She needed to see him again.

Huguette entered the office. On the director's desk she looked at the files. Nothing about her baby. Then she tried a drawer, where she found a half-empty bottle of wine. Then another drawer—files marked *adoption*. Huguette's heart leapt and her stomach lurched.

She scanned the files for dates. Only one adoption today:

male, Caucasian, four weeks old. The surname of the family that had adopted him began with an *R*, the rest hardly more than a scribble. But she squinted until she made the name out: *Renadot*.

This had to be Huguette's baby. Her heart pounding, she tried other drawers in the desk but found them locked, with no keys in sight. She rifled through the drawer with the wine bottle again and there it was, an envelope with today's date hastily jotted on it. Within the envelope, a wad of fifty-franc notes and a church donation receipt with the name *Renadot* and an address.

The answer came to her. A cold sensation ran down her arms as she understood the director's phone conversation. The woman had pocketed a commission on her baby.

A great ache opened in her.

But she had a plan. She'd take the money, return it to the family, and get her baby back.

HUGUETTE HAD TO MOVE QUICKLY. She packed the little she had—somehow she'd lost her mother's second aquamarine hair clip—into a laundry sack and whispered goodbye to Lena. Before she could respond, Huguette put a finger to Lena's mouth. "Shhh."

Next, the staff cloak room, where Huguette took a thick wool cape, hat, and muffler off the coat rack. From there, she just had to make it to the massive entrance door unnoticed.

"Huguette!"

Huguette whirled back to see Madame Silot approaching down the corridor.

"Come back and sign your papers," called Madame Silot. "Where are you going?"

"You sold my baby." She slammed the door. Ran and ran.

Early May 1945

Outside Sceaux

—

Huguette pulled the wool hat low and cape tight as she hurried through the village. At the bus stop, she scavenged in her bag and found two francs—the only money to her name, apart from the five thousand francs in the envelope.

Her stomach twisted, and she touched the knotted butterfly scarf—the last remembrance of her mother, who'd hand-embroidered those delicate wings—around her neck for comfort. Would the family understand? The director had said they were good Christian people; surely all she needed to do was explain that it had been a terrible mistake and return the money. She needed her baby back. Of course they would understand. Sympathize. Then she could find work as a wet nurse and keep the baby with her.

The bus arrived, and Huguette slipped on, pressing her two francs into the driver's leathery palm. The old woman beside her on the crowded bus clutched a straw basket full of eggs. She checked the eggs continually and glared with suspicion at Huguette as if she'd steal them. Huguette tried sending her a smile, but when she was only met with another glare, she gave up and looked the other way, rubbing her sleeve on the condensation-fogged windows to see out.

The country road held carts pulled by horses, bicyclists whose scarves trailed in the wind, a burnt-out German truck by the roadside. No private cars or taxis in sight.

Or gendarmes.

When the clouds broke over the lush forest, sunlight splintered on drooping fir tree branches laden with melting snow. Roadside clumps of green grass peeked from the mud, and each time the bus stopped, the open door let in brisk air warmed by the sun heralding spring.

For the first time in months, Huguette felt free. A little scared. But ready to start anew.

In the Sceaux train station she rushed to the departure board tacked on the high-ceilinged station wall. The weather had disrupted the rail line, and there hadn't been a train departure since early this morning. The couple who had adopted her baby must be waiting for the next one. All trains went to Paris.

And one was leaving in five minutes.

She flew up the stairs and down to the platform before the train pulled in.

She scanned the passengers on the platform. Then she saw a couple, a suitcase between them. The woman, wearing a chic blue wool suit, held a tiny baby.

Even from that distance, Huguette could see the downy fuzz on top of his head and the squashed mushroom of his nose.

It was her baby.

Hurt and anguish spread through her as she ran down the platform, nearly colliding with the couple, who didn't seem to notice her until she was right in front of them. "*Excusez-moi,*" she said, struggling to catch her breath.

The couple looked up. The man, in wireframe glasses, wore a tailored coat with a Cross of Lorraine hanging from a blue ribbon pinned on his lapel. A war medal. His gaze wasn't unlike that of the woman on the bus—cold and distrustful. Huguette couldn't even begin to imagine what a mess she looked with her unkempt hair, ill-fitting cape, red cheeks, and eyes beginning to fill with tears, but when the man didn't immediately call for the police, she felt hope swell.

"*Oui*, mademoiselle?" he said impatiently.

"Monsieur and Madame Renadot, you've come from the maternity home, *non*?"

He studied her more closely. "Why do you ask?" he said, suspicion in his voice. He took his wife's arm.

Huguette's gaze drank in the baby. He'd begun to cry.

The woman stepped back. "Who are you?"

"His mother." Huguette reached out for him. "He's hungry. There's been a misunderstanding."

"Young woman, this is our child."

The husband picked up the suitcase, held his wife's elbow more tightly. All around them the passengers watched, cutting their eyes to the source of the unfolding drama.

"He's my baby." Huguette's voice came out in a cry. "Mine."

The woman looked frightened. "Leave us alone."

"He's not for sale." Huguette withdrew the envelope of cash, thrust it at the man. "It's a misunderstanding, like I said. Here's your money back."

The man shook his head, stepping away as he put his arm around his wife's shoulders, and raised his voice to shout, "Police!"

Two gendarmes, blue capes over their shoulders, broke away from the wall, muscling their way through the crowd to Huguette. Smoke and soot billowed above as the train arrived at the platform. A conductor's piercing whistle startled her baby, who burst into screams, his face red and crinkled.

The sound went right to her heart. Racked with anguish, she yelled, "He's scared. There's been a mistake—please listen."

The train cabin doors creaked open. The man began to guide his wife toward the carriage steps.

"*Non, non.* You can't take him." Huguette was begging, following them, and when she saw the woman pause to mount the steps to the train car, she saw an opportunity and grabbed at her sobbing baby, trying to wrest him away. His little hand caught hers, chubby fingers clinging tightly. She craved that sweet milky smell wafting from him. If she could just hold him—

The woman pulled away, screaming.

"Officers, please control this young woman." The man was showing a tall gendarme papers. "She's utterly deluded. Look, we have legal documentation proving this is our child . . ."

The other gendarme had taken her arm. Pulled her away. "Come with me, mademoiselle. Let's discuss this at the station."

She saw the gendarme handing the paper back to the man, saluting, then picking up the envelope of money that had fallen onto the platform. He tucked it into his coat.

"You can't take that," Huguette cried.

Then she didn't see the couple anymore—the train's doors closed behind them. The conductor's whistle blew again. *Chug, chug* as the train's wheels began to turn. Taking her baby away from her.

She kicked the gendarme in the shins, broke away, and ran toward the train. Panting and shouting, she pounded on the train's siding as it gained speed pulling out of the station. The woman held her baby at the window. He was still crying, even when the woman turned away and vanished from view.

And then the train was gone.

May 1945

Commissariat Sceaux

For an hour, Huguette pounded the jail cell door, yelling herself hoarse.

"Why don't you believe me? The *directrice* sells babies. The nuns help her."

Eventually, she collapsed, shivering on the gouged wood bench under the slit-barred window open to the air. Exhausted and hoarse, she sunk into a fitful sleep.

Finally, the next morning she heard the scraping metal of a key as the lock turned and the heavy scuffed door opened.

"The magistrate's here." Without ceremony, the gendarme she'd kicked yanked her outside into the dark hall and forward.

Taken upstairs to a dark wood-paneled nineteenth-century judge's chamber, she was put in a chair to face an old gray-haired man holding a file. He wore a blue striped suit, definitely prewar, that hung on his shrunken frame.

"You're accused of theft and assaulting an officer," he said.

"They bought my baby," Huguette said, still furious even through her exhaustion. "That's illegal."

"Contrary to your allegations, the couple who adopted

the infant followed the legal pathways to parenthood. Their contribution to the church orphanage fund—also legal and aboveboard—was a sign of their appreciation for Madame Silot's work." He shoved a paper across the bar. "You signed this maternity agreement renouncing any claim to this child, and no name is listed on the birth certificate. See?"

Under *Mother's Name* was an X.

Panicked, Huguette felt herself grasping at straws. "Madame Silot? You can't trust her! She's a drunk—she runs the maternity home as a business and takes a commission—"

"I called Madame Silot. She says you're distraught, delusional, and belligerent, and consistently fabricate tales."

Of course he'd believe her over Huguette.

Her father had dealt with these types: lawyers, government officials, and businessmen. Ones holding power and position— happy to benefit from his black market deals. Yet at Libération when he wasn't useful anymore, they distanced themselves, afraid to dirty their name, acknowledge their dealings, or compromise their power.

But she needed to adopt a meeker tone and make her case.

"Monsieur le Magistrat, I wanted to return the family's money and get my baby back. That's all."

"Mademoiselle, you're seventeen years old, a minor with no lodging or income to care for a child. According to Paris police records, you're an orphan suspected of theft and collaboration. Your family café, previously run by your father, Remy Faure, now deceased, was reported to be a hub of illegal black market dealings."

The hypocrites.

Huguette hadn't expected to hear her father's name—not here, not now. A lump swelled in her throat, and the meek mask she'd only just put on slipped away. "Papa did what everyone did," she said. "I'm not saying it's right. It's wrong. But that has nothing to do with my baby. And right or wrong, when people are hungry they trade on the black market."

Hadn't this judge ever bought anything on the black market? Punishing someone like her was easy. He'd make his quota.

She remembered the words embroidered by her mother and framed in their living quarters above the café.

People don't like the truth when it's inconvenient.

"Dealing on the black market's illegal, young lady."

"What about beating someone to death?" She stared down at her mud-spattered boots, trying to banish those mental images of vigilantes dragging her battered father through the streets. "Is that legal? Because that's what they did to my father. They murdered him and they took over our café."

The magistrate still didn't seem impressed. "Is that all you have to say?" he said. "None of this qualifies as a defense for these charges against you."

"But it's true!"

A sigh. "Mademoiselle, I'm duty bound to take legal action." He closed her file. "However, Madame Silot took pity on you and prefers not to press charges. She feels you're immature and deserve a second chance. We came to an agreement and decided it would be fair for you to work at the maternity home to pay off your debt."

Huguette blinked. "What debt?"

"The money you stole, mademoiselle."

The way he was looking at her with a mixture of pity and disgust made her skin crawl. Fury flared again. "The gendarme picked it up from the platform. Ask him for the money."

The magistrate consulted the file. "The gendarme's report

states two thousand five hundred francs were discovered. The family donated five. There's a discrepancy."

He'd pocketed half.

"You believe that? Ask him if there wasn't five thousand francs that I was trying to return to the family. Ask anyone who stood on the platform!"

"A sworn officer of the law has given his statement. There's no further action. Later today you'll be returned to the maternity home."

She tried one last time, genuine tears filling her eyes. "Please don't send me back there."

"The alternative is Pentonville. If it weren't for Madame Silot's mercy you'd be headed straight there."

She'd heard of the notorious prison that accommodated underage offenders; the brutal living conditions, the abuse by the guards. The prison reformers had tried to close it down before the war, but somehow, things had only gotten worse.

The judge's knobby arthritic fingers tapped the file.

"Consider yourself lucky, mademoiselle."

He called that *lucky*?

The corrupt gendarme would get away with robbing her. So would the *directrice*, who stole her baby and sold it, and the family who had bought him.

How did she stand a chance against them all?

Outside in the drafty hallway, a *flic* had arrived with a prisoner. Her cell was needed. With her departure imminent, Huguette and her laundry sack of belongings were put in the gendarmerie's kitchen to wait for her escort back to the maternity home. The kitchen had sad tobacco-stained yellow walls bearing a single tattered calendar, a cold stove, a large farm table, and mismatched chairs.

Tears rimmed her eyes. Facing her lay a future under the vindictive *directrice*, years of work in the laundry to pay off a corrupt gendarme's take. Every day seeing the babies who'd remind her of her loss. She'd seen the girls who'd given birth and were kept like indentured servants, some of them for years. Gaunt, lifeless—no hope in their eyes.

She saw no way out.

And all this started because she'd just wanted to say goodbye to her baby.

Huguette wrapped her one treasure, her mother's soft butterfly-embroidered scarf, around her for comfort, and rocked, sobbing, on the cold tile floor until she had no more tears left. Then she noticed her breasts were soft. Nothing leaked. Her milk had dried up from shock. Hadn't the *directrice* said it could happen just like that?

"*Excusez-moi.*"

She looked up at the *flic* she'd passed in the hallway. He was young, fresh-faced, with a sympathetic look in his deep mocha-colored eyes.

"Don't mind me. I'm making coffee for the *commissariat*."

She covered her head with her arms and burrowed deeper into herself. Miserable, she couldn't wait for him to leave.

A scratch of a match, the *thuk-whoosh* as a gas burner flickered, then caught. Water rushing from the tap. The sounds of normal life.

The intoxicating aroma of fresh coffee filled the kitchen. Real coffee. She hadn't smelled it in years.

She heard the clattering of cups and saucers, the tinkle of spoons on a metal tray. The sounds of coffee being poured into cups. Then the door opening and closing.

The aroma lingered. She stretched her head up. Steam rose from a cup on the table.

He'd forgotten one.

But he came back in and sat at the table with a cup and some paperwork. Following her gaze, he smiled slightly. "Help yourself."

She knew nothing came free from a *flic*. "No, thank you."

"Suit yourself." He shrugged lightly. "If you don't drink it we'll give it to the prisoners."

Wasn't she a prisoner?

Wary, she battled the urge to grab it.

He turned the knob on the radio on the shelf. Classical music drifted through the kitchen. It was almost peaceful—until the staccato peals of a news bulletin interrupted the symphony, and a crisp-voiced announcer declared that the Russians were continuing their takeover of Berlin. Driven into his bunker like a rat in a trap, the Führer had died.

The war would truly be over.

The *flic*'s jaw had dropped, and he'd abandoned his own coffee to listen. Huguette uncurled from the corner and moved closer.

"About time." The *flic* listened to the radio for another few seconds, then shook his head, turned the volume down, and picked up the stack of paperwork he'd brought in with him.

Since he was ignoring her now, Huguette judged it safe to move, approaching the table and taking up the coffee. She cupped the warm chipped mug in her hands and sipped.

Heaven. Definitely not ersatz crushed chicory, but the taste of another life, of prewar times in the café. She pictured the waiter Luc winking at her from behind the counter, her smiling mother offering her a *religieuse, choux* pastry stacked with sweet hazelnut crème.

She couldn't let her mind wander. She came down to earth with a sob.

It was all gone. Libération had brought her nothing but heartache and loss.

Tears flowed down her cheeks.

"The coffee's not that bad, is it?" the *flic* said.

Consideration showed in his eyes. Sincere or not, it was the first humanity anyone had shown her.

"It's real coffee. *Merci.*"

"But not as good as in Paris, eh?" he teased. "You're Parisian. Typical snob."

She shrugged. Dabbed her eyes with the butterfly scarf, sniffled and wiped her nose with her sleeve. "It takes a Parisian to know one. But you sound like an Auvergnat."

"For my sins." He grinned.

Huguette struggled to smile back. Everything was sinking in all at once—that she'd never be able to go back and see Paris how it once was. "My father owned a café in the fourth *arrondissement*. I grew up there."

"So an expert," he said. "Where exactly is the café?"

"Across from the prefecture. On the corner."

He blinked. "Café du Soleil? My boss goes there with the rest of the top brass. A little pricey for ordinary *flics* like me."

Huguette wanted to slink away again to nurse the wound hearing the café's name had reopened, but his jokes, his warm smile, and the fragrant coffee lulled her. She couldn't remember when she had last bantered like this. She opened her mouth to retort, but then the door banged open again as the thieving gendarme from the train station strode into the kitchen.

"Leduc!" His small eyes took in the scene. Huguette hid the cup and put her head down. "Paperwork finished, I hope. You've got a new prisoner to escort back to Paris."

"Understood," said Leduc.

"You." The gendarme pointed at her. "Keep to yourself. You're being transported as soon as another officer's available."

The door slammed shut.

"You're going back to Paris, too?"

She shook her head. Set down her coffee before her now-trembling hands could spill it. "Back to the maternity home. It's because of that corrupt gendarme."

"Blaming the gendarme? Come on."

"You don't believe me? But it's true."

The story tumbled out amid a new wave of tears. Her parents dead. The baby. She left out who the father was and her papa's betrayal—after all, Leduc was a *flic*.

He passed her a handkerchief to wipe her face. She took it, bracing for his pity or castigation. Instead, "How old are you?" was all he said.

"I'm almost eighteen," Huguette said, a little hoarse from crying.

He looked confused. "You're seventeen—a minor—and they put you here?"

"They ran out of cells."

His brow furrowed and he took a notebook out of his inner pocket. "There's a new law. Isn't the magistrate aware?"

"What law?"

He looked down at his notebook, thumbed through several pages, then read aloud, "'Juvenile offenders must be treated in accordance with the Ordinance of February 2, 1945.' De Gaulle's put the law into effect."

Huguette didn't know what to think. "But what does that mean for me?"

"Penalties imposed upon minors aged between thirteen and eighteen years old must take into account their situation.

Especially war orphans and homeless minors. We worked on a juvenile case last week, that's how I know." He took another sip of coffee. "You should be in school. Get a slap on the wrist. Know your citizen's rights, as they say."

Her mouth widened in an O of surprise.

He poured her another cup of coffee.

"If you're ever in Paris again . . ." He reached into his pocket. "We use these now."

He set a Métro ticket on the table. It was different from the ones used during the war, with a new price and stamped with the letter K. And a pocket-sized red book—a bilingual Paris map by *arrondissement*.

"You'll fit in great with the GI tourists."

He winked and was gone.

The coffee was still hot and she drank it.

"Time to go," said the gendarme from the door.

Huguette gathered her bag, the ticket and book safely tucked inside, and stood. "I want to see the magistrate."

"Don't waste time."

"There's something important I must discuss with him."

"He's not here. Hurry up, your transport's ready."

"I'll wait for him."

Anger showed in his small eyes. "You'll follow the law."

"Yes, I will," Huguette shot back. "The new penal code effective February 2 says my situation must be assessed in light of my war orphan status. Also that minors must attend school and be under supervision."

He grabbed her arm and pulled her forward. "Troublemaker."

"Wait till I get started," she spat. "The minute you spend a centime of that money, I'll see."

Her grandmother used to frighten her by talking like that.

When she was little, she'd wake up with nightmares of *grand-mére* with eyes in the back of her head.

He sneered. "No one believes a thief."

"You're the thief," she said, using her quietest voice as her grandmother used to do. Stared at him. Tried for the evil eye. "As an officer of the law, you should return it."

A flash of uneasiness showed in his gaze. Then he shoved her out the door. "You'll get what you deserve, crazy eyes."

The hall led out to the temporary annex next to the bombed-out courthouse, a crowded room stuffed full of gendarmes and the public awaiting their hearings. She yanked her arm free of his hold and threw herself down to squat on the floor. When the gendarme tried to haul her up again, she shouted, "I demand to see the magistrate. He must rule according to the new penal code. Until then, I'm not moving."

Angry rumblings of "Haul her off . . . little slut . . . thief."

"She's correct." There was Leduc, the Paris *flic*. "Even this backwater has to follow the law."

The gendarme at the admitting desk shot him a dirty look but raised his voice: "Summon the magistrate."

THAT EVENING A TIRED SOCIAL services worker escorted Huguette to a foster family on the outskirts of Sceaux. She was given a franc fifty for school supplies, which the work-worn mother pocketed immediately. Stonemason father, five children. A bowl of weak soup was plopped in front of her at a rough-hewn table. She shared a bed with a small girl who sniveled all through the night. The next day, Huguette discovered the one-room schoolhouse held forty children, and she was the oldest. The desk was so small her legs wouldn't fit under it.

Her hopes dived.

How was this any better than the laundry?

She swallowed the fear, the resentment, in her throat and kept quiet.

That night, after a day of toiling to clean the house and dodging the father's lingering stares, a nightmare woke her—she was hungry and living on the street.

She clutched her baby's knit vest and battled tears. Small comfort in the long night. She couldn't stay here—she'd be better on her own, and she'd find her baby.

Dawn found her trudging, feet numb from cold, on the muddy road bordered by melting snow. A wash of ochre rust stained the sky. She kept on through village after village until, mid-morning, she passed a road sign pointed toward Paris.

At the Red Cross clinic on the outskirts of Paris, Huguette joined the crowd. Women in wood-soled shoes and prewar clothing stood with children and old men checking the Red Cross lists of the missing and the dead. So many had been displaced during the war.

It took the afternoon to track down the Renadots using the regional phone books. Their home lay only a forty-minute ride from the Paris outskirts. Huguette's heart leapt—her baby was so close. She couldn't wait to cradle him and inhale his smell. To put on the little vest she'd knitted for him.

For two nights Huguette hid from the guard in the Red Cross clinic, planning and sleeping in the storeroom. Early the second morning she took a health worker's uniform and a bike from the clinic. Promised herself she'd return it all.

Near the Renadots' manor, a burnt-out Mercedes sedan sat in the adjoining wheat field.

Had she gotten this wrong? What if something had happened to them, and her baby?

Iron clamped her insides.

Non, non . . . he had to be here.

Praying she'd find him, she walked past the open gate into the manor's courtyard. She clutched the Saint Christopher medal her friend Marina had given her around her neck. Her senses were hit by fragrant greenery. Shooting tulips bordered the limestone wall.

Here spring had bloomed.

A chestnut-maned horse snorted, his white nose visible from the stable door. An old timbered washhouse had been transformed into a school, with a handwritten sign reading ÉCOLE DES FILLES ET GARÇONS DU VÉSINET hung above the large wooden door.

Huguette heard children's voices singing a nursery rhyme she'd loved in her childhood. Her arms dewed from a welcome spray of splashing water at the pump in the yard.

The place felt alive. Vibrant. Welcoming. Not the prison she'd expected.

"Ah, mademoiselle, come here." A doctor wearing a white coat beckoned her from a doorway.

Just the person who would break her cover! *Zut alors*—she was dressed as a Red Cross health worker, after all.

"Where's Jeanine?" he said, giving her a quizzical look.

Her plans veered toward disaster. She had to act quickly. Struggling, she managed a smile. "I'm sorry, but . . ."

"No matter if they sent you instead," he interrupted. "Thank you for coming. Follow me."

"But I'm looking for Madame Renadot," she said.

"Of course you are. This way."

Panic lanced her. She hadn't meant to confront the woman. Her plan was to snatch her baby, leave her letter of explanation in his place.

"Doctor, emergency call from the clinic," said a voice from inside the house. "They need to speak with you."

He turned around.

"Here's madame's injection," he said. He handed Huguette a kidney-shaped aluminum dish containing a syringe, a vial of alcohol, and a brown bottle. "Take it to her in the back garden. I'll join you when I can."

The next minute he'd gone.

Her stomach wrenched. What if the real health aide he was expecting showed up? Her plans seemed impossible now.

But she had to find her baby. She'd come too far to turn back.

Hurrying, she reached the entrance to the back garden. She paused at the door and took in the scene: Madame Renadot, the haughty nervous woman she'd last seen on the station platform, sprawled laughing on the grass. Beside her on a small blue blanket, Huguette's baby lay kicking his feet. Huguette recognized him right away.

Her hands were shaking. She grabbed the doorframe, watching, transfixed. The woman pulled him into her arms and kissed his little fists. His azure eyes bright, his cheeks and skin a rosy glow. A little bundle of health—he was already filling out. He gurgled as the woman blew on his toes.

Breathless, she held still in expectation. The long cypress branches swept the grass framing the idyllic scene of the blond mother and her blond baby. A longing so strong came over her. She squeezed her hand into a fist so hard her fingernails cut into her palm.

"Made for each other. Wonderful, *non?*"

She almost nodded. Startled, she turned and realized a nurse had joined her in the doorway.

"I'll take that. I'm Jeanine." The nurse reached for the kidney-shaped dish. "Did the wires get crossed at the *clinique*?"

Quick—she had to think and act like it was a mistake.

"I'm not sure," Huguette said. "Isn't this the Renadots' house?"

"You're not the baby's regular nurse," Jeanine said, eyebrows arched.

The baby had a nurse? This was proving more difficult than she'd thought.

"That's right. Where is she?"

"I don't know," said Jeanine. "Who are you?"

Belatedly, Huguette remembered the clipboard she'd brought and pulled it out from her satchel, determined to act the part. "I'll talk to her later," she said. "But I'm glad you're here to answer a few questions. My department checks on how adopted babies adjust to new parents."

"You're awfully young," said Jeanine.

"I'm trained, if that's what you're worried about."

Jeanine, dark haired and in her early thirties, sighed. She stretched her neck and leaned against the doorframe, but at least she didn't look hostile—Huguette felt herself beginning to exhale. "No one said you were coming."

"We make unscheduled visits. The procedures were all explained during the adoption process," said Huguette. "So, if it's all right with you, I'd like your observations before I speak with her." Huguette pasted on a smile and continued before she lost her nerve. "Just a few questions. How long has Madame Renadot been treated for her condition? Her physical ability to raise a child is important."

"Madame Renadot's anemic," said Jeanine. "Nothing unusual to get iron injections, *n'est-ce pas?*" Jeanine smiled, watching the two of them on the grass. "She suffered three miscarriages. Despaired until they found a little Catholic baby through the nuns."

The Renadots had been conned. Would Renadot, a hero awarded a war medal, want a Nazi baby? Of course not, and he had no idea.

Still, Huguette had to maintain her calm exterior, and she scribbled on her clipboard, nodding thoughtfully. "Of course it's not unusual. We simply have to look at whether the environment's in the baby's best interests, and how he's taking to it. Examine if he's fussy, takes to a bottle well, has colic or sleep issues."

She hoped she didn't sound too word for word like the Red Cross manual she'd studied.

Every fiber in her strained to know more about her little baby, who looked a picture of contentment on the blue blanket as Madame Renadot's silver laughter joined his gurgles of delight.

"Fussy? I rarely hear him cry. Babies adapt. And he took to the bottle right away. Madame gives him goat milk from the farm—she says it's better and prevents allergies. Seems like he's gained a little weight since he came. Very happy, I think." Jeanine tucked a stray strand of hair back into the bun at the nape of her neck. "Look: He's a picture of health, mademoiselle. Thriving."

Huguette pretended to check a list. All of a sudden, Monsieur Renadot appeared at the end of the garden. He hurried over, threw down a briefcase, kissed his wife, and then lifted the baby. Cradled him. The face, stern and angry, she remembered from the station platform, now split in a smile.

"How's my big boy?" His tone was warm and proud. "Have you and *maman* been silly?"

Laughter erupted again from Madame Renadot.

Jeanine took a pack of Gauloise from her pocket, tapped out a cigarette, and offered Huguette one.

"*Non, merci.*"

Jeanine slid the Gauloise back, flicked open a Zippo lighter, and lit her cigarette. "He's one lucky baby you've placed."

Huguette's heart stabbed in her chest. "Would they be concerned if the child's real mother showed up?"

Jeanine's eyes flickered over to her. "That's an odd word to use." She tapped the ash in the gutter. "The *birth* mother gave him up, and Madame Renadot adopted him to give him a good life. She loves him, as you can clearly see. I hope that goes in your survey. Babies need love. Safety. Protection." She took a long draw from her cigarette. Exhaled a plume of smoke. "A mother puts her child before herself. Say a birth mother chooses to give up her child when she can't provide for it. To me, that's love. That's brave."

Huguette caught her breath. Felt tears brimming. She pretended something had gotten stuck in her eye and wiped at it hard. Kept trying to find anger at this woman.

Jeanine looked at her. "Don't you think so?"

"Not everyone has that choice."

Jeanine inhaled and nodded. "I know you're doing your job, but he's her son as if he came from her."

"But he didn't."

"*Alors*, it's for the best. You only have to look and see he's, well . . ."

Huguette put down the clipboard. "What?"

Jeanine hesitated. Exhaled. "Never mind," she said.

"Say it," said Huguette.

"He's a *Boche* baby," said Jeanine, lowering her voice. "People spread rumors. Me, I don't care. But no one will ever think that now."

"What do you mean?"

"There's blond babies born in my village who'll always be branded bastard *Boche*. But this one—he's got a Resistance hero for a father and a blond *maman*." Jeanine gently touched Huguette's arm. Huguette looked into her eyes. They were kind. "I applaud the mother who had him adopted. She was thinking of what's best for him."

The doctor had appeared on the grass.

"I better go," said Jeanine.

Another nurse, a young one, had scooped up her baby from Renadot's arms. "Nap time, little one."

Seconds later she was passing Huguette in the doorframe and giving her a smile. The baby's eyes were heavy. Huguette felt drawn like a magnet to follow them into the house and to a cozy, plain room with a crib. Unable to tear her gaze away, she watched the nurse check his diaper, lay him in the crib, and put a stuffed bunny beside him. Huguette ducked into an alcove as the nurse pulled the shades and left the door halfway open.

She'd never said goodbye to him. It wouldn't hurt to touch him. To hold him.

To take him.

She didn't know how long she stood there, just watching as eventually his wriggling slowed, and his little chest began to rise and fall with breaths of sleep. Finally, when she was sure he was asleep, she lifted him up, inhaling his smell. So different from his sweet milky nursing scent she remembered. He felt soft, his skin like velvet.

She snuggled him in her arms. His closed eyelashes fluttered like a kiss on her cheek. Her baby was perfect.

All of a sudden he arched his back. Kicked his little legs.

Was she holding him too tight? Perspiration broke out on her neck.

She took the bunny from the crib, nestled it with him. It was easy now, just how she'd planned it. She left the letter and headed toward the nursery door. He startled and his heavy eyelids blinked open. He burst out crying.

Shocked, she didn't know what to do but hold him tighter.

"Don't worry, you're with your *maman* now. We'll go and—"

His cries reverberated against her chest. Full-throated howls, his face going beet red. She rocked him back and forth. Trying to hug his tears away.

"It's all right. You'll be fine," she whispered, kissing his hot forehead. "I'll take care of you like before."

She heard voices. They had to leave. Quickly, she turned to rush out with her screaming baby.

Madame Renadot was hurrying down the hallway. Sunlight speckled over her face, which was knit by worry. "Why did he wake up? Is he sick? Wait . . . who are you?"

"He'll be fine. He'll get used to me again. I'm his mother."

Sweat poured down her spine.

"What?"

Desperate, Huguette tightened her arms, protectively turning the baby away from Madame Renadot. "It's all in my letter. I'll pay you back but right now . . ."

"You're that crazy one," Madame Renadot said. "I remember you and your strange eyes. Like a witch." She crossed herself, then kissed the crucifix around her neck—and held her arms out to Huguette. "Please give him to me. He's innocent."

"My baby was never for sale," Huguette said. "Let us go."

The baby's screams curdled her thinking. What was she doing wrong? He was struggling, flailing out with his little fists.

"But you're a child yourself. Too young." The woman's lips quivered. "You don't know how to take care of him. He's overheating, and you're holding him wrong."

She was?

"Don't you understand? He's all I have."

Monsieur Renadot stepped between them. "Please let go," he said. "I don't want you or the baby hurt."

She pulled the baby tighter. His cries rose. "His father was a Nazi," she confessed, desperate, though the bitter words burned her throat to spit. "You don't really want him. Sooner or later you'd realize that and hate him."

"Is that what worries you?" Renadot shook his head. "*Au contraire*. We want him because he's god's child. Innocent. We promise to give him a good life."

Before she knew it he'd snatched the baby and handed him to his wife. Immediately her baby's cries stopped and he settled down. Madame Renadot cooed, holding him over her shoulder, rocking him, and patting his back.

Huguette's arms felt a cold emptiness. She knew he belonged with this woman. Her bond with him was broken.

The nurse had been right. With a blond mother and hero father he'd have more than Huguette could ever give him.

The sight of him happy now seared her.

He'd always be hers. But she'd be the best mother she could and not think of herself. Put aside her hunger for him, the only family she had left.

She took one last look at him: the pink pearl-like toes, chubby fists, a little yawn. Familiar. So like her own mother.

"What's his name?"

"He was christened after the saint on the day he was born . . . Hugues, but Hugo for short."

The feminine version of her name. Now they would always share that.

"Please leave. We don't want you to be hurt, either. But please, please leave us."

Huguette was nearly blind with tears. Numb, she turned, walked down the hallway into the courtyard. Didn't look back.

Jeanine, having another cigarette, waved to her.

She didn't want pity. Her hands shook but she kept her eyes straight ahead. Focused on mounting her bike, riding out the gate and down the rutted road. Willing herself not to break down. She felt light, too light—she wanted Hugues's weight in the long scarf she'd brought to carry him wrapped on her chest, feel his soft warmth.

She pedaled through the bombed-out village, past the roofless thirteenth-century church, its open fresco walls pocked by bullet holes, its backless wooden confessional. Her wheels crunched over the broken glass by the *commissariat*'s blown-out windows. The *mairie*, the town hall, had boards nailed over the door.

The war was over. Things were supposed to get better, weren't they?

A village in ruins, broken like her.

A kilometer, three, five until her legs gave out and her heaving lungs wouldn't let her breathe.

She crashed on the grass verge. The wrenching pain howled up from deep inside her and she screamed. She lay there on that remote road, pounding the dirt, sobbing, for she didn't know how long.

Finally, exhausted and spent, she rolled over and looked at the soft pale blue of the spring sky. Felt the fresh breeze and remembered her mother saying, *When one door closes, another opens.* Tears rolled down her face into her hair as she watched the white clouds dancing through the sky. She thought about all that had happened to her in just a short time. Thought about her baby, Hugues. Thought about being Huguette . . . and knew she had to let it go.

MAY 1945

Paris Morgue

—

Claude Leduc donned a gown to enter the morgue's white-tiled autopsy lab. The air was cold, laced with putrefaction antiseptics couldn't cover; Claude's nose started running as soon as he crossed the threshold. Each time work brought him here, he found himself both physically and emotionally uneasy.

Bile rose in Claude's throat. Memories assailed him from the street fighting at Libération: the corpses bloated in the heat, his best friend lying on the cobblestones, riddled by German sniper bullets. The battle in Dijon where they'd fought for every street.

But he had a job to do. The sooner he finished it, the sooner he could leave this stinking place.

On the porcelain table lay a male, sheet up to his chin. His swollen face was tinged black-purple; his parted blue lips revealed black stumps of broken teeth. The skin at the hairline hadn't been realigned properly after the scalp was separated from the skull at the autopsy. Poor *mec*. Not a great way to end up.

What injustice had brought him here to this slab?

The doctor's voice cut through Claude's musings. "You're here about number 321, *n'est-ce pas?*"

Claude nodded.

Dr. Cendrars looked just out of medical school—like many here, and in the force these days. All with something to prove.

Like Claude.

Claude checked the corpse's toe tag, and his heart accelerated. "Remy Faure, found in Saint-Cloud."

Immediately he recognized this name. At first, Faure's name had been on a collaborator list recovered by the police in August 1944, nailed to a tree. His subsequent disappearance pointed to possible revenge by a lynch mob. But Faure's body had never been found and there had been no official police report of his death. Why would his body surface now, months later?

The longtime cashier at the Café du Soleil had identified Faure by his missing fingers: the pinkie finger of the right hand and partial loss of the left hand's ring finger. Claude had met Faure's daughter in the *commissariat* at Sceaux—the sweet sad girl with the strange eyes who had drunk his coffee. Here before him, in her murdered father's corpse, he saw the tragedy that had driven Huguette Faure to the unwed mothers' home in Sceaux. Or at least part of the tragedy.

"Remy Faure is on my list, but Saint-Cloud's not our jurisdiction," Claude said regretfully. "He's not ours." He loosened the gown's ties and turned to go.

"Two bodies, 321 and 322, were found on the same day in Saint-Cloud," said the doctor, weary. "The municipality couldn't handle it and sent the bodies to us. Since 321 was a Paris resident, we were told your department was assigned to the job."

First he'd heard. Why hadn't the Sûreté's homicide division been informed?

"Take a closer look, detective." The doctor pulled down the sheet and pointed to the body's neck. The skin was mottled with midnight blue and purplish veins like tree branches and revealed an indentation around the neck. "That furrow marks where a rope was. There's no bleeding associated with it, so this occurred postmortem."

Claude's curiosity was piqued. "Strangled after death?"

Dr. Cendrars nodded gravely. "It's one of the inconsistencies I discovered in the autopsy. Decomposition can't hide that. Yet Remy Faure was found in the river."

That was the underlying smell Claude noticed: algae and river grasses.

"He didn't die twice," Claude said. "Meaning, what . . . he was murdered and much later thrown in the river?"

"You're the detective."

"Where's the evidence? Do you have something else to show me?"

The doctor's gloved hands pointed to a damp woven cord in an evidence tray.

"This cord was around his neck," said the doctor, "the other end tied to that."

A damp gray cobblestone in the box caught the light.

"So he was dead before being weighted down."

"*Exactement.* The autopsy revealed a skull fracture. Severe facial trauma. Recent fauna contact and minor insect infestation. I'd guess the body was resting in cold water and then washed up. But he had a rope tying his wrists, like the other."

The hairs on the back of Claude's arm prickled.

"Can I see the other?"

"This way. We have a new *frigo.*"

"What happened? The old one break down?"

The morgue's ancient freezer workings made a joke of efficiency.

"We ran out of space with all the bodies from the *épuration.*"

Street justice and reprisals against collaborators ran dark currents through the Libération. Kangaroo courts in the street, vigilantes taking matters into their own hands and settling scores. Women accused of sleeping with Nazis had their heads shaved. This so-called people's justice stank of revenge. Few talked about it; no one wanted a finger pointed at them.

"You know Remy Faure was a collaborator," said Claude.

"Not my business. He was long dead before he washed up on the bank."

Dr. Cendrars led him to a room with a thrumming refrigerator unit. About twenty-five metal drawers with handles were built into the wall. The doctor pulled open one of the drawers on the left, then drew back the sheet on the corpse to reveal a man, waxen faced with a red-black bullet hole in his temple and similar rope marks around his neck.

"Both cadavers—321, Remy Faure, and this one, 322, who we've yet to identify—were recovered on the same day from the Seine in Saint-Cloud. The Prefect's conclusion was they were dumped together. They bear the same ligature marks and were weighed down by cobblestones in the same manner."

Claude surveyed the corpse and jotted some brief notes. "This body seems less decomposed than the first."

"I wish I could tell you more. A lot of factors make it difficult to know what happened." Dr. Cendrars handed him a slim binder. "In this file you'll find information; identification, ballistics, preliminary autopsy findings and photos."

Now all dumped on him and his unit.

He felt the chill in this room reach his bone marrow.

"Any other similarities between the two?"

The doctor nodded. "Limestone traces were found on the clothing."

The execution-style murders carried a signature: corpses weighed down with a cobblestone in the river, necks tied with rope. One suffered blunt trauma, one was shot.

The killer or killers were intent on sending a message. Who was next?

May 1945

Boulogne-Billancourt

Outside Paris

—

Huguette trudged along the roundabout as a jeep driven by two smiling GIs paused.

"Are you lost, miss?"

At least that's what Huguette thought they said. Her spotty English learned from *maman* and BBC Radio broadcasts would need to improve for her to survive.

She showed them the film studio address on the smudged IOU from her father's black market contact.

"No problem. We're headed to the base next door."

The GIs gave her a Hershey's chocolate bar and a ride to Boulogne-Billancourt. As they crossed the Pont d'Issy, her nervous gaze registered bomb sites and the piled rubble of the distant Renault factories. The Americans were chatty, and Huguette pieced together what she could: Most importantly, Ralph, their buddy, was stationed at the supply depot on the grounds of the nearby Château Rothschild occupied by the army and it seemed he had lots of things like these Hershey's bars for sale.

"Tell your mom and your friends to visit Ralph," said the grinning driver with a silver front tooth. He took a hand off the steering wheel and gave her a thumbs-up. "Okay?"

Did he expect her to do the same? "Okay, monsieur!" she said, returning his gesture.

On the tree-lined quai she thanked the GIs, waved goodbye as the wind gusted the wool cape around her. A walled cemetery flanked the studio. She made a sign of the cross as she passed it. Set her jaw and strode through the imposing entry of the Étoile film studio.

Huguette's nervous fingers played with the film studio's crumpled work order. She hoped Papa's former black market contact—the Italian with big ears like cauliflowers—remembered her. Would Enzo even be here after all these months? And if so, what if he alerted the black marketers on her trail?

Her shoulders sagged. Her legs ached from walking all morning. Her resolve was growing shaky, but Enzo was her last hope. Otherwise, she'd keep living on the street.

As she walked into the compound, her eyes bulged at the flurry of activity around her. Workmen pushed carts piled with props, a woman in a tall white wig and rose-pink brocade dress à la Marie Antoinette stood taking drags of her cigarette between presses of a powder puff across her face. Could she find Enzo among so many in the WWI buildings transformed into film studios?

She felt a creeping awe.

Everywhere were signposts with arrows pointing to fantastical places, some of which she didn't even understand: WARDROBE DEPARTMENT, DRESSING ROOMS, SMALL PROPS, ART DEPARTMENT, PROP ROOM, MAKEUP, SCENE SETS, CARPENTRY SHOP, PROJECTION ROOM, LABORATORY, WRITERS ROOM.

Her mind spun.

She stood lost in a sea of people rushing back and forth amid shouts and laughter. Things blurred. All she'd eaten today was a bite of the chocolate bar.

The swollen rain clouds opened. Huguette ran for cover below an overhang.

"An extra?" a man holding a clipboard asked her.

She shook her head. Held out the work order form. "Where's this place, monsieur?"

"*Là-bas.*" He pointed to a wall directory. "Building four."

She scurried through the pelting rain until she found building four, the set design workshop, a cavernous metal-sided building like an airplane hangar. Inside, a crew in overalls hauled in worn lumber, while another hammered the reused wood to construct sets. Others still painted a château on a huge canvas backdrop—so real her jaw dropped. Transfixed, she watched, not even noticing her wool cape dripping on the floor.

"May I help you, mademoiselle?" asked a young man in paint-spattered overalls.

"I'm looking for Enzo."

He shook his head. The cigarette hanging from his mouth barely swayed. "Not here."

She'd come all this way; was her only chance gone? She pressed her hand to her temples. She couldn't give up.

"Where did he go?"

"No clue."

She shivered in her wet clothes. "But I have to find him."

The young man ground out his cigarette on the cement floor with his toe. "Wait . . ." He craned his neck and shouted. "Umberto."

A man painting clouds on the canvas looked around. "*Si.*"

"Go ask him. They're friends, I think."

Umberto's French was passable. It turned out Enzo had suffered a work injury over at the sound stage fixing equipment, and he hadn't worked there since. Huguette's bad feeling mounted. Umberto was suspicious at first; it took five minutes before he relented and gave her Enzo's whereabouts—the kitchen.

Tired, wet, and cold, she finally found Enzo. He stood alone at a stove in the steamy kitchen of the workers' dormitory, leaning heavily on a crutch. His big cauliflower ears had gone pink from the heat of the boiling pot of pasta he was stirring.

"I remember you, signorina," he said with a grin. "Your papa I remember better."

"That's right." She showed him the signed IOU. "You owe him money."

"Eh, look at me. You think I can do real work with this?" Enzo pointed to his leg—bandaged from top to bottom in a thick white cast. "But I feed you pasta, okay?"

"You're saying you don't have this money?"

"Sit down. *Prego.* We eat. We talk."

Starving, she watched him drain the pasta with dexterity, spoon it in a bowl, douse it with olive oil, and ladle a bubbling tomato sauce over it. She took off her damp cape and boots, stiff with mud, and perched near the stove's warmth. After a quick *bon appétit,* she stuck in a fork and tasted.

Hot, savory, made with canned tomatoes and laced with herbs. Nothing had ever tasted so good in her life. Enzo laughed at her, and she realized she'd smeared sauce all over her cheeks.

"Wonderful." She wiped her mouth with her sleeve and tried to eat slowly.

Enzo gave her seconds.

She ate.

"More, signorina?"

"*Non, merci.*" That had been precisely what she'd needed; now her mind felt sharp again. Time to concentrate on the present.

But she accepted another spoonful at his insistence. "Where's your friend with the freckles, Enzo?"

"*Cosa?*"

She pointed to her nose and tapped.

"Ah, Manfredo."

"He's your partner, right? Manfredo? Ask him to loan the money to you." Back at the café, during the happy days she could barely stand to think about, she'd seen them together all the time. Manfredo had dealt with her father, too. The more she thought about it, the more it made sense. "Then you can pay me."

"*Sì*, but is not so simple. Your father and I, we have arrangement, signorina."

A forkful of pasta lodged in her throat. "You deal with me now." She swallowed. "What arrangement?"

"Arrangement," said Enzo. He had returned to the stove for another batch of pasta. "It work this way. He front me merchandise, I sell it and give him his cut. A good deal for him and for me. But my contact moved, I broke my leg and, *allora*, couldn't finish the business."

Excuses.

"Where's the merchandise, Enzo?"

He smiled. "I like you. You keep his accounts, I remember. He call you his smart daughter."

All the Italian charm and pasta in the world wouldn't budge her. "Tell me."

He shrugged. "Not here. But I help you."

"I'll stay here until that happens."

Tired actors and stage crew entered, clamoring to eat. Enzo shot her a look.

"You go now. I work. Don't get me in trouble."

— — —

Dejected, she tramped out into the twilight. Wandering with nowhere to go. Tiredness weighed her down.

The haloed apricot sunset faded as the sky darkened into night. Streetlights flickered on and off from the electricity shortage, twinkling on the Seine below. Promises wouldn't put a roof over her head.

She had no choice but to curl up on the quai. She nodded off to sounds of gurgling water but kept waking up. The worn wool cape insulated little against the cold, hard stone.

Laughter came from a band of men. She could practically smell the alcohol on their breaths from here. Their silhouettes appeared through the dense charcoal night, walking her way. She heard shouts of "Mademoiselle, it's cold, let us warm you up."

Gathering her cloak, she hurried up the riverbank steps. She thought she'd try her luck at the studio, sneak in again, but a guard stood checking a night crew in at the gate.

No help there.

Terror-stricken now, she kept to the shadow of the cemetery wall on the tree-lined street. The men were following her, whistling and catcalling. Her knees shook. They were gaining on her.

All she saw ahead was rubble, the open expanse of bomb sites, and the bridge. Too far and exposed. Behind lay the studio and the men, and to her left the high cemetery wall.

Nothing for it but to try to scale a plane tree and climb over the fence into the cemetery. Grabbing a branch, she swung, then braced her foot against the wall. Little by little, she climbed her way up. Slipped, only managing to catch a toehold at the last minute. Breathing hard, muscles straining, she reached the top, which was crusty with pigeon droppings.

"Come back, mademoiselle, share a drink," called a slurred drunken voice from below.

Not on her life.

Trembling, she let herself down the other side, finding footing on a cracked mausoleum roof slippery with moss and sliding slowly, somehow keeping her balance. At the bottom, she was surrounded by dark tombs. Shadows. The lifelike statues on the graves reached out arms as if beckoning her.

No way could she sleep with the dead. The studio's bright buildings poked their way, fingerlike, over the cemetery wall in an odd configuration. She could at least sneak in there and demand Enzo's help for the night, if he wouldn't make good on the IOU.

Trying to estimate where the studio kitchen must be, she crossed the graveyard, her footsteps crunching on the gravel, and used a lichen-covered headstone to grasp the wall. She slid over onto the studio grounds.

The lingering smell of fried onions guided her to the kitchen, which was empty—no Enzo or anyone else.

She crept inside the back door. It was so warm inside. Quiet. She huddled by the ceramic tiled stove. Steam came off her damp clothes.

A bright light flicked on.

"The kitchen's closed. What are you doing here?"

An older guard stood inside the door.

"Getting warm," she said. "Please let me stay."

"Who are you?"

"A friend of Enzo," she said. "He said I could stay here."

"Not on studio property, mademoiselle," he said, and knocked on the kitchen back door.

A rumpled Enzo entered, rubbing his eye with one hand while the other leaned heavily on his crutch.

"What's going on, Enzo?"

"You wake me up for this?"

"Tramps can't stay here. The studio has rules. It's a business, not a shelter." He gestured roughly, as if meaning to throw Huguette out.

Huguette shrank back, huddled shivering in her damp clothes.

"*Si* . . . but . . ." Enzo motioned the guard over. Whispered loud enough for Huguette to hear. "She's good in bed, eh, so . . ."

A tutting noise came from the guard. "Do it at a hotel. Not here." The next moment the guard was helping her up. "We'll forget it this time, young lady. You'll be escorted to the Dominican sisters' shelter on Place du Marché. It's warm there, too. Safer."

He threw a disgusted glance at Enzo.

She pinched herself not to cry.

HER FIRST THOUGHT WAS TO run away again. But the nuns who sold her baby weren't Dominican, and she was so tired.

She fell exhausted onto the canvas army bed. At least she had a soft blanket, and heat dribbled from the charcoal burning stove. The shelter was in a high-domed side chapel lined by statues of the Virgin Mary. Rows of beds provided for the bombed out, the displaced, mothers and children, and camp survivors.

The human flotsam from the war.

The nun had informed her she could stay three days. Temporary, she'd said, to help you on your feet. Then she'd need to move on.

The watery soup and chestnut flour bread didn't fill her up. How could it?

In the middle of the night she woke to cries—a Jewish woman having nightmares. A few had trickled back to Paris, blank-eyed scarecrows, some mute with terror.

The next morning, when Huguette was returning from the

crumbling showers, she found a young woman going through her satchel under her bed.

The young woman backed away, fear in her eyes. Feral. "Please don't tell . . . I didn't take anything. I'm hungry."

Her ribs poked from beneath her thin dress and her cheeks were hollow. Numbers were tattooed on the inside of her arm.

Huguette dug through her bag and handed her several coins and the last remaining Hershey's chocolate square. "Don't worry, I won't."

The woman looked away. "Thank you," she mumbled. Wary, her eyes flickered to Huguette again. "Why?"

"What happened to you wasn't right."

"Do you care?"

"A girl in my class never returned," said Huguette. "She didn't do anything wrong. You didn't, either."

Rachel, her classmate, hadn't come to school one day and her parents' apartment was empty when she and Marina had gone there to drop off Rachel's homework.

"Deported," whispered the concierge, with a furtive look.

That afternoon she and Marina joined the Catholic youth group who passed the priest's messages and warnings to those in the underground and Jewish people in hiding. Just small actions against the Germans. She should have done more, not gone along with her father, who sold to the Nazis on the black market. After school one day she heeded the warning to avoid the post office roundup of Jewish workers and bystanders by the Gestapo and scurried down another street. She'd been guilty of looking the other way.

"You pity me, *non*? Pity's useless. My family's gone."

"Mine, too. I understand."

"Understand?" A shrug of her thin shoulders. Her eyes dulled. "I don't think anyone can understand what happened in the camp."

What could she say?

"I understand losing family. But the rest—"

The young woman interrupted. "I can't unsee what I saw. You're lucky."

Shame filled her.

"I'm sorry."

The words felt so inadequate.

"It's easy for you to say sorry and pretend. Just like her."

"Who?"

The woman—now Huguette saw she was scarcely a girl, like Huguette herself—thrust the rumpled paper into her hand.

And then she was gone.

Huguette smoothed out the paper.

A photo of a woman on the first page assaulted Huguette's senses. Dark clothes, no makeup, eyes downcast—but recognizable.

It felt like the air bent in the room, and Huguette's throat filled with the taste of bile, so like the Champagne this very woman had forced her to drink . . .

The headline read: NAZI MISTRESS FILM STAR TESTIFIES.

Underneath the photo was an article:

Corinne Lelouche, actress at the former German-run Studio Étoile in Boulogne-Billancourt, will take the stand this week in her own collaboration trial. The French-born actress, 26, is accused of aiding and abetting the occupying German forces for four years during the Occupation. At Libération, Lelouche is alleged to have fled with her Nazi lover to Germany; she returned to Paris under guard . . .

The newspaper dropped from Huguette's hand as she ran to the bathroom to vomit.

EARLY JUNE 1945

Studio Étoile, Boulogne-Billancourt

~

A different guard stood at the studio gate. Huguette took no chances; she mingled with the evening worker shift on their way into the kitchen, joining the line. Enzo was doling out ladlefuls of stew to the workers, and when she reached him, he immediately looked wary.

"*Bonjour*, Enzo," she said, catching his gaze. "You owe me. Pay up and I leave."

He slopped chunky stew into her bowl and waved for her to move on. "Sorry, signorina," he said. "Manfredo's in jail. But when he come out, I get you money."

"My pockets are empty and the shelters are full. I have nowhere to go," she said. The line behind her was starting to grumble about her taking so long. Her heart pounded. She knew she had to confide in Enzo if she really wanted his help. "My papa's dead."

"Dead?" Enzo's jaw dropped briefly. He glanced down the line, gestured to Huguette. "Wait. I come to you after dinner. Eat, signorina."

Huguette stepped aside, finding a corner seat at a long table where she could hunch over her bowl and wolf down the hot, rich stew. The workers sitting around her took no notice—probably assuming she was just another extra—as they jabbered about the films currently in production, the directors and their grand visions, the actors making outrageous demands. These were the people who made the magic happen. Huguette remembered going with her *maman* to the Saturday matinee double feature. As a former dancer, her mother had loved musicals—it had been their special treat until the tuberculosis took her. The memories were bittersweet, made all the more bitter as Huguette recalled the newspaper article and looked around at these workers, wondering who of them had met Corinne Lelouche on set just a few years ago.

Finally, the canteen began to empty. Huguette stayed where she was until she was the last person remaining, just another shadow. Had Enzo forgotten about her? But there he was, unsteadily crutching his way over to sit with her. He got straight to business, too, a frown pinching his brows. "You say your papa is dead?"

"Murdered." Her mouth trembled. She leaned closer. "As a collabo. I'm next."

"I'm so sorry, signorina."

"You owe me, Enzo. Please."

"Eh, like I'm the only one who owes? The notary, Gisors, he work with your father, you know, big deals. Ask him."

The crooked *notaire*, evil incarnate? She wanted nothing to do with the traitor. She wasn't going to let Enzo pawn her off.

"My father said I could trust you, Enzo. He said you'd make good on this."

Enzo sucked in his breath.

"Does anyone know you're here?"

"How could they?"

"You say you're next," he said. "Did anyone follow you?"

She shook her head.

Enzo regarded her with a terrible mixture of pity and guilt. She squirmed under the gaze but didn't flinch. Finally, he sighed heavily, his mind evidently made up. "I have plan. I pay you back, you have place to stay. But only when you do what I say, *si*?"

"Tell me," she said.

"Promise me you do what I say, signorina?"

Apprehensive, she clutched the small satchel with her few belongings. He wasn't exactly in a position to make demands. But nor was she in a position to refuse them—she had nowhere else to turn. "I promise."

"There is a man here. Monsieur Louis. He needs extra help. I fix it you sleep in dormitory with lady workers, eat here. Mornings you help me in kitchen, serve on studio set. Then, afternoon and nighttime, work for Monsieur Louis."

She heard something in Enzo's voice. Suspicious, she asked him, "Monsieur Louis will pay me to do what?"

Enzo shook his head. "Quiet money. Like your papa do, *capito*?"

Her stomach lurched. She hated what her father used to do, scrounging black market deals. And all for what? She knew how it had ended for her last time. She couldn't risk that happening again.

But she was hungry. No roof over her head.

As if Enzo could see her apprehension on her face, he added, "Better now. Safer than during war. Dealing with GIs is easy. Trade American stuff for Monsieur Louis. You agree?"

Her mind went back to the GIs who'd given her a ride—their friend Ralph who had Hershey's bars. They had been rambunctious but kind. Definitely better than the shady characters she remembered coming through the café—Enzo himself included.

Her jaw set tightly, she nodded. "I agree. But I expect you to repay me, Enzo. *Capito?*"

"Like father, like daughter," he said with a grin.

She winced. She wasn't like her father. Was she?

"I ask Monsieur Louis tonight. If he say yes, then tomorrow you help me in the kitchen, then for Monsieur Louis after in the evening. Now come."

She followed Enzo to the long room off the kitchen with ten or so curtained bunk beds.

"*Allora*, signorinas sleep here. Come and go. Like train station. Keep your head down so no one notices you. It's crazy. Big filming right now, they work all night."

AFTER ENZO LEFT, PROMISING HE'D take her to meet Monsieur Louis in the morning, she found blankets, settled in an empty bunk, and pulled the curtain shut.

It was nothing like the shelter. In the distance, she heard happy voices, laughter, and the clang of pans. Around her, the rustling of curtains, yawns and then snores. Like at home above the café. A lifetime ago.

She clutched the tiny vest she'd knit for Hugues. All she had of him apart from the ache of missing him.

Her eyes grew heavy.

THRILLED BUT TRYING NOT TO show it, Huguette served breakfast to a well-known actress, her hair in metal curlers as she studied a script. Next to her, a stagehand in overalls read the horse racing news at the long wooden table for the crews and actors. No one paid her the slightest attention.

When the serving was done, Enzo pulled her aside. He smiled, passed her a chipped cup of steaming café au lait, part of a crusty baguette, and a slab of butter, pale yellow as if kissed by the sun.

Her eyes widened at the bread made of white flour, not ground chestnut meal. Real coffee, too. The milk was frothy.

France's fields lay fallow. Few crops had been planted since the Germans melted agricultural machinery for arms during the Occupation. Food rationing continued.

But these studio employees ate like kings. What a treat. She'd enjoy it while she could.

She spread the creamy butter on the bit of baguette, dunked it, and savored the familiar taste. For just a moment, she luxuriated, rubbing her toes over the worn tile floor. Enzo was stirring pots simmering on the stove. Her stomach was full; she felt safe, warm. Then Enzo sat down across from her.

"Bad news, signorina."

Her grip tightened on the cup of coffee.

Enzo looked around, then leaned forward to murmur, "This morning, people come looking for a girl. The guard man told me."

Her? Social services sniffing around? Or the Paris police?

"Maybe it's you, signorina, but I say nothing."

Enzo put his finger over his lips.

Now he was covering for her? He'd want something. To cancel his debt?

"But no one knows I'm here."

Her food threatened to come up—she was sick to her stomach with anxiety. She wanted to run, but she had nowhere to go. Or hide.

The kitchen door opened; a woman wearing dusty overalls strolled in, and Enzo quickly leaned back from Huguette. "Ahh, *buongiorno*, Marie," he said. "Perfect time to introduce you. This is Marie, stage set director here. Meet my little cousin. She helped my uncle in the café. Smart, hard worker. She's the one, Marie."

"Ah, the Parisian orphan who's good with numbers?"

So that's how Enzo had explained her, vouched for her. He cast her a meaningful look. *Go along with it.* Never mind that obviously he was Italian and she was French—all kinds of things happened in the war, and people understood there were multiple kinds of family. Huguette nodded.

"What's your name?"

"Huguette, madame."

"Huguette, how do I know you won't steal from an almost blind man?" said Marie.

Anger flared up in her. "Accusing me of being a thief?"

Enzo laughed. "Such spirit."

Marie joined in the laughter. Poked her and winked. "Can't take a joke?"

Joke?

"She's a spirited little Parisian all the way," said Enzo. "But I see her in action. Smart girl. I know this sure, Marie."

Marie smiled again, sizing her up. "Let's go meet Louis. He might just like you."

"**Forget it**," **Louis de Jouvenal** said.

On the walk over to Louis's lodgings, Marie had explained to Huguette who, exactly, Monsieur Louis was: Studio Étoile's most famous film director and producer. In his heyday, he'd run the studio with an iron fist in a velvet glove. Now he was an old man, pulling the strings from afar. Huguette could see that power still in him, hear it in his commanding voice, even as he sat in a sagging wicker armchair, his hair more salt than pepper, moth holes in his silk bathrobe.

Sunlight drifted over the gray-whiskered German shepherd who cocked one ear, then fell back asleep on the tile floor. Huguette watched Louis feel for an ashtray to stub a cigar that had already gone out.

"Louis, the film's behind schedule. Again." Marie took Louis's liver-spotted hand. "This girl will do the jobs I do: read you the scripts, the newspaper, go to the post and bank. *And* she'll assist you with Enzo's jobs."

Louis lived in a *passage* lined by small but exclusive limestone houses surrounding a postage stamp–sized cobbled courtyard with an old well. Not far from the studio, yet village-like and secluded. The dark-paneled rooms smelled fresh. Sunflowers nodded at the window. The house gave off a whiff of old man smell, but Huguette liked how the furniture was polished, the floor gleamed, and framed movie posters lined the walls.

Movies he'd directed with big stars. Stars like Corinne Lelouche. The woman who—

"You've got a mouth, haven't you?" said Louis, interrupting her thoughts. "Speak."

He'd turned in his chair and faced her. She tried not to focus on his clouded right eye. Something in his strict demeanor reminded her of her father. She had to focus on her meal ticket.

"I'm a good worker, monsieur."

"How old are you?"

"Almost eighteen."

"Why aren't you in school?"

Huguette shifted on her feet. Birds twittered outside the window. "No family left. Only my cousin, Enzo." A little lie, but otherwise why would he trust her? It was the same thing Enzo had already told Marie—best to be consistent.

"You didn't answer my question."

"It's complicated, monsieur."

He snorted. "Life's complicated. Can you read and write, calculate sums?"

"Yes, monsieur. I was top of my class. I served in my parents' café, and *maman* taught me bookkeeping. When she got ill, I took over the café accounts."

"Accounts?"

She nodded. "I kept track of all the books for Papa until . . ." Her throat caught. "Libération."

Marie put her hand on Louis's shoulder. "Enzo already vouched for her, too," said Marie. "I'll check her work at the end of the week."

"And how will I pay for this? You think I'm made of money?"

"I'm taking care of it. But something tells me she'll earn her keep."

Huguette and Marie walked back in sunlit air filtered by damp greenery, sounds of birds and a horse cart clomping over the cobblestones.

"Is Louis your relative?" she asked Marie.

"We're all family at Étoile," said Marie. "Louis fed us and our families during the war. We hardly had wood or nails to build the sets but he'd find it. He taught me everything I know. Somehow, he kept the studio running under the Germans."

A collaborator.

Her stomach jumped.

"So you know my idol, the actress Corinne Lelouche. Did you work with her?"

Marie stopped dead in her tracks, fixing Huguette with a sharp glare. "You think it's glamorous here—movie stars strutting all over the place? And I'm some gossip who'll tell you all their secrets?"

"*Mais non—*"

"My world is production. Not actors," Marie said coldly. "And Louis is a genius, a world-renowned icon in the film industry. If you're starstruck, fine. But if you can't handle working for him, tell me now before I waste my time on you."

A world-renowned icon? All Huguette had seen was a haggard, half-blind man with a temper. And did she really want to be painted with the same brush as yet another collabo?

"He doesn't like me," Huguette said. "He thinks I'm too young."

"*Non*, that's just his way." Marie exhaled a taut huff of air. "I wish I didn't need your help, but . . . you heard me. We're about to miss our deadline, and I can't do my job on set while helping Louis with everything he needs."

Agitated, Huguette rubbed her wrists. It didn't matter if she stayed here or left—she needed money.

"*Alors*, if you don't steal or mess up, you'll get forty francs on Friday."

Marie had just made a mistake in telling Huguette she was desperate. So she took a chance.

"Fifty?"

Marie hesitated.

"You better be worth it."

That decided her.

"I am."

June 1945

Louis de Jouvenal's house, Boulogne-Billancourt

―

"I won't hide the money anymore, Louis," said a raised male voice. "The studio's different now."

Huguette, taking off her muddy boots in the cloakroom, almost dropped her string bag of baguettes when she heard the man shouting in Louis's salon.

"Jacques," Louis was saying, "be reasonable."

She couldn't hear the rest. She moved closer, peeking past the stacked equipment boxes that clogged the way. Through the salon's half-open door, she saw Louis sitting across from a man she recognized from the studio compound as the accountant with the bad combover.

"*Mais oui*, the money I stole from the *Boches* kept the studio running, didn't it?" Louis pounded the table. "You got a paycheck. So did everyone I kept on payroll. What's your problem?"

On the table, two glasses and two empty bottles: one Cognac, one Calvados.

Jacques's mouth curled with derision. "My problem is that your numbers don't add up. The account's empty. I can't do this anymore."

A snort of disgust. "You did it before."

"That's different."

"You're too picky, Jacques."

"Picky?" Jacques slammed a fist on the table. "Stealing from the Nazis is one thing, but robbing Étoile's different. The studio's getting audited because of your court investigation."

"Then get creative, like you always do."

"No more." A sarcastic laugh. "You'll have better luck with the black market."

Huguette tried to get closer to hear more clearly, but she slipped and the boxes toppled with a loud crash. Caught eavesdropping—now she'd get fired.

"*Excusez-moi . . .*"

She didn't finish as Jacques whipped past her in a huff, stepping over the boxes carelessly to grab his coat. He slammed the door shut on his way out.

Hesitantly, Huguette emerged and made her way over to Louis, who was staring into the dying fire. He was always cold. When she got close enough, she wanted to shrink away again; Louis reeked of liquor. He swiped the empty Cognac bottle onto the floor. "I stole that filth from the *Boche*. No wonder it tastes like piss."

Huguette took a rag and wiped the wet rings on the table.

"Coffee, monsieur?"

He grabbed her wrist, his grip tight like wire. "Listen, my little girl, you're going to do Enzo's jobs, *n'est-ce pas?*"

Her throat caught. "*Oui*, monsieur."

"Seems like Enzo and Marie trust you. But why should I?"

Her pulse raced. He was drunk, unpredictable.

"Why? Well, why wouldn't you, monsieur?"

"During the war, I learned the hard way not to trust anybody." He tapped his cloudy eye, and she realized that he meant the First World War—before she'd even been born.

She thought yesterday had been the interview, the trial. But evidently, she'd have to defend herself again today. "I can speak GI English, and I'm good with numbers. You've seen the housekeeping budget Marie gave me, and I kept my father's accounts in the café since I was thirteen. And . . . after *maman* went to the sanatorium, my father had me keep two ledgers."

Louis's face barely changed. He nodded slowly. "One ledger for the tax man and another for himself, *oui?*"

"You could say that, monsieur."

Louis reached in his silk bathrobe pocket. Handed her a key. "Unlock the bottom drawer in my desk. Take out the two ledgers in there."

She did.

"Now make coffee. We've got work to do."

DESPITE HUGUETTE'S MISGIVINGS, READING THE ledgers came as second nature to her. The feeling was as familiar as attending Mass and feeding pigeons on the Seine.

Louis and Jacques had cooked the books as her father had taught her—but they'd made mistakes. Maybe it had fooled the Nazis during the war, but now there was a reckoning.

"There's discrepancies, Louis."

He sipped his coffee. "They need to disappear," he said. "Show me how smart I think you are. Work some magic."

She grinned. Magic? Put that way, it sounded fun, and she liked a challenge. She got to work on the back of an old envelope while Louis drank his coffee, occasionally flipping through the script in his lap—which she doubted he could see at all, even with the magnifying glass he clutched like a lifeline. Huguette didn't care why Louis wanted the books cooked: debts, medical bills—he'd have a reason like her father. She had little choice.

Again.

After twenty minutes, she looked up. "There might be a way."

"Eh?" Interested, he leaned forward. "How do you mean?"

"There's legitimate loopholes in accounting."

"Legitimate loopholes." Louis laughed. "That's a new one."

"My papa said that's what accountants do all the time. You know, professionals, who know what to look for and avoid—not like that Jacques."

Louis raised his demitasse in a toast and clinked against hers. His hand shook with a slight tremor.

"Play your cards right, *ma petite*, and I'll teach you what I know. Films, life, it's all the same. Survival."

Survival. Huguette knew a thing or two about that already. Could she stand to learn any more?

"Go ask Enzo for his GI contact. Let's try you in the field."

THE WIND CUT LIKE GLASS through the uncommonly wet June afternoon. Huguette's eyes hurt from squinting against the rain by the time she reached the grounds of the former Château Rothschild, requisitioned during Occupation by the Nazis and now by the Americans. The once-formal garden was a forest of army tents. She followed excited schoolchildren and housewives carrying baskets through the back gate in the wire fence. She passed war-torn, bullet-scarred château outbuildings, a dry ornamental lake, and headless statues.

A short GI, smiling and red-cheeked in the wind, handed out small boxes labeled Lifebuoy and Ivory soap, cans of condensed milk.

She'd found the GI easily. Enzo had said it would be difficult. Maybe he'd underestimated her.

The GI quickly pocketed the francs the housewives thrust

in his hand, and when a few latecomers tried to approach, he made a mock sad face. "All gone . . . *fini*," he said, lifting up an empty box.

"Butter tomorrow, monsieur?" asked one of the housewives, covering her basket contents with a checked dishcloth.

"Same time, same station," he said. He tapped his wristwatch, pointed to the gate. "Okay?"

The housewife grinned. "Okay, monsieur."

Every GI seemed to end his last sentence with an okay.

Huguette nudged forward.

He glanced at her. Piercing gray eyes that matched the sky, a reddish-blond mustache.

She smiled. "You're Ralph?"

"I might be."

"*Excusez* my English. I'm rusty."

"Sound pretty good to me."

She smiled and showed her teeth, like the GIs did. "Nice Americans said to ask for you, Monsieur Ralph. They said you have real chocolate. Hershey."

"Kids." He grinned back. "Come back tomorrow and bring your mama, okay?" He slipped a chocolate bar into her hand. "Between us, shhh."

"*Merci*, Monsieur Ralph, too kind," she said. "But I'm not here just for chocolate." She glanced back over her shoulder—the housewives were leaving, paying no attention. "My cousin Enzo has something for you."

He raised his furry eyebrows and lowered his voice. "The Italian, he's your cousin?"

"*Si*," she sniffled. Looked down. "My uncle died. Monte Casino."

"Monte Casino? That's tough. I'm sorry, kid."

"My cousin my only family now. But Enzo broke his leg. He ask me to help his business with you. Cognac."

She hoped that's what came out. That he understood.

"Listen, kid. I'll go half on the Cognac, say that. Enzo will understand. Make sure it gets here tomorrow night."

She remembered to give a thumbs-up. "Okay!"

Evening, June 1945

Boulogne-Billancourt

In the Woods by Former Château Rothschild

—

Huguette pushed a wobbling baby buggy through the woods. Louis's Cognac clanked inside.

With each step, Enzo's words rang in her ears. *Like father, like daughter.*

This was wrong. Roped in again, she felt dirty.

In the forest's chill, sweat streamed down her back, her hair plastered damp on her scalp. Her breath shot vapor, her leg muscles strained, her arms ached.

The muddy earth fought her every step. Fleeting images of her baby boy blanketed inside, instead of contraband Cognac for the black market, filled her mind.

She hit a rock and grasped the buggy handle before it could overturn.

And then she sensed someone was following her. She'd been so intent on her mission, she only now registered leaves crackling, a twig snapping.

A fizzing shiver in the small of her back traveled up to her neck. Someone or something was there, watching her from the darkness.

"Monsieur Ralph? It's me. Enzo's cousin."

An arm wrapped around her neck. The stink of cheap whiskey hit her face, and hot breath brushed her ear.

Her scream got silenced by a hand clapped over her mouth. A man's body was thrusting against her.

"Calm down," said an American voice.

She squirmed hard, trying to fight her way out. Wild panic filled her.

He crooked his elbow to lock her neck tighter. So tight she couldn't breathe. The air felt ripped from her lungs.

He took his hand from her mouth.

"Stop . . . let me go . . ."

He slapped her.

She lost her balance; she felt him pulling her coat off, ripping her sleeves. The baby buggy overturned, bottles spilling out against the forest floor.

When he tumbled down onto her, she bit his arm.

"Oww—hey!" He slapped her again.

Each time he hit her, she withdrew into herself. She wanted to fight—she strained forward to bite him again—memories were surfacing, another pair of hands holding her down.

"Quit moving or it'll hurt more . . ."

With her weakening legs, she tried to kick him off her.

She felt another stinging slap, then a whoosh of chill air. He'd let go.

Dizzy, she dove away, scraping herself against the branches of the underbrush. She heard shouts and thuds of fists pounding flesh. She scrambled to her scratched knees, shaking as she curled around her stomach.

"Hands off the locals, soldier."

The downed man yelped, sounding like an animal in pain.

"You ship out at dawn. Get to the barracks or I'll throw you in a cage where you belong."

The huddled figure of the GI took off, limping, through the crisp night.

"Are you okay, mademoiselle?"

In the dim moonlight she recognized a soldier who'd stood patrol near the base gate.

"Did he hurt you?"

Her face burned and her palms bled. Steeling herself, she sucked out a pebble from her torn palm and spit it out with blood. Trembling, she shook her head.

"Go home. Not safe for you out here."

Her fear turned to frustration.

"But I'm meeting Monsieur Ralph."

"Ralph? He's not coming. His girl left him for a damn sailor."

Huguette struggled to keep up. Her mind was still spinning, her body still ached with the man's phantom hands grabbing her. But she could piece together enough. "Ah, his *amour* and another man . . . So he is gone?"

He glanced back in the direction of the base. "You should go home. My unit's going home, too."

"Going to the USA, monsieur?"

"Tomorrow," he said.

Through her fog, Huguette realized with alarm she'd have no way to sell the Cognac for Louis. She imagined Louis's wrath—she couldn't let this deal slip away. "You know, Monsieur Ralph and I did business."

The GI looked at the overturned buggy, a broken bottle of Cognac dripping. "It's not a good idea anymore," he said. "Not for the likes of you. You're a nice girl. Just a kid."

Did he think she did this for a hobby? Fun?

"Ralph owes me, monsieur."

"Sorry, kid." He reached in his pockets and thrust a handful of fifty-franc notes at her. "Worthless to me now."

The wind whipped the notes away. She ran after them and picked them up, disregarding the brambles.

The American was already marching back toward the fence. She couldn't let him go without a contact.

"*Merci*, thank you, thank you," she said, running back to him. "You've been kind. Please, my cousin's sick and I must sell Cognac to buy medicine. Now it's all we have. Monsieur Ralph said he knew people."

He shrugged.

"Please, I need to sell this," she said, desperate, and reached to tug at his sleeve. "Can you give me a name?"

Finally, he slowed, and she saw hesitation in his eyes. "Well, there's the Voltaire gang."

That sounded promising. "Help me. How do I find them?"

He sighed. "Dang, okay," he said, "Pete's here on Tuesdays. He's the contact."

"Pete's a GI?"

"Went AWOL."

"I don't understand."

"Look, be careful. Promise?"

This GI seemed to really worry for her. Touched, she nodded.

"Pete left the army—not a GI anymore. But he acts like he is. And before he left, he stole guns."

JUNE 1945

Boulogne-Billancourt

~

Huguette waited in the crowded post office at the Poste Restante window, distracted by the man behind her in line, his racking cough and the old red wine reeking from his jacket.

"Hélène Foy?" called the bored postal clerk from the grilled window. He held an envelope. "Hélène Foy?"

Remembering her new name, Huguette stepped forward to claim the letter.

After she'd explained to Louis about the GI market drying up, she'd told him about the new contact, Pete, and how she'd strike a deal with the Voltaire gang.

"You're a smart girl," said Louis. "I reward smart people."

Thanks to Louis's seemingly endless connections, she'd become Hélène Foy—a name from the Red Cross missing list. Twenty years old, born in Boulogne-Billancourt. Hélène was ready to sell Louis's Cognac without the baggage of Huguette Faure weighing her down.

Pleased, Louis also suggested a new look for the ID photo. When Huguette had admitted she couldn't afford it, he'd laughed—reminded her where she was. That there was always a way. He told her to ferry dinner to the makeup artists, wig makers, and wardrobe crew on the backstage lot during night shoots. To keep the dishes warm and make herself useful.

To her surprise, it worked.

The coiffeuse laughed. "So you want a new hairdo? You must really want to work in films, eh?"

Huguette faked a blush, shook her head. "I want to go incognito, you know, start over," she said. "To avoid my old boyfriend."

The women of the crew looked at each other, understanding passing between them. "We'll take care of you."

And they had. In the mirror, Huguette saw not only a whole new young woman, but a whole new chance at life.

"Mademoiselle, your identification, *s'il vous plaît*," said the postal clerk.

Calmly, Huguette showed her new identification card. No one paid her any attention. She clutched the letter and thanked the dismissive clerk.

At last, a letter postmarked from Paris. It could only be from her friend Marina. Finally news from her one connection to home, to what she was before, to people she knew.

And to who was after her.

Overjoyed, she found a park bench and eagerly slit open the envelope.

Marina's reply to her letter was brief:

Chére Hélène,

I like your new name. Chic. School is so boring. The nuns put me to sleep. Rafael thinks he's a big deal because he got shot—a graze of shrapnel—annoying—remember? Our youth group will volunteer in Chartres this summer. It will be no fun without you. Your life in the movie world sounds more exciting than mine. That actress you asked about is facing prison at Frésnes, that's all I could find out.

Your café reopened. It's that man Monsieur Gisors who owns it now, not that he runs it. Lucky for him he managed to buy it from your father before he died, I guess. The whole thing is so sad to see. I don't stop there, I don't like him at all. I see Yvon, the Commie, a lot on my way home from school. Céline from the flower shop, too. She's got a GI boyfriend who gives her lots of presents, Chanel perfume, a fur coat. He's in some gang but I didn't tell you, okay? She asks about you and wants to make contact. But I didn't breathe a word.

When they painted the café, I found your father's old blue briefcase thrown in their trash heap. I took it for you. There's his notebook I remember him always writing in, and some business stuff inside. Stuff you'd know about. I grabbed it before anyone noticed. It's "safe."

There was another collabo denounced on my street. But a lot of collabos buy people off, my father says, and it depends on who you know.

Be careful out there. It's still not safe in Paris. Not for you or lots of people. Keep safe where you are.

I miss you! Write back when you can!

Love, Marina

Huguette clutched the letter. *It depends on who you know.* Some things never change.

But her father selling the café to that man Gisors? Never. She would have known.

Then again, her father had lied to her and betrayed her in the worst way possible. Maybe he had lied to her about the café, too. Maybe he had sold it right under her nose.

Life in Paris continued without her, of course it did. Huguette battled encroaching homesickness as she washed dishes in the studio's staff kitchen. Pushed little Hugues from her thoughts. Like always.

Survived.

In the dining area, actors were drinking coffee and reading *Le Parisien* at the large table. One pointed to an article and the others gathered around.

Huguette was bussing the table, stacked the dirty cups as she half listened to the conversation.

"That slut's trial is almost over. Pierre, didn't you work with her?"

"Corinne Lelouche? *Bien sûr*," said the lighting tech.

Alert, Huguette scraped crumbs off the plates and stacked them on her tray.

"Not a bad camera angle to her face," said Pierre. "The camera loved her."

"Wasn't she dumb as a post?" asked Huguette.

Had she really asked that out loud?

Everybody was looking at her; Pierre laughed. "Funny, she always said that. I guess she was no genius. It was all instinctive. You can learn to act, but the good ones are born with instinct."

The dirty glass she held fell shattering to the floor.

Pierre and the others stared.

Huguette, cheeks burning, ran to grab the broom. By the time she returned to sweep up, only Pierre remained.

She blurted out her question before she could stop herself. "Did you see her Nazi lover?"

Pierre snorted and stubbed out his cigarette. "Which one?"

His offhand tone sickened her. Huguette's hands tightened on the broom handle, and her voice quavered. "The one with an eye patch."

Pierre opened his mouth to answer, but before she could hear it, she was running outside to dry heave into the bushes. The nightmare was back.

June 5, 1944 • One Year Earlier

Île de la Cité, Paris

—

Outside Café du Soleil, a black car pulled up on the quai, rare these days. The blue-painted streetlights, camouflaged against aircraft, caught on the dull sheen of the roof. Huguette, clearing off a table, had been watching the car through the window, so she watched as a stocky man in a double-breasted suit and fedora entered the café and made a beeline for her. He handed her an envelope.

"What's this, monsieur?" she said, surprised.

"An invitation to a party. For you."

Huguette stood a little straighter and opened the envelope to see a thick card with embossed gold letters reading *Treasure Hunt, 16 Place Victor Hugo*. She was just a schoolgirl with no connections—who would possibly invite her specifically? "From who?"

"Let's go. Your father gave his permission."

Huguette turned back to see her papa behind the counter. "What's going on, Papa? Is this some sort of special surprise?"

He was concentrated on uncorking a bottle of Burgundy. "You heard the man. It's a party."

She wanted to be excited, but there was something strange in the way he wouldn't meet her eye. She guessed, "Does this have to do with that German?"

This morning, her father had met with a Nazi with an eye patch; they'd talked for at least an hour in the cellar where Huguette couldn't hear. It had seemed like a big deal, as afterward her papa had promised all the workers in the café a pay raise.

"Just go, Huguette."

His hands shook and he spilled wine from the bottle.

He was normally so deft, despite his missing pinky and partial ring finger. You'd miss it unless you watched him closely. Huguette frowned. "Is something wrong, Papa?"

The man in the fedora had come up behind her and tapped his keys on the counter. "Hurry up, or you'll be late."

Several Wehrmacht officers raised their empty glasses from a table. "Where's our wine?"

Huguette's father turned to serve the soldiers.

The fedora beckoned her. "It's almost curfew. The soirée's already started."

Huguette watched her father for a moment before looking down at herself. She was still in her school uniform and couldn't imagine going to a party at all, let alone in this state. "But I have nothing to wear."

"You'll do fine," the man dismissed. He smiled at Mylène, the cashier. "Where's your lipstick?"

Mylène raised a quizzical eyebrow. "Not your shade, I'm afraid."

"Share it with her, eh?"

Mylène pulled a lipstick from her purse, handed it to Huguette, then turned away to take a waiter's bill.

The next thing Huguette knew, she was in the black car riding along the quai. Soft leather seats and the hint of stale perfume.

The yellow headlights were covered, with only a middle slit emitting dim light through the charcoal haze of the city.

How in the world could the driver see his way?

During the Occupation's four long years, she'd never left the Île de la Cité after curfew. This evening it seemed like another world. She smelled the Seine on her right, that familiar waft of algae. So quiet apart from the gears shifting. Few people were on the streets and the city felt asleep. Unconscious.

"Who invited me?"

The man was surveying her in the rearview mirror.

"I'm just the driver. Put your lipstick on and relax."

Mylène's lipstick was carmine, a brash red that looked like a stoplight on her face. Huguette felt absurd—like she was playing dress-up. Whoever had invited her to this party, they'd be sorry.

The driver cursed as he slowed down; a police control was stopping them. Huguette's pulse skittered. Would they be arrested?

He showed a pass, a stamped *laissez-passer*. A flashlight beam poked in the car, then they were waved on.

"Where are we?" Huguette asked meekly.

"The sixteenth."

The poshest *arrondissement*—no place Huguette had ever been before. She gazed with wonder at the beautiful buildings with intricate balconies and even window boxes full of flowers until the black car turned and pulled under a porte cochere. The hulk of a big house loomed behind it.

The car door opened. A broad-chested man wearing an old-fashioned red uniform took her arm to help her out.

"Your card, please, mademoiselle?"

Huguette handed it to him.

"This way."

A tall door with blackout curtains revealed a circular

cloakroom. On the black-and-white tiles stood several people looking as lost as she felt.

"*Bonsoir*," she said, her manners kicking in.

A dwarf in a tuxedo smiled and returned the greeting. The other two, a barefoot vagabond with torn clothes and a woman with a curled mustache, ignored her.

A bell rang and the red-uniformed man motioned the group up a short flight of stairs to a large landing, which was sparsely peopled. The Gestapo officer who'd visited Huguette's father this morning stepped forward, still wearing the eye patch and his black SS uniform.

"You're here," he said to Huguette. "Excellent. I'm glad you got the invitation in time."

Something about this man—his confidence and wandering gaze—bothered her. Her hands trembled.

"Why me?" Huguette asked.

The officer caught her arm and steered her into an expansive salon with a dripping chandelier, the largest she'd ever seen.

"Don't you like parties, Huguette?"

Women dressed like pages from fashion magazines glided by in shimmery sequined slips, slinking satin gowns, laughing, drinking, and smoking.

"Siggie! Over here!" one of them said.

Siggie, the German, smiled and joined the women by the window, leaving her alone.

Huguette didn't belong here. She felt so out of place—stranded, a fish out of water in her school uniform.

"Champagne?" A chilled coupe was thrust into her hand by a brown-haired woman wearing a gold scarf and matching beaded dress. It glittered and rustled as she moved. "You'll need it, *ma petite*. Make yourself at home."

"Is this your party?" Huguette said, unsure what the woman meant. She sipped. Bitter, and the fizzing bubbles burned her throat.

"The countess—well, she calls herself a countess—she says it's a treasure hunt. I think you might help win the prize."

"*Moi?*" Huguette sniffed. A sickly sweetness rose from a burning pellet resembling tar. Transfixed, she watched as two women inhaled its spiraling smoke through long pipes.

"No opium for you. Siggie's determined to win, but you have to put up a fight. That's his nature, you know that."

Siggie, the German. Where had he gone?

"I'm not sure why I'm here."

"Ah, another one," said a blond woman in green satin and beads that left more of her exposed than they covered. She touched Huguette's collar. She smelled of something expensive, reminding Huguette of *maman*'s scent for special occasions. "He adores Catholic schoolgirls."

"I'm . . . confused."

"Even better." She grinned. "I went to Catholic school, too."

Huguette felt dizzy. Their faces wobbled. "Who are you?"

Another coupe replaced the empty one in her hand. "You don't recognize me? I'm an actress." The blond laughed. "Corinne."

Corinne pushed Huguette's hand, tilted the coupe back to her lips. Powerless, she drank more, coughing against the bubbles.

Maybe the actress looked a bit familiar. Huguette's thoughts fuzzed as she tried to think.

"Weren't you on a movie poster at the Rex?"

The blond laughed again. "Probably. Who can keep track of that sort of thing?"

"She has the memory of a goldfish," said the dark-haired woman, grinning at the blond, Corinne. "Don't you?"

"I'm dumb as a post, but the camera loves me. We use what works, eh?"

The dark-haired woman yawned. "I'm bored." She'd lifted a small mirror with what appeared to be powdered sugar across it. "Want some?"

Corinne shook her head. "Lay off, Misia," she said, protectively putting her arm around Huguette.

"Why? She might like it."

"She's just a kid."

Huguette felt odd being discussed as if she weren't there.

"Live and learn," said Misia. "Life's tough."

Someone turned on the radio, a big brown mahogany piece. Static sounds, then the blare of horns.

"Let's dance."

Corinne peered at her. Up close, under the makeup, Corinne's skin looked dimpled and bumpy.

"Did Siggie pick you for your eyes?"

People constantly commented on the different cast to Huguette's left eye. The pale topaz contrasting with her other eye, an olive green. Heterochromia, the doctor had called it.

"You're marked—that's a sign," Corinne said, giving a knowing smile. "Look, kid, whatever happens, make sure to get something out of the sturmbannführer."

At least that's what she thought Corinne said.

"What?"

"Gestapo Sturmbannführer Sigmund Muller." She winked. "Your patron, Siggie."

Misia, the dark-haired one, rubbed white powder from her nose. "She's right. Make him pay. Otherwise you climb up the same rope every time."

She heard their tinkling laughter. Her legs buckled. The coupe was empty. Is this what champagne did? She caught the velvet drapery, trying to stand upright.

Everything swirled, moved in slow motion. People were turning toward the front of the room, clapping.

Above the noise, one voice rose: "After hunting in Paris I found all my treasures," said Siggie.

He pointed to the dwarf wearing the tuxedo, the vagabond, the woman with the mustache.

The partygoers applauded. The woman next to Huguette wore only a mauve scarf; another woman had shed her dress. A man wearing lipstick kissed a man in a top hat and tails on the divan. The radio blared.

"Tell us who wins, Countess," said Siggie, smiling.

The countess, an older woman with heavy makeup, jeweled rings on every thick finger, and a silk red dress encasing her stout body, returned the smile. "But the grand treasure hunt prize—one of my little Renoirs—depends on if you brought a virgin, Siggie."

Siggie was pulling Huguette over, holding her shoulder hard as he raised his glass in his other hand.

"I've got her."

Huguette stiffened. "What are you talking about?"

"A Catholic schoolgirl virgin. I win."

She slapped him so hard her hand stung.

"A feisty one, too." He pulled her tight. "Bet she's the last one in Paris." Hoots of laughter, cheers, and more applause.

She struggled, screaming, as he dragged her through the crowd into a bedroom.

The partygoers laughed louder.

HUGUETTE WOKE UP SHIVERING ON a cold soaked sheet. Darkness. She heard voices, the crackling of a radio.

Shaking, she stumbled off the bed, crawled across the floor, feeling around for her clothes. Her body felt raw, torn, and bruised. Defiled.

So ashamed. A sob escaped her.

"This is the BBC Home Service . . . the Allied Command . . ."

Huguette lay on the floor, listening to the radio somewhere down the hallway. Concentrating on the barely familiar words helped quell the roaring within her.

Siggie found her like that. Grinned and adjusted his eye patch, reached down for her. "I missed you, my little virgin with the strange eyes."

Rallying herself, she scrambled away. She would jump out of the window before she let him touch her again.

But before it came to that, a knock sounded. The Nazi answered the door, where a soldier handed him a telegram. A brief conversation followed.

Invasion was the only word she caught.

He sat down on the bed and dialed a number on the black phone. The telegram dangled from his fingers. Siggie carried on a guttural conversation in German, then slammed the phone receiver down.

"Did the Allies invade?" she asked.

His laugh sounded like a bark. The last thing she'd expected him to do.

"Has the invasion started? Is the war over?"

"You'd like that, wouldn't you?"

Maybe she should shut up. But she couldn't stop herself.

"My papa will get you."

From outside the window came soldiers' shouts and the rumble of trucks in the street. Strength filled her.

He shook his head. "I don't think so. You wouldn't want him to get in trouble for the work he did with me, would you?"

"But the Allies—"

"I think we keep this between us. Otherwise I'll have him shot for breaking the law. He is, after all, an infamous black marketer." He grinned in the charcoal light of the overcast morning. Grabbed her hair so tight her scalp burned.

"Now let's have some fun."

June 6, 1944

Île de la Cité, Paris

Bone tired, Huguette slipped into the bright-lit Café du Soleil. Not only did her raw skin sting, her senses were sharpened. Had it only been yesterday evening she'd done her homework at the cashier's—munched a *tartine* and worried about her assignments?

It must be plain as day to everyone. They'd see through her. Mark her as defiled after the night with a one-eyed Nazi monster.

Around her the café hummed with clients. The bus driver sipped ersatz coffee, the delivery man pushed his beer dolly toward the dumbwaiter, its wheels clacking over the worn tiles. Like any other morning, but it wasn't.

Her world was forever different.

She quivered with guilt. She felt dirty.

Luc served clients while her father joked with a patron as he swiped a towel over the zinc counter, gleaming in the sunlight.

"*Ça va*, Huguette?" Mylène said from behind the cash register, a deep scrutiny in her eyes.

She couldn't return Mylène's gaze. Or answer.

Hot with shame, she ran past the cash register and upstairs

to their living quarters. Mylène knew she hadn't come back last night—probably everyone else did, too.

It must be written all over her face.

Her hair was matted with him, she stank of his smell. The insides of her legs were sticky. She wanted to throw up.

Under her ripped school uniform, her torn heart weighed on her chest like a stone.

"Huguette." Her father stood tapping his watch at the bathroom door. She hadn't heard him. "You're late for school."

Was that all he could say?

"I'm not going to school like this," she shouted. "Or ever again."

He entered the bathroom and shut the door. His mouth tightened. His eyes were bloodshot. "Don't raise your voice to me, young lady."

Where was the Papa she'd trusted? The father who had been the closest person to her in the world, besides her late *maman*?

"Just a party, you said." Her voice rose. "Go along with it, you said."

"Quit making a scene," he said between his teeth. "People can hear."

The water faucet dripped. Steam fogged the mirror.

"How much did you get for selling me, Papa?"

A vein in his forehead pulsed. "What?"

"How could you send me with that Nazi when you knew what was going to happen? Why didn't you tell me?"

"It was a party," he said. "That's all I knew. Simply a party, Huguette."

She didn't believe him.

"Do you know what he did to me, Papa?" A sob rose in her throat. She couldn't stop shaking. "I trusted you."

Her father looked away.

"Answer me."

"Huguette, it wasn't supposed to be like this."

Her lips trembled. "You know what happened at that party." She took a deep breath. "Tell me why you didn't protect me. Tell me why you took their money and let him . . ." Her throat caught.

Sweat beaded her father's brow. "There were huge bills for *maman*'s operation and sanatorium. I went into debt."

"Why didn't you pay for that with all the expensive Champagne you hide down in the cellar?"

"Try to understand."

In the bulb's harsh light she saw her father's slumped shoulders. He'd buried his head in his hands. When he looked up, tears ran down his cheeks. "He would've shot us both if I didn't cooperate."

She'd lost her virginity and her innocence. All trust in her father had shattered. Now she didn't know what to say.

"We're alive, Huguette. We survived."

"At my cost. I paid for it, Papa."

He wiped his cheeks with the back of his hand.

"How do you think I kept us afloat?"

So she was sacrificed. But that was all wrong. Cutting through her rage and humiliation was the nagging worry over the one-eyed Nazi's threats. "One-eye threatened to have you shot as a black marketeer. But I won't go again," she said, gathering her courage.

She grabbed a washcloth to scrub her face.

"You have to do something. Tell the commissaire, you know him."

"Monsieur Remy?" Mylène's voice was calling upstairs. "You're needed."

Her father grabbed her shoulders tight. "Tell no one. It's not just my life but yours on the line, *comprends*?"

He meant she had to live with this. Carry this secret shame.

"The nuns will find out and so will everyone at school, Papa." Her chest tightened.

"That's the least of our worries right now," he said. "We'll get arrested if I don't cooperate. You and me thrown in prison."

Huguette's hands shook but she nodded.

"The Allies are coming, Papa. The war is going to be over. The *Boches* will run."

"Not soon enough, Huguette."

June 1945
Studio Étoile, Boulogne-Billancourt

Huguette woke to hammering from the soundstage. The studio shot three films a year here, as it had during the war. If one film wasn't in production or post-production and editing, it was in pre-production preparation. Film schedules hummed in the face of union demands, supply shortages, a crew member's broken arm, irritable cameramen, or a drunk screenwriter. It was precisely this nonstop bustle that enabled Huguette to thrive—nobody looked twice at her when there was so much work to do.

At Étoile's makeup department, Huguette delivered afternoon coffee, Enzo's renowned almond biscotti, and Louis's script notes for Béa, a famous theater actress. Without makeup or wardrobe, Huguette wouldn't recognize Béa on the street. She winked at Huguette in her lit mirror and gestured to Tonette, Étoile's makeup director, who was sipping a coffee.

"We're on break. Why don't you freshen her look, Tonette?"

Tonette, a short, middle-aged woman with a red bob, was a studio legend. A genius, she'd given famous actresses their "look." She had done top stars like Arletty, Danielle Darrieux, and Marlene Dietrich before the war.

"*Moi?*" said Huguette. "I just help in the kitchen. Where's the time?"

Tonette put her cup down and took up the challenge.

"There's never time to look mousey." Tonette surveyed her. "Smile."

Self-conscious, she did.

"Good teeth, that's a plus," said Tonette.

All thanks to her mother's insistence on the dreaded annual childhood visits to the Institut Dentaire. Sweetened by an ice cream afterward at a café with her mother's friends, other ex-dancers who still lived in that neighborhood, where *maman* had danced in a famous revue before she married Remy Faure.

"My dear, you're too young not to highlight your features. Pull your hair back and pin it up, for a start," said Tonette. "Curly hair like yours needs to be tamed so it doesn't frizz in the humidity. *Zut alors*. Accent your good bone structure. All it takes is a few strokes."

Intrigued, Huguette nodded.

Tonette illustrated on Béa, shading below her cheekbones with a stubby makeup brush. "To define the shape of your face, subtly contour the blush here, and dot and pat the apples on your cheeks with rouge. To narrow your lips or make them fuller, use a lip liner. Like this."

Tonette stepped back, gazing at her handiwork, then resumed: shaped the brows with a few strokes, wet a cake of mascara and lengthened the lashes. She snapped her fingers at an assistant who was powdering Béa's nose. Tonette smiled.

"Simple. See?"

Mouth open, Huguette nodded.

"Of course with Béa, it's how she becomes the character by immersing herself in the role. Makeup and costumes alter perception and create a look."

Béa's simple look was defined, natural, and put together.

Tonette glanced at her watch, then pulled out a scarf-like wrap.

"For Béa's next scene, she's a spy and will wear a turban." She rifled through a drawer at the mirrored makeup table. "Round sunglasses will make her look totally different. Garbo did it all the time. No one ever recognized her when she went incognito."

A buzzer sounded from the sound stage.

"Showtime," Tonette said, and winked at the actress.

HUGUETTE'S LAST ERRAND WAS DELIVERING another of Louis's corrected script memos to the head office. Hurrying down a narrow corridor illuminated by a small skylight, she bumped into a woman.

"Ah, *excusez-moi*," Huguette said, bending to pick up the pages she'd just dropped, and when she looked up, she froze.

It was Corinne Lelouche.

Paralyzed, Huguette stared dumbly up at her.

"You're late," Corinne said.

That same petulant voice. The one that had coaxed her to drink glass after glass of Champagne, admonishing her about how to act with Siggie.

The actress was thinner. Lines etched her brow. The blond hair, now mouse brown, was pulled back in a chignon. Instead of a sleek emerald-green beaded gown, she wore a navy blouse and wool skirt. She looked like an office secretary.

Or like she was playing one.

If the camera once loved her, would it again? How long had she been back at the studio?

Huguette swallowed hard—was the memo she was delivering intended for Corinne's own hands?

Above her, Corinne huffed. "What's wrong with you?"

Huguette's fear bubbled into anger, helping buoy her to her feet. They were nearly the same height. "What do you mean?"

"Where's my check?" Corinne said, speaking slowly as if Huguette were having trouble understanding her. "The accountant said it would be waiting. I made a special trip."

"I don't work in that department."

Corinne huffed. "I'll miss my deadline."

"That's not my problem."

"How dare you speak to me that—" Now Corinne looked at her sharply, as if seeing her for the first time. "Where have I seen you before? Who are you?"

The rage was fading again, and Huguette was shaking. "You really don't remember?" But a hallway was no place for this conversation—anybody could come upon them. Huguette, no longer able to think clearly, grabbed Corinne by the arm and pulled her.

"You're hurting me!"

It served her right.

The first room down the hall was dim, but when they entered, Huguette heard the cry of a baby.

Corinne dropped her bag, wrenched away from Huguette, hurried to the side of the foldable crib. She sternly shushed the wriggling baby.

Huguette looked down at the fallen bag. In it were cloth diapers, a bottle.

All of a sudden Huguette understood. Corinne had a Nazi baby, too.

"We're a lot more alike than you know," said Huguette.

Corinne's coral lips narrowed. "I don't think so."

"Remember the treasure hunt in Paris?"

"What?"

"The night before the Allies invaded. You plied me with spiked Champagne. Siggie won first prize finding a virgin, remember? He got me pregnant."

Corinne's shoulders sagged. Her haughty look crumbled. She picked up her mewling baby.

Huguette stared at her. "That's Siggie's baby?"

"*Never.*" Corinne shook her head. "But her father's dead, too."

"You mean Siggie's dead?"

Corinne's gaze wandered. "All of them: my father, my former husband, my lover. Executed." She set down the baby, who began to cry again, but Corinne made no move to comfort her. Strange.

"If you're asking for pity, I'm the wrong person," Huguette said. "My father was killed because of Siggie. And I—" Her voice broke off, furious, hurt.

Corinne looked at her deeply for the first time. Studied her. "Those strange eyes. I remember now. Siggie spoke about them again and again."

Corinne's pale ringless hands worried her sleeve.

"How did you find me?"

"Find you? No, I'm . . ." Huguette stopped herself before she said she worked here. "I'm delivering a package. You're front-page news."

A sharp bark of laughter. "As if that feeds me or my baby." She cast her assessing eyes over Huguette. "Where's *your* baby?" she asked, suddenly interested.

Why had Huguette told her? Idiot. Corinne might pretend to be dumb as a post, but sly fit her better.

"Better off where he is than with me."

"A boy? Siggie always wanted a son."

Huguette's insides turned. The baby cried.

"I was seventeen. He humiliated me and hurt me. Now you're saying he'd planned to use me like a brood mare?"

Corinne looked away. "I'm sorry."

The baby's cries raked her nerves. Corinne seemed oblivious.

"No, you're not."

Now Corinne said nothing.

"But"—Huguette swallowed hard again—"he's dead?"

"I heard he'd managed to flee Paris with trunkfuls of loot. Art, some said gold. Apparently, he hid it and buried it before he got caught."

"How could he flee Paris?"

"With enough money anything's possible, *non*? I'd hoped he'd be more generous with his friends, but . . ." The sentence hung in the air.

Expecting a handout for her services? Huguette was repulsed by this seemingly remorseless woman, but she needed more information. "What happened to him then?"

Corinne shook her head. "He was in a POW camp. He tried to escape and he got shot."

"You're sure?"

"I told you." Corinne jerked her chin. "They're all dead."

Huguette should feel vindicated. Yet now she'd never be able to confront him. He'd gotten away from punishment.

As the baby wailed, Corinne picked her bag up, withdrew a small mirror to check her lipstick. Her eyes flickered over to Huguette. "You won't mind if I put you in my memoir?"

Newly horrified, Huguette stepped back. "What do you mean?"

"I won't use your name," Corinne assured. "I don't even know it. I'll just call you 'the virgin.'" Playing another part— writing a sensational tell-all about her life as a Gestapo mistress, a demimondaine who'd profited from the Nazis, dined on oysters while others lined up for rations. Huguette couldn't believe that Corinne would be getting rich from these stories—including hers. Disgusting.

It was as if Corinne could see Huguette's thoughts; her lip curled in disdain, wide-set eyes narrowing. "Do I have a choice now with a baby to feed? It's all about survival."

Let the woman rationalize. "Are you lying about Siggie?"

"Why would I?" Corinne said. "We're alive, and he's not."

TRUDGING BACK TO LOUIS'S HOUSE, Huguette wondered why it still mattered to her. The monster who'd fathered her son was dead; the innocent child she'd had to give up was with a better family, leading a better life than she could ever have provided him; and Corinne Lelouche was washed up, bitter, and facing life in prison. Worthy of pity rather than hatred. And what of her poor baby?

How useless to look back. Huguette's life had changed.

She reread Marina's letter, which she'd hidden in an old trunk discarded by the prop department. Marina said Céline at the flower shop kept asking about her. Why? Something sparked in Huguette's mind—half suspicion, half hope. She had unfinished business in Paris, the contents of her father's case at the "safe" place in Marina's house. But could she risk going back to Paris?

If she truly wanted to outrun the past, she would first need to return to it.

Early July 1945

Left Bank, Paris

—

Scenarios flew through Huguette's head. Would she see someone she knew? Someone who could identify her? She kept her head down.

She could hardly believe she was breathing the Paris air again—the whiff of cologne mingled with the baking of bread, the dank wet smell drifting from the sewers. She battled the urge to see the café. Her home where she'd grown up.

The oatmeal-colored Haussmanian limestone buildings of the Left Bank reflected the afternoon heat. Above peeling circus posters, a seventeenth-century sundial, rusted in time, clung to a wall. She hadn't missed the humidity, and as she walked through the streets, she fanned herself with the Métro map booklet that nice policeman Leduc had given her.

Nice—but still a *flic*.

She found a corner café that would sell her a *citron pressé* for a few francs. The tang of fresh-cut lemons made her mouth water, and the flavor of the drink was divine—a perfect mixture of cold, sweet, and sour.

How long had it been?

After she drank at the zinc counter, she consulted the phone book.

Her finger skimmed the flower shops on Île de la Cité until she found Céline's shop off Boulevard du Palais.

She bought a *jeton*, the same old phone token from before the war, slotted it in, and dialed the rotary phone.

"*Atelier des fleurs*," said a voice.

"Céline?"

"Who's this?"

Huguette hesitated. "A friend of Marina."

A quick conversation sounded in the background—Huguette couldn't make out specific words, but then Céline's throaty voice came on the line. "*Oui*, who's this?"

"Céline, it's Huguette."

"*Mon Dieu*, where are you?"

"In Paris. What do you want to tell me?"

A pause. "Not on the phone." Céline cleared her throat. "I'm sorry your delivery didn't arrive, madame."

"What?"

"No problem at all, madame," said Céline, "I'll deliver it to you right now. Let's say Place de Furstemberg in ten minutes?"

Huguette read between the lines. Someone was listening to Céline. She couldn't talk there but wanted to meet.

The phone cut off.

GRATEFUL TO LEAVE THE CAULDRON of heat on Boulevard Saint-Germain, Huguette was about to enter the small eighteenth-century square of Place de Furstemberg when her gaze caught on the rose brick facade of Delacroix's former atelier. Leafy plane trees rustled in the faint breeze under the candelabra-like light posts. The street was deserted, quiet apart from the strains of a violin drifting from a partially open window with a lace curtain, green shutter half closed in the dense heat.

A woman pedaled a bike into the square. Huguette recognized Céline: a stylish blue head scarf, platform sandals, a chic purse that her GI gangster boyfriend probably gave her. And the bicycle. It was Huguette's.

The last time Huguette had seen her, at Libération, Céline had been sitting in a jeep, drinking champagne with the GIs. Huguette had been fleeing the crowd. Running for her life.

But they'd been friends, *non*? Céline had been a café regular with her little Chihuahua. Or had she turned on Huguette like the rest of them? Yvon, the communist who had denounced Huguette and her father to the mob that day, had claimed Céline had been telling everyone Huguette played mattress for the *Boche*. Huguette knew Yvon was a liar and a hypocrite, but what if he hadn't been lying about that?

No flowers lay in the bike basket. Something stopped her. Made her turn around before Céline could see her. Her heart hammered—it felt all wrong.

Fighting the urge to speak to Céline, she hurried back to the crowded Boulevard Saint-Germain, melted into the pedestrians and kept going.

THIRTY MINUTES LATER, AFTER BACKTRACKING several times, she was at Marina's block in the Latin Quarter. She hoped she wasn't followed.

Wood-soled shoes clumped over the cobblestones; leather was still rationed. But at least there was no longer the hated slap of jackboots.

Huguette wondered what else had changed since the

Occupation. The new American soldiers robbed them blind, just like the Nazis.

On Marina's floor, the tall windows' shutters opened to the twisting thread of the street. Someone had to be home.

Huguette walked into the cobbled courtyard like she had every Friday after school for Les Éclaireurs, their Christian youth meeting. Nervous, she glanced around. Only the cinnamon cat. The concierge's door bore a sign: FERMÉ. From the garlic smells she must be having lunch. Huguette passed the marble statue, ignored the wire cage elevator, and mounted the stairs. She paused at each landing, listening for anyone.

She hesitated to knock on the carved double door. To the right stood a service door and the back stairs. Would Marina be home? She longed to see her friend, confide in her. Then again, hadn't Marina warned her not to come? What if Marina wouldn't see her? Or said she didn't want to get involved?

She delayed, wishing somehow Marina would just appear. The wood floor creaked as she shifted her weight. She unbuckled the sandal strap cutting into her ankle and rubbed the red mark. Took the other sandal off and relished the cold polished parquet on the soles of her feet.

Voices came from below. She peered out the windows overlooking the courtyard.

She recognized Marina's brother, a pain, and her father. With them, Rafael Croix, that grasshopper of a classmate. He looked taller and ganglier than the last time Huguette saw him. The Grasshopper had a chip on his bony shoulder; he'd resented her before he'd gotten shot and now probably blamed her.

Just who she wanted to avoid.

She turned the service door handle, slid inside, and bumped smack into a sack of coal, which tumbled to the floor with a loud thumping. Stupid. She should have looked where she was going! As fast as possible she scooped the coal chunks back into the bag, tried to brush the coal dust into the stair corners. She took the coal rod, shut the door, and padded up the back stairs barefoot.

The stairs led to the fifth floor *chambre de bonne* and the "safe" place Marina mentioned in her letter, where she'd stashed Huguette's father's briefcase. Working with Les Éclaireurs during the Occupation, they'd hide messages and Resistance newspapers here.

The stairs had been painted in the months since she'd last opened the secret compartment. That seemed like a bad sign. She hooked the coal rod into the second to the top step and pried a floorboard up. A pop and it opened. Cobwebbed and musty, the bulging blue briefcase was there. Thankful, she reached in, grabbed it.

She felt a hand on her shoulder.

"What do you think you're doing?"

July 1945

Left Bank, Paris

—

No way could she say she was recovering her father's things. But, caught red-handed, what could she do?

Huguette turned and faced Rafael Croix, her former classmate, towering over her. When in doubt, be brazen. He hated her anyway so she had little to lose.

"*Bonjour* to you, too, Rafael," she said, deftly sliding the riser back in place.

She got to her feet and shouldered the bag.

"Why are you sneaking around here?"

"Sneaking? I'm meeting Marina, not that it's your business."

Rafael's eyes narrowed. "People are looking for you, Huguette."

Panicked, she clutched the case tighter. Looked for a way out. But *non*, better to redirect him. She had to get him off her tail before Marina's brother and father overheard.

"I'm trying to find my cousin." Thousands of people were searching for lost family. "Remember, he went missing at Libération? What are you doing here, anyway?"

One of the lenses in his glasses was cracked. His cheeks reddened.

"I stay upstairs. It's temporary, during vacation."

Staying here was quite a step down for the Grasshopper. Surprised, she wondered if Rafael's family had lost their townhouse and fortune due to his father's collaboration.

"But what did you hide?"

"Hide?"

"Let me see."

"*Alors*, Rafael, I'll be honest," she said, perspiration pooling under her eyes. "I thought my things would be stolen if I had them on me. So Marina hid them here and now I need them back. Please don't say anything."

True. Yet he could make it hard for her. Tell the family Marina had hidden her things, had been helping a fugitive.

God knows what they'd think, and she hadn't even told Marina she was coming.

Voices sounded downstairs.

"Look, Marina kept this quiet from her parents. Please don't get her in trouble, Rafael. Keep this between us three."

"You can't tell me what to say," he said with a huff. "Your father was a collaborator and I don't believe you."

She'd tried to stay neutral but that did it.

"And yours wasn't?" she snapped. "I think the same man who got my father caught yours. Mine died, did yours?"

Rafael looked away.

She wondered if she'd hit the mark. He'd hated his father, who'd lived openly with his German mistress during the war.

"Look, I won't ask why you're living here. Or why you haven't gotten new glasses. It's not my business."

She stepped closer to him. Made him look at her and stared him down.

"But if you breathe a word I'll destroy the myth of your courageous wounding while shooting German snipers. Tell them what really happened. You only joined us the twelfth hour when the *Boches* were running away."

He stepped back.

"Do you want that? I'll make sure it follows you all your life, Grasshopper."

Rafael hated that nickname.

"Shut your mouth."

"I can. But it's up to you, Grasshopper."

He looked away again.

She grabbed his elbow.

"I saved your life. You would have bled out if I hadn't used my dress hem as a tourniquet to staunch your blood and gotten the Red Cross nurse to you, remember? You owe me."

That hot afternoon when the German snipers hiding by Notre Dame shot at her, Marina, and Rafael as they ran for cover.

Not even a grunt of protest. Rafael owed her and he knew it.

"It's your choice. So which is it?"

She caught Rafael's nod.

"Say it. Say you'll keep quiet."

"I will." A pause. "Someday, somehow, I'll pay you back."

This would have to do. Then she was running past him down the service stairs, slipping through the door and out into the courtyard. In the shadowed coolness she tore a page from her notebook, wrote Marina a message, folded it, and knocked on the concierge's door.

"*Bonjour*, madame," she said, "may I leave this for Marina?"

One smiling face in Paris greeted her. Madame Joubert had a sweet spot for Huguette and the other members of her youth group.

"*Bien sûr.* She's coming back later."

"*Desolée*, I've got to go."

Madame Joubert handed her a brown paper package tied with string. "I meant to mail this to you, couldn't find your address, but *voilà*." She winked. "Marina said you'd like these. The laundress mended them, they're good as new."

Inside was a pair of sandals and her favorite dress of Marina's. Definitely better than the stained and threadbare dress she hid under her kitchen work smock.

"But it's so generous. *Merci*."

Madame Joubert tucked a stray gray hair in her bun, then leaned forward to whisper in Huguette's ear. "People have been asking Marina's family about you."

"Who?"

"Troublemakers. *Desolée*, but it's dangerous for you to be here."

Pain lanced her. Her one friend, and she'd put her in danger.

HUGUETTE WALKED OVER THE COBBLES, turned the corner, and almost ran into the fruit cart piled with a small mound of rare peaches. Ripe fruit, like jewels furred with fuzz. Their fragrance reminded her of a family Sunday picking peaches in Montreuil's orchards in the heat of summer.

She felt a hand grip her shoulder. Torn from her memories, she winced. She'd been caught.

Fists raised, she whipped around.

A snort of laughter met her.

"If you could see your face." Marina grinned.

Marina stood on the cobbles in navy espadrilles and a matching sundress, her glossy hair straight. A carefree Parisienne on a summer evening ready for *vacances*. From her straw bag peeped a textbook.

But now her brows knit. Her face turned serious. "What are you doing here?"

Huguette pulled Marina into a courtyard.

"Why did Céline want to talk to me? Do you know?"

"I can't be late, but . . ." Marina glanced behind her. "Look, that man Gisors remodeled the café after the looting. That's how I found your papa's case. So you recovered it from our 'safe' place, eh?" Her voice lowered to a whisper. "Did your father steal money? Or something valuable? Loot, art? Or did you?"

What a question. Her mind went to Siggie.

"*Moi?* Why?"

Marina shook her head. "That's what Gisors has been saying, that he's heard rumors like that. People are looking for you, Huguette. Céline's one of them, I guess."

Huguette wondered what mess her father had left behind for her.

"You know I never stole anything, Marina. What do you know about this man Gisors? You said in your letter he claims he bought the café from Papa?"

Marina grimaced. "Who knows what the truth is. He took over right away when you were gone. I overheard the postman telling our concierge that Gisors's related to de Gaulle. He's protected. He can do whatever he wants."

A quiver went up her spine.

Shop awnings shadowed the narrow street. The horse hitched to the dairy man's cart nickered, and the sound echoed off the walls.

"Madame Joubert gave me your package, *merci*. And she warned me to stay away. She said it was dangerous."

"Good. Be careful, she's a gossip. I'll ask my cousin if you can stay *chez elle* when they go *en vacances*. But I'm going to be late, I need to study."

"School starts next month, Marina."

Marina rolled her eyes. "My parents insist I bring up my

grades or I can't go on the youth group outing to Chartres." A pout. "I have to study every night. I promised."

Huguette wished she had parents, had to study for school. A home.

But clearly she couldn't stay here. Or keep Marina longer.

Huguette didn't know when she'd see her friend again. She unknotted the scarf embroidered with butterflies and tied it around Marina's shoulders. The last thing of her mother's.

"Here, you've always liked this."

"*Non, non*, this was your mother's. I can't accept this."

"Of course you can. You've been so generous to me." Huguette smiled. "Gifts are for sharing, *maman* always said."

She'd missed Marina. Now she'd miss her again.

A church bell pealed.

"I'm in deep trouble now. So late."

Huguette hated to say goodbye. She pecked Marina's cheeks, hefted the case, and caught a bus. Then another. She rode past the Eiffel Tower and finally got off near the Pont de Billancourt. All around her were the scents of the Seine.

In the distance she saw the Renault factory's entrance, sprinkled with bullet holes. Weary, she wondered what to do.

JULY 1945

Police Prefecture, Paris

―

In the Suréte's office, Claude Leduc rolled up his sweat-dampened shirtsleeves and hit the fan. Nothing. Hit it again until it sputtered to life.

Tepid air sent a feeble ruffle through the papers on his desk. Not a window was open, even in this unseasonable heat, but he'd learned well from his mother that drafts from open windows weren't healthy.

Ten more minutes until he could leave for his well-deserved vacation.

It was all hands on deck with a skeleton crew during the approaching annual vacation, when Parisians would flee to the country while the city shut down. He looked forward to farmhouse cooking, fresh eggs, figuring things out with his wife. His young son Jean-Claude's smile.

Despite the impending joys of vacation, Claude was bothered by the lack of progress in the river victims' investigation. He hadn't gotten anywhere with his own research, and nobody seemed to want to answer his questions. He was cross-referencing a report against his notes on descriptions of one of the victims when a shout came from the reception desk.

"Leduc. Urgent memo for you!"

The bells pealed at Notre Dame a block away. Six o'clock—time to go.

Before he could say he was *en vacances* as of this minute, a flush-faced young officer thrust a memo on his desk.

ALL STAFF LEAVE AND VACATION CANCELED UNTIL FURTHER NOTICE

"There's been another body found in the river. Same as the others. It's not pretty."

Victim three. The third body might hold clues to cracking the first two murders. Adrenaline rippled through Claude. He grabbed his jacket. "Anything else?"

"No more details. But the boss has been called back from vacation. He says you and Alain should meet him in his office."

Claude hurried to send a telegram home.

CLAUDE RARELY STEPPED INSIDE HIS boss's office overlooking the Pont Saint-Michel and the Seine. Newly promoted to the homicide ranks, he would remain a rookie until a new hire joined.

He found his boss standing at his desk holding a large café crème. Inspector Marchal wore a white suit that gave off the scent of sun-dried linen. His suitcase was on the floor.

On a tray lay a steaming *cafetière*, cups, and napkins from Café du Soleil across the street. The belle époque café the police brass frequented. The former business of his murder victim Remy Faure, and of his daughter, Huguette.

"*Un café*, Leduc?" Marchal pushed a demitasse toward him.

"Sir, the café where this coffee came from—it was run by the first river victim, Remy Faure. I've been studying the case. There's got to be a connection."

"Eh?" Marchal sipped his coffee. "All in good time. First we need to handle the crime scene at the river before it's compromised. A suspect's been arrested."

Claude pulled out his notebook. Pondered what this could mean. Case solved?

Alain, his partner, appeared at the office door, panting and with a tennis racket poking from his bag.

"The killer's caught? Who is it?"

Marchal grabbed his hat.

"Let's go find out."

It was going to be a long night.

JULY 1945

On the Bank of the Seine
Outside Paris

—

*B*uzzing flies hovered like a black cloud.
 Claude raised his arm to his nose to quell the stench. It reminded him of his father's words about Ypres in the First World War: You smelled the frontline trenches long before you got there.

No one had informed them this one was fresh.

A young female lay face down on the muddy bank with a black wound in the back of her head, a rope tied around her neck. The rope was tied to a cobblestone above her torn, waterlogged dress.

The crime scene officers turned her over and Claude, Alain, and the inspector all groaned at the sight of her ruined young face.

Claude wondered if this could really be the work of the same killer he'd been pursuing; those deaths all followed a pattern that culminated in finding a body in the river, but this young teenager hardly matched it. She wasn't in advanced decomposition like the others, either.

Awful job, thought Claude, pinching his nose shut.

"Another muddy stinking mess," said Inspector Marchal.

"Who found her?" Claude asked.

"A barge captain reported seeing the body tangled in debris," said Marchal, consulting a police logbook.

"And the suspect?" asked Alain.

Marchal sucked his teeth, lifting his chin to indicate a sullen young man in a blue work coat and clogs beside a horse-drawn milk cart.

"A milkman?" asked Alain.

"He's no angel."

"But how's he a murder suspect?"

Marchal again consulted the police logbook.

"Cart tracks, horse feces, and footprints, identified as the suspect's clogs, led down to the riverbank where the body was discovered. Upon questioning, he admitted that yesterday on his delivery route, he got paid to dump a sealed package in the river. No idea of the contents. Like he did during the war 'supplying' the 'Resistance.'"

Alain spit, coughing. Swatted a fly off his chin. "Disgusting."

Claude studied the slow-moving brown-green river. Noted the sluggish eddies rippling to the mud-caked shore. The water was shallow. The body hadn't been weighted down enough, so it had gotten stuck. If not for that, who knows how long the poor girl would have drifted?

Marchal shrugged. "He swears he didn't know what he was dumping. And he seems a slice short of a baguette, according to the gendarme."

As the body was lifted onto a stretcher, an evidence collector lifted a torn scarf with a stick from the river grass. In the canopied sunlight, green algae clung to dripping pale blue fabric.

Hand-embroidered with butterflies. Unusual. Claude sucked in his breath.

He'd seen this scarf before. But where?

"Find any ID?" asked Marchal.

The *flic* took a wallet from a soggy straw basket. "The student card in here says Marina Roussel, 5 rue Galande, Paris."

He suddenly remembered where he'd seen the scarf: on Huguette Faure, who'd sat on the gendarmerie's kitchen floor wiping her tears with it, whose father was also found in the river. There had to be a connection—otherwise, how did her scarf wind up on a young corpse?

Two plainclothes officers from Renseignements Généraux, the domestic intelligence agency, escorted the milkman toward an unmarked car.

"What the hell? What are they doing with our suspect?" asked Alain.

Marchal took them aside.

"It's turned political. The RG have taken over this investigation."

Claude rubbed his damp neck. This journey in the humidity for nothing? If the Renseignements Généraux had taken over, then he would have nothing to do. The RG's ranks came from wartime insiders, POW buddies, and de Gaulle's former Free French forces. They played by their own rules.

A dawning realization glowed on Alain's face. "So we can go back on vacation, *oui*?"

"We're assigned to assist them. That means turning over all the river victims' files to the RG."

Alain's smile faded.

Marchal looked angry enough to kick a horse. Claude understood. Canceled vacation, the heat in deserted Paris with hardly a café open, and now assisting the RG—bad to worse.

"Assist how? It's our case," said Claude. "And I think I've found a connection."

"You'll have to furnish it to them."

Like hell he would.

July 1945

Studio Étoile, Boulogne-Billancourt

—

Run off her feet, Huguette only managed to find ten minutes to herself before kitchen duties the next evening. Shut up in the studio's makeup-cramped supply closet, she examined the contents of her father's case with a flashlight. Her father had called it his insurance; she remembered the greed in his eyes.

Inside she found his thick lined notebook in the handwriting she remembered so well. Names, dates, locations. The ledger contained notes scribbled on café napkins clipped to lists. It made her eyes fill with tears.

Non, she couldn't take this in now. She felt dirty just touching this—but she knew this must have been valuable, his "insurance."

A much-folded receipt had gotten stuck in the corner of his notebook. It was from her mother's tuberculosis sanatorium, indicating a Monsieur Honoré Gisors had paid for her mother's last medical bill and burial in 1944. Why would the man who forcibly took over her father's café have paid this for her mother?

— — —

THE STUDIO SCREENING ROOM FELT like a sauna. Huguette had been perspiring from the moment she walked in with the drinks tray. Regis, the director, a squat fireplug of a man, beckoned her over.

"Hurry, please."

"Lights dimming in one minute," shouted the projectionist from the upstairs booth.

"*Bien sûr.*" She caught her breath, uncorked the wine, poured, and served the production crew: the skinny intense editor who cut his wine with water, the redheaded actress wearing a makeup smock, the horse-faced cameraman. She tried to avoid Marie's accusing looks, but without success; when she set a wine glass in front of her, Marie hissed, "Don't be late again. You're making us all look bad."

Huguette nodded and hurried along to empty the ashtrays. This group smoked up a storm during the nightly screening of daily rushes and rough cuts. She topped up drinks, half listening to the crew's chatter.

"It's a masterpiece, Regis," said the editor, sipping his watered-down wine. "What are you still worried about?"

"Is this really the film I want to make? A film people want to see and buy tickets for?" He exhaled a plume of smoke. "We need Jean Gabin back on set for retakes, but I can't afford him for a reshoot."

"Gabin's Marlene Dietrich's lover," said the redhead. "Won't come up for air, if you know what I mean."

A collective sigh went around the stuffy room.

The redhead laughed. "Redo my closeups with better angles and no one will miss Gabin."

Pause. "She's onto something," said the cameraman, adjusting his thick glasses on his nose. "It's not difficult and much cheaper.

If I smear the lens with Vaseline, blur the shot, and use a stand-in, his presence will be suggested, and he'll never have to set foot in here again."

"Cheaper sounds good. I need this in the can Friday or we'll go even further over budget." Regis nudged the editor to take notes. "The distributors are hounding me for an early release date. Roll the newsreel, then we'll go over the rushes."

Regis insisted screenings began with a newsreel as if this were an audience-filled theater. Just like those Saturday matinees Huguette used to go to with her mother.

The images flickered and rolled: a military band marched on the Champs-Élysées, a minister cutting the ribbon of a new school, police conferring near a reporter standing on a riverbank.

"The latest victim found in the Seine is confirmed to be an eighteen-year-old schoolgirl, a member of the Christian youth organization Les Éclaireurs."

Huguette's breath caught.

"Her parents are asking the public for help."

The reporter handed the microphone to a man who held a scrap of fabric—a scarf patterned with butterflies. Her hand stiffened on the wine bottle. That was Marina's father.

And her butterfly scarf.

"My daughter never did anything wrong. She never even came home late, until the other night she didn't come home at all. Please, if you have any information about who might have wanted to hurt my Marina . . ."

The wine bottle crashed to the floor.

HUGUETTE CLEANED UP HER MESS, made excuses, and ran shaking into the cemetery behind the studio. She'd as good as killed Marina, her best friend. Her only friend.

She fingered Marina's Saint Christopher medal hanging on her neck, begging him to bring her back. But how could he? It was clear Marina's murder was her fault. Huguette had made Marina stay out late—and the scarf she'd given her as a gift had been used to identify her body.

She couldn't stop shaking.

Her fault. She clung to a moss-covered tombstone and cried until the tears dried up.

JULY 1945

Studio Étoile, Boulogne-Billancourt

―

Birds trilled. Outside, leaves spread in a green carpet. Last night's rain dewed the trees.

Huguette's heart lay heavy as she wound her way through the woods to where she'd buried the last of Louis's Cognac. Low mist wisped through the branches. Her old blouse clung damp to her skin.

Marina's death shadowed her every step. Conscience-stricken, she'd hardly slept. Every morning she had to force herself to do her job.

She didn't understand this game the Americans played. If they showed up at all, they'd be serious one minute and silly the next. Today she needed to meet this Pete and sell him the Cognac. She had to make Louis a decent profit. He depended on her. She tried to shake off her feelings and concentrate.

Sheep bleated and the soft air carried the scent of wildflowers. As usual an assorted crowd lined up at the fence. Cotton puff clouds hovered in the crisp blue sky.

The supply depot looked quiet. No activity or soldiers. Huguette wondered if she'd gotten the day wrong. Pete was supposed to be here on Tuesdays, but no one had shown last week. If no one showed again today, she'd be late for her job at Louis's with nothing accomplished.

Her mind went back to the newsreel and Marina's father's appeal. Guilt flooded her. Why hadn't she listened to Marina?

It didn't appear as though anyone would be coming to the gates any time soon. Huguette proceeded back to the forest, to the copse of trees she'd buried the Cognac in—the rustling oak shaded the spot, the fir branches covered the entrance. She looked around, then slipped inside.

Two men in civilian clothes huddled in conversation at the base of the oak tree. Right where she'd buried the Cognac.

She twisted her braid, worried. Had someone followed her the other night? Dug up the Cognac? The men were speaking English and hadn't noticed her. Who were they?

She ducked before they could see her. Leaves crackled and she slipped in the mud, landing right on her behind.

Before she could pull herself up, arms grabbed her tight. A thick hand went over her mouth, gagging her with its salty metallic taste.

"What are you doing here, kid?" said the thin one.

Huguette's eyes widened. It couldn't happen again. She kicked out, and he caught her legs. Panicked, she jolted her foot back, hitting him between the legs.

"*Owww.*"

The hand let go. She was roughly turned around to face a young bearded man with a knife. Some sixth sense overcame her.

Don't show fear.

Act like you know what you're doing.

All this shot through her head in a split second.

She stood up straight, brushed down her skirt. "Are you Pete?"

"Eh?"

If only her English were better.

"Watch out. GI Ralph taught me this." She stuck her index and middle finger in the sides of her mouth, puckered her cheeks, about to whistle.

"Hold on, kid," said the bearded one, slipping the knife in his pocket. He sounded like Ralph, with a flatter accent. He kept his voice low. "Why'd you interrupt us?"

"Does it say 'private,' monsieur?" she said. "Is there a sign here in the woods saying 'keep out'?"

The thin one rolled his eyes. "What a pain in the ass," he said. "Get lost."

She itched to look down at the earth, see if it had been disturbed. But couldn't draw attention to the spot.

"Not worth it," said the bearded one. He slung a sack over his shoulder. She heard clinking, like sounds of metal. "Let's go."

Black marketers, maybe deserters. Huguette's heart pounded. It was now or never. "GI Ralph told me Pete does business. That I should meet him here on a Tuesday. Is that you?"

The bearded man looked back at her. "What kind of business?"

"What do you think?" She pointed toward the supply base chain-link fence visible through the leaves.

"Butter, Hershey's bars. That kind of business?" he asked.

The bearded man was testing her. Had he expected someone else?

Huguette shook her head. "I'm disappointed," she said. "Too bad."

"Why?"

"Who do you think introduced Enzo to GI Ralph?"

A lie, but she couldn't come up with anything else. Would it make her seem impressive, or did she sound ridiculous, like a little girl playing pretend?

He turned to the thin man. "Wait over there."

While the other man trudged away, Huguette flicked her gaze to the oak tree. The ground looked untouched. She exhaled faintly.

"Yeah, I'm Pete," he said. "You can get me Cognac? A crate, like Enzo promised?"

She nodded. "If you pay me in cash and cigarettes."

No surprise on his face. He nodded. "Fifty cartons. The other half in francs."

She quickly added it up and swallowed her shock—he was trying to undersell her. "Seventy-five cartons and the rest in francs," she said.

Pete grinned. "You've done this before."

No, but she could add and multiply. She just smiled. "I'm Hélène. You deal only with me now, okay, Monsieur Pete?"

He looked her up and down. She read his eyes.

To him she was just another hungry French girl. Like so many.

"Fine, Hélène." He pronounced it with a hard H. "If that's how your boss likes it. Safer, too."

Again, a man who underestimated women. Never saw them coming. He figured she worked as the go-between. Good. Let him think that.

"My boss likes it, *oui*. He watches everything. Okay, monsieur?"

"Deal, Miss Hélène. No hard feelings?"

Was that some kind of apology? She'd let it go. For now.

"We keep it business. Tonight. Here, Monsieur Pete."

He winked. Then handed her two packs of Chesterfield cigarettes. "For you and your boss."

JULY 1945

Louis's Home, Boulogne-Billancourt

—

Marie blocked Huguette's way into Louis's cloakroom. Her pointed finger prodded Huguette's arm.

Huguette had left her muddy boots near Marie's by the coat rack. The soft wet mud on Marie's boots indicated she'd just beaten Huguette here. Lucky they hadn't crossed paths in the woods.

"What's going on? I pay you to be on time."

Startled, Huguette did her best to hold her ground. Her mind had been running in circles over Marina. "I'm sorry, Marie," she said. "Everything will get done, I promise." Beads of sweat broke out on her brow. Her lungs heaved from running.

"Why isn't everything prepared?"

Of all days to be late . . . This was the day Marie went over the weekly accounts with Louis. She had evidently worked all night and not slept. Huguette could kick herself.

"I'm so sorry," she said again, sincerely meaning it. Marie had expected Louis already drinking his coffee and a warm house. Louis was always cold, even in summer. Huguette hurried to light the stove. "I'll get the fire going and make coffee. It won't happen again."

"You're right, it won't." Marie scowled, padding over the old tiles in her wool socks. "If I can't rely on you, this isn't going to work."

With an angry flounce, she stomped out.

Louis shuffled in wearing his silk bathrobe and plopped down heavily at the kitchen table. "We need to talk, Huguette." He sounded hoarse.

Mon Dieu! "Louis—"

Marie's shout interrupted her. "You've been robbed, Louis. Your cellar—"

"Just listen to me," he interrupted, rasping. His breath came in spurts, and suddenly, he clutched his chest. "Huguette, you need to . . . hide the . . ." Now his veined hands flailed, trying to point at something. His words choked and his face turned beet red.

Huguette rushed to his side. "What's wrong?"

Her reaching hands couldn't stop him in time—he fell off the chair.

"This is not his first heart attack," said the irritable white-mustached doctor. "If I've told Louis once . . . but he's a stubborn one. Two months ago I sent him home with strict instructions to hire a nurse, adhere to a diet, exercise, and leave the studio alone. Why don't you people follow through?" The doctor shook his head as he consulted his clipboard.

Marie's tired face fell. "He lied. Told me nothing."

"His heart's a ticking time bomb. He needs treatment. We'll keep him here until his condition improves."

The doctor left on his rounds.

Poor Louis. Huguette had had no idea.

A selfish thought crossed her mind: There went her job. Marie wouldn't need her now. No more work in the kitchen, no more place to stay. She'd go hungry again.

Time to move on.

Yet she couldn't leave until after the deal tonight. Louis was counting on her.

"Marie, let me keep helping Louis while you sort out nursing," Huguette said. It was terrible timing—her best friend had been murdered and she'd just made Marie angry this morning—but maybe this changed everything. "I can pay the bills, make deposits, take care of business."

Marie rubbed her eyes. Her sunken cheekbones, chalk-white skin, and drained look concerned Huguette. "Can I really trust you?"

A flame of guilt seared her. But she shoved it away.

"You've trusted me until now," said Huguette. "Have I let him down? I'll read him the scripts and the newspaper to keep up his spirits. Feed the dog, too."

Marie's eyes flickered with relief. "What are you waiting for? Go feed Miki and then deal with the police."

Her insides crashed. Talk to the police?

"The police? What do you mean?"

"Give a statement and list what was stolen."

HUGUETTE SAT BESIDE LOUIS'S HOSPITAL bed as afternoon sunlight burnished the worn floor tiles a glowing honey. He looked frail under a mound of white linen sheets.

Weak. Old. As though he'd slip away and float out the open window and join the clouds.

The nurse removed the thermometer sticking from his mouth. "Your fever's down. Good."

The nurse sponged his forehead with water from the chipped

enamel basin. After she left, Louis pincered Huguette's wrist and pulled her close.

"What's all this about the cellar and the police?"

Her fingers crunched the stiff hospital sheets as she leaned into his ear. She whispered about her Cognac deal tonight and the profit he would make. His filmy eyes batted. He groaned. Good God—she hoped she hadn't given him another heart attack.

Instead, he laughed. "That Cognac's brown piss with a bite," he said. "Inferior quality. But I sold it to the *Boches* and stole it back." Louis pulled her closer. Hissed in her ear. "Just reinvest my cut."

Huguette grinned. Balancing his books was one thing—actual black market dealing was another. But she'd read Louis right.

"Marie made me give a police report. If she ever finds out I took the Cognac to sell—"

"She won't, if you're careful. Just keep the ledgers hidden."

A muffled church bell rang in the distance, and Huguette jolted, suddenly noticing the shuffling of other patients in the corridor. What if somebody overheard their conversation?

Nervous, she stood and checked for listeners in the hallway. Only nurses and doctors on their rounds. She closed his room's door, then returned to his side.

"But here's the thing, Louis—you've run out of Cognac."

"There's more buried in the neighbor's cellar next door." He smiled. "That's where I hid my Jewish screenwriters. A door in my wall connects them."

She blinked.

"The key's stuck behind the door frame, on the right."

"What if I get caught taking it?"

Louis fixed her with a look, oddly lucid considering the clouds over his retinas. She understood that to mean: *don't*. "Once you've sold it, you must protect the cash. Clean it."

"Like cooking the books. I know."

"No, no. It's more complicated than that." Exhausted, he lay back, a small grin parting his lips. "Think, Huguette. Use fruit stands, cafés, laundries. All cash, quick turnover. Use the profit to buy up, keep it moving, flowing. Diversify."

She didn't know what that meant. "*Quoi?*"

He was happier than she'd seen him for a while. He was enjoying himself, as if directing a new production. "You use the money from selling the Cognac for something legitimate. Buy a small cinema, like I said, a laundry, café, the *boulangerie* in the next village, a market stall. Then another and another."

She got the concept. "All this with cigarettes and Cognac?"

"We go bigger."

Huguette liked the ambitious shine in his eyes. But was she out of her depth? "I don't have the connections you do, though."

"I'll introduce you. You must always sell through connections—never let it trace back to you. Use this profit to buy GI gasoline. You sell the gasoline marked up 100 percent to garages and taxi drivers. *This* profit is what you invest in another business."

Like her father. Fingers everywhere. Part of her was disgusted she'd be doing the same as him.

"You make it sound easy, Louis. But it's not."

"*Ma petite*, it's the law of supply and demand. No one can buy gasoline even if they have the money. Rarer than gold and everyone wants it. And the GIs who steal from their supply depots can't move it themselves, they need us to fence it for them."

Us?

"How do you know this?"

"You read me the newspapers, don't you?"

Sickened, she wanted to pull away from this. She couldn't go back to how she'd lived before—her heart ached to remember what her father's black market dealing had done to her in the end.

Yet Louis depended on her and she'd lose the little she had if he fired her. She was stuck again.

"This is just like the old days."

"Yes," Huguette said, eyes lowered.

Louis didn't seem to notice that Huguette had a different reaction to the *old days* than he did—he was still grinning. "You can do it, Huguette. People believe anything. But *you* need to believe it. Play the part."

Once the director, always the director.

His bony veined hands grabbed hers so hard it hurt. "You can save me. I need the money or I'll go to court. Lose my property, my studio shares and distribution dealings. Everything."

Pleading shone in his milky eyes.

"Please, promise me."

She did.

"Now let me tell you exactly what you're going to do."

Early August 1945

Police Prefecture, Paris

—

Inspector Marchal slapped the latest issue of the American magazine *LIFE* on Claude's desk.

He flipped through the magazine to an article with a photo of a smiling GI driving a jeep by the Arc de Triomphe.

"Read it, Leduc."

"I can't, Captain. It's in English."

Marchal snorted. "You speak GI," he said. "I've heard you."

Claude shrugged. "I picked up a little GI slang at the end of the war. But I can't read it."

"You'll figure it out with all those pictures. Like you did in nursery school, eh?"

Claude was sick of being picked on, but what could he do as a rookie? He huffed, sliding the magazine toward himself. "What am I looking for, sir?"

"Don't you continually bend my ear with your theory that there's a connection between the river corpses and the black market, collaborators? So read this and find it."

Marchal pointed to the article's headlines:

CHICAGO SUR LA SEINE?

GANGSTER GIS ROB GASOLINE DEPOT IN BROAD DAYLIGHT

Claude sighed. He knew about these cases, of course: Deserting GIs formed gangs and thrived, using the Parisian underworld gangs to sell on the black market. They ran rampant. In this league, it wasn't cigarettes and butter—it was armed robbery and murder. Lately, they'd gotten even more out of hand, using their doctored or expired military IDs to trick their way onto the US base, saying they had permission to commandeer the gasoline trucks. They'd shoot anyone who didn't cooperate. He could have given Marchal a full rundown himself, no need for *LIFE* articles, but the inspector had a soft spot for dramatics, hence this act with the magazine.

"It's gotten more embarrassing," Marchal said. "The chief's holding the bag and wants these *mecs* caught." Marchal nudged his large behind onto the edge of the desk Claude shared with Alain. "Splashed all over the Paris papers daily. On the radio. Now the international rags. What's your progress?"

"Our investigations are ongoing, Inspector," said Alain.

What they always said when cornered by their boss.

Inspector Marchal rolled his eyes. "In other words, zero, *n'est-ce pas*? Not good enough."

Claude privately agreed. He was frustrated, too. The GIs had guns. His team didn't. They'd all felt burdened with this feeling of helplessness for weeks. "Why are you bringing this up now, sir?"

Marchal looked down his nose at Claude, something smug about his expression. "Since you're not making any progress on your own case assisting the RG, you won't mind being assigned to assist the US military in their investigation into this gang activity, will you?"

Claude's heart sank. "Assist how?" he asked, wary.

"Well, you know the territory—they don't. Think of it this

way: If you were in Chicago and had this problem, wouldn't you want the locals' help with finding the bad boys?"

It made sense; Claude just didn't see how it was his problem. "Will we get the credit?"

Marchal huffed. "Focus on catching the perps first."

To the victor went the spoils.

Typewriters clicked from the adjoining office.

"It's all hands on deck, Leduc. Prove yourself. I won't say it again."

"Understood, sir."

This was a way in.

"Now. How are you going to make it happen?"

Claude looked to Alain, who was already looking at him, as if each expected the other to have all the answers. Finding none, Claude huffed and improvised: "We'll look at local gangs and those in reserved occupations who didn't go to war. Trace their connections, their stockers, their middlemen. Priority will be finding new recruits who speak GI English."

"How about your informers?"

Nothing. He and Alain just couldn't compete with the going market rate for rewards to squeal on the black market connections.

"Ongoing, Inspector."

Marchal's thick black eyebrows crinkled as he sucked in air. A bad sign. No pat on the back from him today.

Alain stabbed out his cigarette to pick up some of the slack. "We'll put out our number and department contact—all anonymous—for tips."

Marchal nodded as if he'd been expecting this. "You're now authorized to offer rewards, thanks to *les Americains*."

While few tips amounted to anything—people were scared of informing on the black marketers—the reward would help.

"Seems there's some bad GI apples," remarked Alain, reaching over to take the magazine from Claude's desk.

"There's bad apples in every barrel," said Marchal. "In our barrel, too. Tread carefully, but get me results. You need to deliver to stay on the squad, Leduc."

Claude swallowed hard. He had to keep this job.

Marchal left after tacking a memo on the board. A ten-thousand-franc reward for information leading to arrest and conviction. No questions asked.

At least this got his boss off his desk. For now.

Midnight, Early August 1945

In the Woods by Former Château Rothschild

—

Huguette watched the two figures at the clearing's edge. This didn't look good. As she approached, she recognized Pete, and the other one melted away.

"Monsieur, you agreed to deal with me only."

"I'll signal him when I see your goods," said Pete.

Play the cards you're dealt, but your way, her father would have said.

"I'll do the same."

She gestured into the woods—a silhouette watched them from behind the birch trees. It could be her boss or his flunky, but actually it was a dummy made up of a costuming torso and head-shaped wig stand she'd "borrowed" from the wardrobe department earlier. *Play the part*, Louis had said. Huguette was no actress, but she didn't have to be to pull this off. She just hoped Pete's cohort wouldn't go investigate.

Pete growled. Low and deep. About to step back, she realized he was laughing.

"We do business now," she said. "Or I walk."

She'd rolled the dice. He'd either play or not.

Fear knotted her stomach. The night birds chirped. Her damp ankle socks, pierced by foxtails, sagged over her boots.

He turned and snapped his fingers briskly, loud and piercing in the misty dim. "Okay, missy."

The next minute two duffel bags were dropped in the clearing. Pete unwound the khaki straps and opened each bag.

She shone Louis's old flashlight inside to see the cartons of Lucky Strike and cash. Once she'd quickly counted, she straightened up, nodded, and leaned by the bush and flicked her flashlight on and off twice as if to signal the dummy.

"Okay, monsieur."

She led him beyond the next clump of bushes, moving the branches and gestured to the shovels in the baby buggy.

Without a word, Pete dug until he could pull the Cognac crates out. She installed his two duffel bags inside the buggy and kicked off the brake.

"*Bonsoir*," she said.

"Nice doing business with you. Same items, same place, same time, tomorrow?"

THEN SHE WAS PUSHING THE buggy, struggling on the path with the weight of cash and the dozens of cigarette cartons. She kept going, not looking back, along the outer fringe of the forest over crackling pine needles. She heard night animals scurrying and the low hoot of an owl, reminding her of the day her baby was born.

For a moment she thought she could have been pushing him in this baby buggy. What a different world that would be. Then her boot nearly slipped on a rock and the illusion was broken.

She didn't pause or slow her pace until she reached the rear of the *boulangerie* at the edge of the village, just like Louis had said she would. Wary, she looked around.

No one.

The unseasonable summer showers made a mess of her boots. She knocked, and the back door opened to a lit cloakroom. Nathalie, the baker's wife, nodded, and Huguette set about brushing pine needles off the baby buggy and unloading the duffel bags, which she proceeded to drop down the outside coal chute trapdoor Nathalie had opened. There was a short rickety staircase that Huguette took to end up in the baker's warm back kitchen, redolent with yeasty smells and the crackling of firewood burning in the oven.

She allowed herself to feel cocooned in the warmth.

Nathalie's husband, Serge, gave Huguette a nod, then ignored her. His muscled hands and arms, dusted white with flour, rolled doughballs into long cylinders. All the while he balanced against the marble-topped table, his leg prosthesis on, his face flushed from the fierce heat of the bread oven.

Wordlessly, she loaded the bags back up onto a cart that had been waiting nearby—she assumed they used it for bread deliveries. She followed Nathalie to the rear storeroom, which was full of sacks of flour. Here, Huguette extracted a fistful of cash and two cartons from a bag, stuffed them into her coat, and transferred the bags into an old WWI metal trunk. Nathalie put a padlock on the trunk.

"*Bon*," Huguette said. "I was never here."

"*Bien sûr*," said Nathalie. "I'll sell to customers I trust. As before. If there are any complications with a customer or the police, I'll remove a geranium pot from the back door." She smiled. "Just like we did in the old days with the Resistance."

That phrase again—the old days. Huguette tried to conceal her shiver as she smiled back.

Could she really trust them? After all, even if everyone dealt on the black market, as Louis pointed out, Huguette didn't know if she could handle their ethics. "And your husband still doesn't have a problem selling on the black market?"

"He's got a problem making the rent while having enough cash left over to buy flour and wood for the oven. Does that answer your question?"

Huguette nodded. "Louis wanted me to double-check."

"Thought so."

No one imagined an eighteen-year-old girl could run a black market business by herself. Fine by her. She was her own perfect cover. She wondered if perhaps Nathalie was doing the same thing.

"I don't want to know where this comes from," said Nathalie, "but for things to work, it has to go both ways. Give us ten percent on what we sell."

Louis had prepared her to give twenty.

"Fifteen, including the cellar storage and your complete silence. If not, I'll find others eager to keep their mouth shut and business flowing."

"*D'accord.*" Nathalie nodded and handed her a key to the coal chute. "Come and go that way, but please stay quiet for my baby."

A pang hit her—what she wouldn't give to be saying those words.

In the low moonlight, Huguette followed the tank treads in the rutted road back to the studio. Traffic was nonexistent. Cattle lowed in the surrounding field, which was filling with mist. She envied Nathalie's baby, hardworking husband, and business. She kept to the shadow of the trees, watchful and wondering how long it would take until something went wrong.

Mid-August 1945

Hospital, Boulogne-Billancourt

In Louis's hospital room overlaid with antiseptic smells, Huguette sat down by his bed. He pulled her close. His spidery veined hand pinched her shoulder.

"Good work, *ma petite*. Gasoline's where the money is, and those GIs have it, eh?"

Again, this gasoline. She shrugged. "You know better than me."

"You don't get to where I am without connections." Louis caught the eye of a thickset orderly in hospital whites by the door. A look passed between them. "You'll work with him, Roc, my go-between, on the gasoline. Trust him, Huguette."

Roc nodded at her.

"What gasoline, Louis?"

"Keep meeting the GI and say you want to buy gasoline. I'll get you front money to purchase the gas."

A big jump from Cognac and cigarettes.

"Wait, what would do I do with the gasoline, assuming these GIs have it to sell?"

"Listen well, *ma petite*. I'm arranging for Roc to coordinate transport and line up buyers. Smoother for you. He'll handle my old prop department and location crew, who'll move and sell the gasoline."

Louis had a network. Middlemen who shifted on the black market.

Roc was summoned by a doctor and slipped out of the room without a sound.

From under the blanket, Louis's hand shoved papers into hers.

Glancing at them, she saw her fake name on an ownership deed of a cinema, complete with a notary seal.

"What's this?"

"A reward."

"But Louis . . ." Stunned, she didn't know what to say or what this meant.

"Play your cards right and count this as the first of many."

"Wait, what do I do with a cinema?"

"Shh . . ." Louis smiled.

Flustered, she leaned close to his ear. "Louis, you bought this for me? I don't understand."

"The cinema's been operating successfully for years—I've just transferred it to you so you can use it to launder our cash."

As if Huguette knew how to do that. Louis had explained it to her, but that had been in theory—could she really do it in practice?

Almost like he'd read her thoughts, Louis said, "I know you can do this. Like me, you're a survivor. Now let's go over the details."

She took notes until twilight deepened the shadows of his room. From small to large, any cinema operated on the same financials: film distribution networks, concessions, staff, wages, taxes. He gave her information on his key contacts, on limited partnerships, on unions and how to negotiate with them, on licensing. He told her he was working on getting her a frontman who had a bank account.

Her mind felt alive as she wrote everything down. Instead of coming across as daunting or impossible, it all made sense. Maybe he was right about her—maybe she *could* do this.

THAT EVENING, PETE TOOK HER aside in the forest clearing. His partner, Vince, chain-smoked as he stood guard. Wispy clouds obscured the moon.

"I'd like to meet your boss," Pete said.

Stall for time until she understood what he was getting at.

"My boss? Why?"

"I want to work out a business opportunity with him. Beneficial to us both."

Huguette tipped her head back, equal parts haughty and confused. "He trusts me to run daily operations. What is this business opportunity?"

Pete grinned at her as if to say, *nice try, little girl.* "Just tell him I'd like to talk. He's in Paris, right?"

She wondered where he'd gotten that idea. Or did he think all French gangsters lived in Paris? Either way, she couldn't stand being condescended to like this. "I don't see my boss much. He prefers that. You understand our agreement, *non*?"

"I do," said Pete. "But this is a real opportunity to grow his business. I need to meet him. Can you get me an appointment?"

For once he sounded polite.

"He's busy," she said. "Doesn't deal with day to day. It's too small for him. I won't risk a message if I don't know more."

He leaned in and told her, "I've got a connection with the SHAEF."

He said it as if she knew what he meant. As if everyone knew.

"*Quoi?*"

"Supreme Headquarters Allied Expeditionary Forces."

This should impress her?

"Specifically connections to the central command coordinating US supply depots in France. My contact's with the bigwigs headquartering at Hotel George Cinq in Paris. Get it?"

Hotel George Cinq had once been the German high command; now the Americans had taken it over.

"So this means what exactly?"

"*Le* big time, Miss Hélène. Tell your boss we need him to fence a lot of product."

"What product?"

"Truckfuls of gasoline to the right buyer. Your boss will make thousands. We need to talk so I can make sure he can move quantity."

Louis had been right on the mark. Lucky, too, Pete suggested it first.

She paused as if thinking it over. "He'll always agree to experiment. A trial. Bring some tomorrow. My boss will line up a buyer, we move the gasoline, and we'll split the profit sixty-forty."

"Just one buyer?" asked Pete.

"The first of many if my boss thinks it's worthwhile. Agreed?"

Pete grinned.

"Make it fifty-fifty, I meet your boss, and can do, mademoiselle."

Her exterior was calm, but her mind raced. This was a huge opportunity, but there was no boss to speak of—she could hardly sneak Pete into the hospital to speak with Louis. She didn't even know if Roc had set up a network to handle the gasoline yet, if they could move it, if they'd lined up buyers . . .

Too many ifs. And such bad timing.

How could she play this?

"*Non, merci*, Monsieur Pete," she said, regret in her voice.

Pete's jaw hardened.

"Why?"

"My boss isn't going to meet you until he sees how this all will work. He's not just going to jump into a venture of this size."

She had to stall.

"Wait a minute, kid, that's not how we work."

"*Alors*, it's how he works," she said. "I'm sorry, but he's like this with all his business."

Pete snorted. "You mean he's asking for our credentials, right?"

The leaves caught the glint of moonlight on the path. Her jumping pulse betrayed the anguish of walking away from a good deal. But she had to.

However, Pete and Vince had moved to block her way out of the clearing.

"Kid, I asked you if he wanted credentials."

Her unease mounted. "*Desolée*, I don't understand."

Vince flashed an American newspaper in her face. "Credentials means legit connections. We can deliver. See?"

His finger pointed to a photo at the top of page two.

"Call these lugs our credentials."

A group of American soldiers stood by an outside café table. The café's familiar terrace overlooked a cobbled quai. She knew it in a heartbeat. Café du Soleil, her home until Libération.

She looked closer and almost cried out. In the group she recognized the Black GI jeep driver she'd seen at Libération with his arm around Céline. Was that Gisors behind his shoulder? The photo was small, but it looked like him in profile.

"I don't understand. How's this important?"

Vince pointed to a larger picture of American military grouped at the entrance of a hotel. Medals on their chests.

"Our contact, the jeep driver, works with the men in this photo," he said. "We can get the goods in quantity, but we need to move them. Fast."

She nodded. "And you want our help selling your product?"

"That's right, kid. Lots of high-grade product. Regular deliveries. Big profits for your boss."

Exactly what Louis had wanted. But her throat was drying up. Unnerved, she didn't know how to answer.

Vince and Pete exchanged looks.

"How about this? We'll put *you* on the inside."

"*Moi?*"

"Kid, you hafta understand—we can't have a new Frenchie with us until we verify, too. Everyone in the café would get suspicious. So you'll work with us for a bit in the café."

"In a café? I don't understand what you want me to do."

"We operate part of our business out of a café. It's safer with people coming and going, and no one the wiser. You'll do a little work while seeing how we do business and report back to your boss. And we'll see how you do, too. Oh, and you'll get a cut. That'll satisfy your boss, right? We can meet him after that."

Her insides curdled. "What do you mean, 'get a cut'?"

"A commission. Between us. You know, nice pocket money for yourself."

A bribe. Her gut sense had been correct.

He took a matchbox from his pocket, palmed it into her hand. "Here."

She stared at the logo with the name of a café. Café Central in the ninth *arrondissement*. Not her father's old café.

"Tell your boss you start tomorrow. We'll see how you do, then meet and we can all decide. Deal?"

She remembered her promise to Louis.

Better the devil you know than the one you don't—and she'd grown up in a café. A plan was forming in her head. She'd chew her way in, bite by bite. Then escape.

"But how does this café connect to people in those photos?"

Vince frowned. "You ask too many questions."

"I'm only asking what my boss will ask me," she said, playing angry, which wasn't hard to do. These cocky soldiers needed to be shown they couldn't treat her like a kid. Establish authority, her father would say, when dealing with black marketers. "He'll want to know who they are. Will they be dangerous to his operation? There's a risk of leaks, since we're working with outsiders. Make sense?"

Pete grinned. "She's right."

He seemed eager to make the deal. But Vince, the cautious one, held back.

"Of course I am," she said. "Say I put my neck out and present your plan to him and he agrees. I'm still on the line if I work in the café."

"How's that?"

"Who serves two masters, Monsieur Pete?"

"I think you'll figure it out." He handed her a wad of US dollars.

Once it hit her palm, she wanted to take her words back. Run away. She was way out of her depth—this was moving too fast.

Pete must have noticed something in her eyes.

"Cold feet?" he said. "Look, keep half and give the rest to your boss."

He thought she was greedy and holding out for more.

How far from the truth could he be.

"And there's more for you where that came from. But . . ." He narrowed his eyes. Put his finger over his lips and his other hand on the pocket where a knife bulged. "Careful who you tell. We don't like people who talk to the wrong people. They get taken care of, understand?"

AUGUST 1945

*Versailles, Hotel Trianon—
Temporary Adjunct Offices of Supreme Headquarters
Allied Expeditionary Forces (SHAEF)*

—

Claude tried not to look impressed as he sat on a gilt chair outside a US general's office. Versailles, home of the kings, made him feel small, provincial, and every inch the peasant his ancestors were. He sighed, again checking the time. Inspector Marchal had said the Americans had been expecting him, but fifteen minutes had turned to half an hour. No staff. No water. The heat in the place parched his throat dry as sand.

In a side salon, he'd noticed a slashed portrait of Hitler alongside red banners with swastikas in a bin marked INCINERATE. Outside the ornate building a cluster of "snowdrops," military police wearing the white helmets, white gloves, and white leggings that earned them that moniker, guarded the entrance.

Claude loosened his tie, stood, and moved to a tall window to catch any hint of breeze. Somewhere a door shut. He cracked open the slats of blue shutters for air. All he got was a warm ripple.

"This way." A soldier gestured and Claude followed him over a scuffed inlaid parquet floor through a suite of connecting high-ceilinged rooms into a room where two uniformed men were conducting a briefing.

"Naughty boy, Beck. I read the report. You should be court-martialed."

Speaking was an American general with medals decorating his lapels. The dark-haired man he spoke to was of medium height, filling out his uniform. The general opened a drawer of an ornate ormolu desk to pull out a pack of Camels. Lit one with a Zippo lighter, inhaled and clicked the Zippo shut. Claude wished he had a lighter like that.

This silver-haired general, trim in his uniform, blew a spiral of blue smoke.

Claude stood still. He understood more English than he'd let on to his inspector. So far, neither man acknowledged his presence.

"But I could make this go away, Beck," said the general. "On the condition you take this mission and follow my orders. Do that and your foray never gets recorded. You know, General Patton says the only good Kraut's a dead Kraut. But we at the OSS don't see it that way. Agree?"

"Yes, sir."

OSS. He'd heard of them. Undercover American intelligence agents.

"Thought so. I'm pulling you off current POW interrogations. You'll work with the Frenchies on this."

"But sir . . ." Beck had a German accent.

Not a breath of air stirred. Claude roasted in his jacket.

"I know, I know." Sigh. He lowered his voice. "Snail-eating, day-drinking skirt chasers. But you'll mine their smarts if they have any. Didn't saboteur school teach you about making the most of locals?"

Had this general thought Claude understood none of these insults? So rude and arrogant, with his get-things-done attitude. So American.

"Meet Leduc, with the Suréte," said the general, pointing to him. "You'll be working with him, Beck."

So Claude was the local they were going to use.

"That's an order, soldier."

"Yes, sir."

The general turned to Claude, fixing him with a stare. "Leduc, you assist Beck, furnish him contacts, and show him the lay of the land. You won't repeat a word of what's been said in this office. Your boss Marchal called me and says you're skating on thin ice."

Skating on thin ice?

"You understand, Leduc?"

Whatever it meant, it didn't sound good. Claude almost licked the sweat from his upper lip.

"Yes, General."

As if the general hardly cared whether Claude understood him or not, or participated in the briefing at all, he directed his gaze to Beck again. "Another question, Beck. Why go AWOL, risking your career?"

"My wife and son might have survived in Hamburg," said Beck, emotionless. "I tried to follow a lead, sir."

"Family," said the general. A slight pause before he nodded. "I understand. But now's not the time for your own personal crusade, soldier. I'll say it again—no more Nazi hunting. Understood?"

"Yes, sir."

"For today, enjoy your office quarters next to Marie Antoinette's little place while you get to work."

"Yes, sir. What's my assignment, sir?"

"Beck, I'll pretend this once that you asked what 'our' assignment is," said the general.

Claude pulled out the small leather notebook from his inside pocket.

"Post D-Day, a paratrooper named Billy Whitlaw stationed at the depot in Fontainebleau went AWOL—something you know about. He formed a criminal gang of deserters. The gang steals from the depot, sells on the black market, and in general terrorizes Paris. They kill French gangsters who don't cooperate, and citizens have been caught in the crossfire. Whitlaw's gang's co-led by an ex-paratrooper sergeant. Raids are planned like military operations."

The sharp caw of crows erupted outside in the grounds of the Château de Versailles. A warning, a signal? Alert, Claude's gaze scanned 360 degrees, looking for possible places of attack.

Relax. He wasn't near enemy lines anymore.

This German soldier wasn't his target.

"Billy Whitlaw's gang plunders in daylight," the general continued. "Brazen. They'll wear fatigues, stop a transport truck and tie up the driver. Now they're raiding private mansions. Their core business consists of stealing gasoline, cigarettes, liquor, and weapons." He stubbed out his cigarette in the nearest thing on his desk—a Baccarat petits fours bowl—exquisite. "Local criminals fence the products. The gang's ruthless. Kill anyone in their own gang who holds out on takings or skims the profits. The Paris police here haven't been able to stop them."

Claude fumed.

The glorious US liberators looked more than incompetent. Not worthy of trust in a country they'd shed blood for.

"This directive comes from the top. Root them out, stop this gang, and do what you need to. I want military justice."

"You mean a court-martial, sir?"

"Didn't you hear me? Do what you need to, understood? You

will capture them and obtain evidence, and the gang goes to trial. Alive. They'll be poster boys for military justice and ending the black market." The general's gaze was steely. "No time to waste. With six months into the game, we've heard Whitlaw's profits are north of half a million. You need to shut him down as soon as possible."

Claude suppressed his surprise. Was he in the wrong business?

No doubt this GI Whitlaw was getting cocky. Careless. They often did.

With people hungry, the black market would thrive no matter what. Robbing, shooting, murder was another kind of criminality.

"How did you get this info on Whitlaw?"

"I can't say."

"So there's an informer?"

"Go find out, soldier. You and Leduc can speak the lingo in the land of wine and more wine. Find me these sons of bitches, their French connections, the fences, and the deserters. Get details and locations. Accomplish your mission, Beck, and your court-martial-worthy offence goes away. I'll need you for the ongoing Nuremberg International Military Tribunal trials," the general said. "Fail, and you'll be infiltrating the remaining guerrilla holdouts of the Waffen-SS division."

The toughest unit, die-hard holdouts—nicknamed the Werewolves—who still believed in the Third Reich, hiding in scattered pockets of the German countryside.

"You have a week. General Patton's coming and these animals need to be behind bars. Understood, soldier?"

"Yes, sir."

"Leduc, if he sinks, so do you. Remember that. Squeeze your contracts dry and get results."

Merde!

AUGUST 1945

Café Central, Ninth Arrondissement, Paris

~

Juju slammed down her tray. "You're late, Hélène. There's tables to serve and a package you need to deliver."

Not another one.

Huguette bit back a catty reply. She'd worked here two weeks and couldn't wait to be done. Playing this role was back-breaking work, and Huguette was frightened of being caught every day.

Over the past two weeks, while Louis was still in the hospital, she'd been proving her "credentials." She'd promised him she'd work here until Pete's gasoline connection panned out. She'd overheard snippets about gas shipments but no real leads. Pete kept telling her to stay patient.

She tied on her apron, balanced the tray of *aperitifs* on her arm.

"Next time, I'll dock your pay," Juju said. Petite with wispy dark hair, Juju would pass for attractive if it weren't for the way she framed her small eyes with thick black eyeliner, turning them into black holes. She seemed to take particular pleasure in tormenting Huguette with endless small tasks.

The atmosphere in the café was always tense. Kitchen gossip said a new gang was muscling in and these GIs' days were numbered. Staff weren't turning up for work.

But was keeping her promise worth it? If she were caught in a gang war and rounded up, the police would discover she was wanted and she'd be thrown in prison.

She'd give it another day, she decided.

She'd said that yesterday, too.

"Forget this." Juju tapped her arm. Her face was expressionless. "They're here."

It was Billy the GI and Albertine, Juju's bottle-blond sister. Albertine winked and the GI nodded to Juju. The next moment, they'd mounted the stairs to the upper-level banquet room, where his cronies usually waited.

Juju poured ice in a bucket, stuck a bottle of Champagne inside, and loaded it onto a new tray with coupe glasses.

"Take this upstairs, serve them, and wait."

Huguette's insides cramped. She cast a quick glance around the café. Apart from the locals—men in prewar jackets, women in turbans to hide hair they couldn't wash without hot water and soap—only a few demobilized soldiers. Just then two men drifted in and a warning screamed in her head. The air of hawk-like surveillance—just like the Gestapo who'd come into her papa's café and rounded up their neighbors.

Juju snapped her fingers. "Hurry up."

Huguette squared her shoulders and heaved the heavy tray. While the black marketeering was a challenge, at least working in a café felt like second nature. Not much of a silver lining, but better than nothing, she told herself as she stomped up the stairs.

When she reached the wood door, she knocked on it with her heel before pushing her way in.

Acrid cigarette smoke and conversations in pidgin English. Billy and Albertine sat at a booth in the low-ceilinged banquet room. With them were two men she'd seen before, GI deserters recognizable by their well-fed frames, stacking cartons of Lucky Strike cigarettes in a box. Her heart flipped at the familiar sight—she'd helped her father stockpile Lucky Strikes in their café's cellar.

Also on the table were stacks of guns—large and small.

Her jaw locked.

At the next booth sat black-haired Tino, the Corsican lowlife whom Juju had identified as another gang boss "never to cross." His fist slammed on the table. "Took you long enough."

Terrified, Huguette froze.

"Hurry up," Albertine growled. "Pop the cork. We've got business to do."

"That's right," said Billy, watching Huguette with his reptilian gaze. "And you've got deliveries to make."

She told herself not to engage. Just kept her eyes down and poured, careful to let the bubbles settle before she distributed the coupes.

That done, she stood back against the wall in the smoky room. Tino raised the coupe of Champagne, made a toast about how the glass's round shape had been modeled on Marie Antoinette's breasts. Loud laughter drowned out most of it.

Albertine waved her over. "Got a big errand for you," she said. "Listen up."

August 1945

Versailles, Hotel Trianon—
Temporary Adjunct Offices of Supreme Headquarters
Allied Expeditionary Forces (SHAEF)

—

Sergeant Mark Beck scowled as they stepped out of the general's office into the sweltering hallway. Claude felt his shirt plastered to his spine. The hottest day of the year and he was wearing a jacket. Yet Beck wore a crisp uniform and hadn't broken a sweat.

Claude reached for a handkerchief to dry his neck. Aimed for a conciliatory tone. "Looks like we're in the same boat."

"Not in a million years," said Beck.

"What's this about your family, Beck?" asked Claude.

Beck bristled. "None of your business, Leduc." His intense gaze bored into Claude. His eyes were dark and seething. "You weren't in the war, were you?" he asked, suspicion thick in his voice.

Beck was testing him. Claude had no reason to lie.

"My unit got captured in '41. I spent two and a half years in a POW camp," said Claude.

"So like all Frenchies, you sat out the war." Sarcastic and itching to fight.

Riled, Claude kept his expression calm. "I wouldn't say that," he said. "We broke out in spring of '44 and fought at Libération. Later I saw battle in Dijon. And you, Beck?"

"You got a rough idea," he said.

Claude had put it together—parts of it, anyway. Beck was one of those escaped German Jews who'd signed up with the Allies. Became a trained saboteur behind enemy lines, then deserted to look for his family. With his training, skills, and expertise, the general must value him. That's why he held his freedom over him.

Claude filed this away.

Outside they passed hanging willows on the Versailles grounds. Birds sang, a fountain gushed somewhere, and sweet fragrance drifted from the roses the Nazis hadn't beheaded in Marie Antoinette's garden.

"Leduc, I won't pretend to think you care about your role . . ."

Claude put his hand up. "*Bon.* I'm doing my job. Like you, Beck. And please speak English, it's good for me to practice."

"Why don't I believe that?"

"It's true. And also your German accent will give you away in French. Not a good idea right now."

"You have a problem with me?"

Anger vibrated in Beck's voice. His flat gaze warned Claude that violence simmered below the surface. Just his luck.

"It's not whether I have a problem or not," he said. "It's whether you can conduct the investigation and get answers in German-accented French."

Beck, conceding, said nothing until they reached the staff room, where he handed Claude the general's file. "Start with this. Note down any details I might have missed. Chart the locations. We meet in an hour. Then I plan the operation."

Claude opened the pages to find smudged police reports.

"What kind of operation? Will you need my team?"

"Assist means assist. For now you're on the periphery. I'll update you."

Beck thought he'd put him in his place. Fortified with watery coffee, Claude got to work.

Precisely an hour later, as if he had German clockwork instilled in him, Beck looked in on him.

"What have you found, Leduc?"

Claude cleared his throat.

"According to police reports, attacks of US military vehicles happen on the ring roads at four access points that correspond to four of the old gates. There are actually dozens of these gates ringing the city, dating back to medieval times."

"I don't need a history lesson."

Claude was determined not to let Beck rile him. "Chances are they keep a storage depot near these four access points. Most Paris gangs we've discovered do this. I went over a map and highlighted the industrial buildings, warehouses, and farms near each."

"This all you've got? There's a lot more in the report. What do your informers say?"

"Little. We've been running in circles trying to chase gangs all over the city. Better to stake out the access points, then follow them inside and take action."

With a disgusted look, Beck stood. "I thought you were supposed to be the best on your team. I could have come up with all of this myself."

"Oh, and there's a Corsican bar in Pigalle worth checking out."

Beck paused and turned. "That's more like it."

BECK LED LEDUC TO HIS office, which was built near the old stables. The whiff of horses, hay, and wet mash brought a tinge of homesickness for his native Auvergne. Two men were waiting for them there.

"Meet my team. Anatole, he goes by Arnie."

A man with a prominent Gallic nose and sharp brown eyes shook Claude's extended hand, giving him a shrewd look.

"Gilles, known as Jim." Another handshake with a blue-eyed blond. "Both trilingual like me. Now let's hear some more about this bar."

LATER, AS THE SCORCHING SUNLIGHT faded, Beck gave them their broad action plan.

"So what are we?" asked Arnie. "Muscle for hire? Middlemen on a buying spree?"

Jim lit a cigarette. "Or a combo? Play whatever jumps out?"

"Our cover is we sell gas to a supplier in a trucking business," said Beck. "No cigarettes or chocolate."

"Do we execute anyone?" asked Arnie.

He looked the type who excelled at silent killing.

"Our mission's to fish and catch. Remember, the deserters are ruthless—they'll lose everything if they're caught. Orders are to keep them alive for trial."

"The orders always say that. We take care of them our way, *ja*?"

Claude concealed a shudder at the man's bloodthirsty expression.

"We're not behind enemy lines this time," Beck reminded. "We're in central Paris, lots of eyes on us. We'll nab the culprits and lock them up."

"That's a job for the military police."

Claude agreed.

"If they could do that, the general wouldn't need us," Beck said. "He's made it clear he needs poster criminals for a big statement, so we've got to nab Billy Whitlaw and his crew. Listen up and pay attention."

Claude took notes. His job was on the line if the team didn't pull this off.

Claude lingered after Arnie and Jim had left. "I think there could be another angle here."

Beck looked up from his desk. "What do you mean?"

"Not only my job but yours hangs on this, Beck. We have to work together. I need help finding a file from 1944. The US military supposedly recovered many of our police files. I can't access them anymore even though I'm in the force and it was my case. Too sensitive. The one I want's missing. Word is, your military intelligence took them."

Or so he surmised if they weren't at the RG.

Surprised, Beck sat back and knocked papers from his desk. They fluttered to the stone floor. He bent and scooped them up. "I don't assist in vendettas, Leduc."

"That's good because this isn't a vendetta. It's an important file pertinent to my ongoing homicide investigation. Three bodies with the same signature execution style were recovered in the Seine. I think the files are missing because someone's covering them up." He took a breath. "I'm being straight with you, Beck. I think it's the reason I've been sent here on this job, and I don't like being sidelined. I didn't join the force for this."

Beck studied him. Claude felt the scrutiny.

"Tell me more."

August 1945

Pigalle, Paris

—

The team settled into the Pigalle hotel room overlooking the Corsican bar, the known black market hub. Claude admired the team's forged IDs and ration coupons as they unpacked their kit bags. Excellent work.

But Beck's men were rough around the edges, and this assignment required finesse. He wondered if their skills of enemy sabotage and assassinations qualified them to pull off this job. His doubts rose.

Then again, it wasn't called wild Pigalle for nothing.

On their second day, Arnie, who relished the role of a gangster, stationed himself by the kiosk across from the bar they surveilled, reading a paper as if waiting for someone. Jim, on surveillance at the window, set down his customized nonreflective palm-size binoculars. He thumbed through the file's photos. Held one up.

"It's him. He just entered the bar. Wearing civvies."

Billy Whitlaw. Maybe this would happen after all. Or was it too easy?

"Alone?"

Eager, Beck spread out the photos of known accomplices.

"He's with her." Jim pointed to a young blond woman.

The hotel room phone rang and Claude answered.

"You might want to get to the office, Leduc," said Alain. "An informer bit. And they'll only talk to you."

"Good, set up a meet for this afternoon and I'll—"

Alain interrupted, "Bad idea. It's time sensitive."

Of all times.

He should participate in this operation—if Beck would let him and quit treating him like window dressing. Torn, he sensed he'd regret it if he bypassed the informer.

"Let's go," said Beck to the men. "Coming, Leduc?"

Claude shook his head. "Something came up. Important. You can handle this."

He hoped he wasn't making a big mistake.

AUGUST 1945

Police Prefecture, Paris

—

"*Et voilà*," said Alain, waving an opened envelope. "Addressed to Leduc, invitation for a meetup. Incognito."

Claude snatched it from him.

"You opened it?"

"We're partners, *non*?"

As partners, they had each other's backs, but Alain had a competitive streak. "How long ago did you see this?"

Alain lowered his voice. "You mean how long have you been seeing your girlfriend like this?"

He didn't like Alain's grin.

"Girlfriend?"

Alain winked. "So you've got a new *chérie*, eh?"

"*You* need a girlfriend, Alain," Claude said. "I'm married."

He'd married young, before he'd been sent to war. When he'd returned after almost three years in prison camp, then combat, he found he had a son, and that he and his wife both changed. She'd found someone else.

"Who delivered this and when?"

"No idea. The reception had no idea either."

He scanned the message.

"*Merde*, I'm late!"

CLAUDE HURRIED TO THE PLACE Paul-Painlevé in the park beyond the ancient Roman baths. Sun gleamed on the pointed tips of the grilled fence and the dark green leaves. He saw no children, but their laughter drifted from somewhere nearby. A man washed the windows of the bookstore facing the park.

It felt almost like before the war.

He sat down, catching his breath, by a young woman at the farthest bench, as indicated in the note. She was holding a newspaper that shielded half her face; she wore dark tortoiseshell glasses and a cloth beret.

"You're late," she said. "No uniform?"

Where did he know this voice from?

"Apologies, I just got the message." He opened his jacket to reveal his badge. Buttoned it back up. "You said incognito."

"I did. Thank you."

That voice was frightfully familiar.

"Wait," he said, "do we know each other?"

A pause.

"What's important," she said, "is what I know."

Eyes narrowing, he watched her. "First, let me see you."

A slight hesitation before she looked around, then lowered the newspaper and removed her glasses.

He never forgot a face. Hers had imprinted on his psyche. The scrawny, tear-streaked young orphan huddled on the floor of the jail in Sceaux after losing her baby. Those strange eyes, one green and one with topaz glints. Not so scrawny anymore.

"Did you use the Métro map and ticket I gave you?"

She smiled. "You do remember me."

Hard to forget. But he didn't say that.

He'd been looking for her, had put out feelers for her whereabouts. He still had no leads as to why her father's corpse had turned up in the river months after his death.

"Did everything work out afterward?"

"You know it did or I wouldn't be here," she said. "But you took me seriously when no one else did. Gave me good advice."

Had he?

"I'm glad to hear it," Claude said. He eyed her for a moment. "But I'm sure you didn't call me here only to tell me that."

She considered him, too. As if deciding whether to speak after all. "You keep informants confidential?" she asked. "Don't reveal your sources?"

He nodded. "*Bien sûr.*" Was this about to be the big break in her father's case he'd been waiting for?

"I have information on the bandit GIs that are in all the papers these days," she said. "Their hideout, their plans. I can even tell you where their depot might be."

Claude didn't know how to respond. How had she gotten mixed up with gangsters? It couldn't have been the rogues *he'd* been tracking—that would be too perfect of a connection. Could he trust her?

Sensing his doubt, Huguette Faure raised her hand as if to bat away any protests. Reddish knuckles, chapped skin. Working hands. "It was the only work I could find when I got back to Paris. Things were . . . complicated."

Surely there was more to it than that. But her history wasn't his business here. Her information was.

"Please go on."

"No different from the occupation, *n'est-ce pas?*" She took a breath. "I work at a café where the GIs hang out. I hear them talking. They're loud."

"You understand English?"

"I understand enough." She smoothed her hands over the newspaper in her lap—the top article was about a recent large theft of gasoline. "Their operation runs through my boss Juju's café. A GI bought it for her sister, Albertine. Now they use it to launder their profits."

Claude nodded. It wasn't anything he hadn't heard before. He needed specifics, but he had to move slow so he didn't scare her off. "I appreciate your information. Forgive me, but I have to ask why you're telling me?"

"I want to get out," she said. "I help you, you help me. There are gang rivalries—it's getting dangerous. I've seen guns. Hot-tempered gangsters with weapons and thousands of dirty francs disgust me. Scare me, too."

"Understood."

Huguette exhaled thinly. "But I guess you're not interested."

"Of course I am. But I need proof to show my boss."

"Cautious, eh?" Huguette scoffed. "During the Occupation, a little note about a neighbor brought the Gestapo, and now I need a certified letter?"

"You're in danger," he said, hoping he came across as soothing. "But my boss will want a source."

"No one was vetting sources when my father got killed."

Her lids batted. Was it to keep back tears, or a flash of anger?

Claude didn't know how much he could share—how much he *should* share—but he felt he owed her in some way. "Your father—Remy Faure?"

Huguette went suddenly motionless.

"Actually, I've been investigating your father's death," he told her, voice quiet.

"Fat lot of good that does me now."

But he noticed her hand skittered on the bench rail.

He couldn't bear to tell her the gory details about the bodies found in the river. Or the girl with her scarf. He'd lose her.

"I'm sorry."

"Sorry won't bring him back."

Or solve his murder, Claude thought.

A stray cat slunk into the park, scattering the birds from the bushes. A woman pushing a buggy bent forward and cooed to her baby inside. Pain crossed Huguette's face.

"Look, count on my help," he said. He could tell she was weighing up the situation. Weighing him up. For some reason he wanted to measure up, to show he wasn't like the others. "I joined the *flics* to do the right thing. Seemed right at Libération. When it doesn't anymore, I'm putting up my shingle as a detective."

She lifted the newspaper back up to shield her face. "And if I tell you what I know, you'll protect me? You won't let them throw me in jail?"

Warnings prickled up his spine whenever a prospective informant asked that.

"Do we have a deal?" she pressed.

"Deal."

A couple walked past them, their footsteps crunched the gravel.

"An operation's happening soon. People in the quartier know. Juju's getting nervous. They're loud when they're drunk. Indiscreet and flashy, with their big cars and flashy clothes."

"Juju's your friend?"

"*Pas du tout.* She dislikes me, the feeling's mutual. But I can tell she's scared to get caught."

He believed her. Still there was something else she wasn't telling him. "What's holding you there?"

"I told you, it's complicated." She shot him a piercing look. "You think I'm after the reward. If I was a man, would you think that? No one's watching out for me, I watch out for myself. I never wanted to work in the black market after what happened to Papa."

Claude's brain raced. The connections were clicking. "Give me the details, names."

"There's Billy, an American."

Claude sat up. "Billy Whitlaw?"

"Maybe. Also Tino, a Corsican."

"I'll handle it from here. You can get out of it, Huguette."

Her face muscles tightened. Where was the vulnerable girl he'd glimpsed before? "They know me as Hélène Foy," she said. "And their operation is happening soon. Tonight. Tomorrow. I don't know. I'll leave a message at your office. *Rose*, that means it's happening. Agree?"

He nodded. "What do you want in return?"

"Protection."

AUGUST 1945

Café Central, Ninth Arrondissement, Paris

—

"Start cleaning up and come upstairs in fifteen minutes. You've got a job, *comprends*, Hélène?" Juju shot her a knowing look.

This was it—the job Pete's gang had prepared her for. So far she'd seen no undercover *flics* staking out the café. Claude Leduc had kept his word this far—but could she trust him?

There was no one else she *could* trust now.

So far, there'd been no mention of a big gasoline deal and she'd begun to question what she was even doing here apart from hard labor. It felt too dangerous—that's why she'd gone to Leduc. If the gasoline operation had stalled, as she'd begun to suspect, she'd be better off leaving and talking to Louis about another connection for selling Cognac through the black market, and at least Juju and Billy's gang would be off the streets.

She rushed through her cleanup and managed to slip to the pay phone to leave Leduc a message: "There are fresh roses at the market." Her nerves rattled as she climbed the stairs.

Upstairs in the meeting room, she put on the schoolgirl jacket Juju handed her, braided her hair, and wiped off her lipstick. Schoolgirls on the Métro got no attention or scrutiny—who better to carry a bag of cash? Wearing the uniform again left her with a hollow feeling in her chest.

Tino thrust a heavy leather carryall with frayed handles into her hand.

"Bring this to the garage on rue Rambuteau. Right by the Métro."

To the waiting arms of the Voltaire gang contact, who dealt the stolen gasoline and laundered their money. Huguette nodded. Wondered if this would pan out and lead to the gasoline.

Too late now.

"The money's all accounted for down to the last centime. So don't get ideas. They'll call when you deliver. Bring back the item they give you. *Comprends?*"

"Like last time," she said, nodding.

She'd delivered their takings last week, a test, and they'd watched her like a hawk.

Tino looked at his watch. "You've got forty minutes."

Back and forth? He must have noticed her look.

"Or I come after you."

Albertine tossed a Métro ticket at her.

"What are you waiting for?"

Huguette hefted the bag and took the back stairs. Glad to get out of their way. She hoped Leduc had gotten her message—he'd show up while she was out, if she'd timed everything right.

Halfway down the stairs, in a slant of light, she peered inside the heavy carryall and gasped.

Packs of banded dollars and francs. Easily worth hundreds of thousands. She'd had no idea.

From behind her came the familiar sound of a door splintering open.

Shouts. The crack of a gunshot.

A fight? A rival gang? The police?

Leave.

She took the stairs two at a time. Tripped, and felt herself in the air. The bag flew through the dark. Somehow her arms braced against the wall—she winced at the scrape of the wood, but quickly righted herself, grabbed the banister, and felt for the bag. More gunshots.

She found the bag handles and ran like hell out the back door.

In the back alley, she careened into a garbage bin, got a sleeve caught by the wheel of a wooden cart. A splinter pierced her arm; she clamped her hand over her mouth so she didn't cry out. She shook free of the cart, kept to the wall, and headed toward the boulevard. Before her the narrow street glinted with light from the streetlamps. The Métro lay ahead.

"I'll take that for you," said a voice.

A hulking figure stepped from the shadows and blocked her way.

"Who are you?"

"Not important." He reached for the bag. Huguette's gaze caught on the skin where his coat cuff didn't reach his gloved hand. She saw the squiggle of a blue spider tattooed on his wrist.

"Give me the bag."

She kicked him hard in the shin.

"Oof," he grunted, doubling over in pain. But that didn't stop him. He reached for her, tearing at the handle. She kicked his other shin, heard a crack. He let go and she ran.

Dead ahead of her were men in unfamiliar uniforms, loudly yelling to each other in English. But not GIs—military police?

Her breath hitched.

Her quick scan showed no Leduc. The Métro entrance was too far. The *boulangerie* had shuttered. And here came jogging up a gaggle of Parisian *flics*—but still no Leduc.

Were these his men? Could she trust them? What should she do? Hand over the bag of money after her experience with the crooked policeman at the train station? She wouldn't be that naive again.

She needed to stash this bag—she didn't care who the dirty money belonged to. Any second that man would come after her.

But the Notre-Dame-de-Lorette church doors were open, admitting congregants for evening service. The stained glass windows glowed rose and azure from within.

She darted inside, dipped her fingertips into the marble font's cold water, and genuflected on the worn pavers. During the war, her Christian youth group had passed messages in churches, leaving notes in prayer books, niches under the baptismal font, or the bases of saints' statues. She and Marina had even taped messages under the kneeler. The memory of Marina sliced her heart as she gulped in the incense-scented air.

None of these thoughts were helpful to her now—the carryall was too big for any of these hiding places and Marina was gone.

Her gaze caught on the Gothic-styled wooden confessional with carved panels topped by an ornate grill. She slipped past the musty worn velvet curtain. Knelt and crossed herself again, the irony nearly choking her. She hoped no one had noticed her—the priests were busy preparing for evening Mass, not hearing confession anymore. As fast as she could, she shuffled francs and dollars into her socks and underwear. Scuttling patter sounded up the wooden wall. Mice.

Then the noise stopped.

They had a nest. It gave her an idea.

She rose, parted the curtain. Deep organ chords sounded as a small choir sang "Ave Maria." The congregants filled the front pews. No one watched her. Or would hear her.

Slinging the bag onto her shoulder again, she found the dark niche between the church wall and the confessional. Her back pressed against the confessional booth, she used her feet to leverage herself up the wall. Painful and slow. When she'd almost reached the top, a quick glance showed a declivity where the wood roof slat met the grill. Small, but it had to do. She lifted and set the bag down, disturbing the mice, whom she heard scattering and squeaking under the boards.

She'd have to get back before they made a nest with the cash.

OUTSIDE, SAYING A SILENT PRAYER, she kept to the edges of the forming crowd. Eager to put distance between herself and the church, she kept an eye out for the tattooed man as she began to hurry toward the Métro. Time to escape.

Streetlights gleamed, reflecting off the damp pavers. American MPs and *flics* were herding several people out of the café: Billy Whitlaw, Juju, and Albertine, who was yelling at Tino, his arm dripping with blood.

If the American military police had raided the café, then who had accosted her?

She kept her head down to avoid being recognized or pointed out.

"This way, mademoiselle," said a man. He spoke English with an accent she couldn't place.

Before she could get out of his path, his arm clutched her elbow. Steered her aside. She tried to shake the hand off.

"Let me go."

"Hélène Foy, you're charged with crimes against the US military." He flashed an American military ID with the name Mark Beck.

AUGUST 1945

Police Prefecture, Île de la Cité

—

Huguette, Juju, and Albertine sat on a hard bench behind chipped green metal bars awaiting Mark Beck's questioning. To him they were all guilty, deserving to rot in a smelly cell.

Did Huguette stand a chance?

Which one would he halfway believe? Juju the barkeep, with her tight skirt and burgeoning black eye, mascara stains on her cheeks? Albertine, her bottle-blond sister, smeared red lipstick pouting? Or her, the frightened girl wearing a blue school uniform jacket, her brown braids stuck to her damp neck?

Fresh scratch marks bled on her wrist. Juju had attacked her when they'd reached the station—Beck had had to break them up.

"Where's the bag, Hélène?" muttered Juju between her teeth.

Dead. She was good as dead. Juju would garrote her with a silk stocking right here.

She surveyed the small cell. Of the two other women besides them, one was asleep, one filed her nails. Huguette leaned close to Juju's ear. "H-he grabbed me in the alley."

Juju turned and read her eyes. Uncanny, Huguette always thought, her ability to pierce through lies. Smell fear.

"Who?"

"I don't know." Huguette let the terror show on her face—it wasn't hard to do. "I heard the shots and ran fast down the stairs, and this man was waiting in the shadows. He stood in my way and said, 'I'll take that.'"

For a horrible second she wondered if he was the gang's own man, employed to effect a switch. To up the security of the errand.

But they hadn't done it before, so why now?

"It was like he knew I was coming."

Juju narrowed her eyes at her. "And you just *gave* it to him?"

"He took it." She made a snatching movement with her arm. "I'd never seen him before. Do you know him? I saw he had a spider tattoo on his wrist."

So far she hadn't lied. Well, once.

Juju blinked. "That's Tino's cousin," she whispered under her breath. "*Mon Dieu.*" She crossed herself. "Tino tricked us."

A Corsican double cross? The Corsicans were notorious for their brutal killing technique.

Furious whispers between the sisters echoed off the gouged plaster walls.

Beck was approaching the holding cell. "Who wants to go first?"

He spoke French with a German accent. Alsatian?

"All I know is that she's a thief," said Albertine. She pulled Huguette's collar. "A liar."

"Your boyfriend's a deserter, Albertine," said Beck. "He's AWOL from the US Army. This means he's getting court-martialed. So will his little 'buddies.' Desertion means hanging."

Across from them, the screamer in the drunk tank wouldn't shut up.

Albertine blustered. "What's that to do with me?"

"You're his accomplice, his partner in crime."

"*Moi?* I had no idea."

Juju piped up. "*C'est l'amour.*"

"And you're okay with your sister hanging around a man like this? You're aware he uses guns, robs and kills, right?"

Juju shrugged. "He's not *my* boyfriend."

"And he bought her the café," he said. "Put it in her name."

Juju's red mouth opened in a O.

"So you didn't know?"

Of course she did. But her surprise was genuine—she hadn't known anyone else knew. Now it had dawned on her that the jig was up.

And how did Beck know? Claude Leduc must have told him. She felt a wave of relief. Beck was on her side, too.

"I've done nothing wrong," said Juju.

He gestured to the CID guard.

"Hélène Foy, come with me."

SHE SAT ON A SCRATCHED metal chair across from Beck at a grease-smudged table. He poured her a cup of coffee from a blue enamel coffee pot. Steam spiraled from the cup and evaporated in the dank air. She took a sip. Disgusting. But, thirsty, she took another.

"Why do those women call you a liar and a thief?"

"Ask them," she said. "They'll spin a story, just like they are with you. They're no innocents—they run the cover for the GIs' black market business. Shouldn't you know all this already?"

Beck sat up. His dark eyes intense. "How would I?"

Hadn't his intel come from Leduc?

What game was this Beck playing?

"I told the *flic*," Huguette said. She took another sip. How did this pass for coffee? "You need to catch up. Talk to Leduc."

"You're spirited, eh, mademoiselle?" He pulled out a pack of Lucky Strikes. Offered one to her.

"*Non, merci.*"

"Keep it."

She pocketed the cigarettes. On closer inspection, he wasn't as old as she'd thought. Maybe that was why he was going against protocol here. But was that an advantage for her, or a risk?

"Tell me what you know about the gang the GIs work with."

She set the coffee cup down. Eyed him, feeling a mixture of fear and annoyance.

"The Voltaire gang fence the GIs' products. That's all I know. You people need to talk to each other, and you need to release me. That's our deal."

Where was Leduc? He was the one in charge here, wasn't he?

"You and I have no deal."

"Doesn't Uncle Sam work with *les flics français*?"

"You've got a mouth on you." He smiled. "What's your job with them?"

"*Moi?* Errands. Tonight they sent me on a drop-off."

The minute she said it she wished she hadn't.

"So that's why you were outside? Or were you running away with your take?"

Her knuckles clenched. He was smart. "With all the noise, I got scared and ran out."

Would he buy it? He didn't seem convinced. His eyes held hers, something curious behind them.

"What were you dropping off tonight?"

"Please talk to the police. I have a deal with Claude Leduc."

Beck shook his head. "Leduc's not involved in this. Here's *my* deal. You tell me. We'll arrest the gang, stamp out the network, and then you're free."

Huguette's heart had sunk the instant Beck had said Leduc wasn't part of this operation. "*Non*, then I'm dead."

Beck knocked on the wall; a soldier came in. "Take her back to the cell."

AUGUST 1945

Café Central, Ninth Arrondissement, Paris

—

"They call this a joint operation?"

In the deserted café, Claude threw his cap down on the zinc counter littered with smudged glasses, half-full water carafes, full ashtrays. A pigsty. He'd never patronize a place where they didn't empty the ashtrays.

He, Alain, and their team had arrived as the US CID military truck drove away with the suspects they'd "rounded up" thanks to Claude's tip-off from Huguette, a.k.a. Hélène Foy. Mark Beck hadn't kept his part of the bargain; the Parisian police were the last to know what was going on in their own case.

Alain gave a snort of disgust. "We make it look real."

Alain gestured to the photographers outside. Reporters blocking the entrance.

Central dispatch had told them over the radio that arrests had been made. Twenty minutes late to the party and it was over. Insider knowledge? Or had the wires gotten crossed? Deliberately?

What a waste of time. And what had happened to Huguette?

RETURNING TO THE PREFECTURE, CLAUDE saw the black Citroën van by the side door on the quai. Memories of SS roundups hit him. But these were *les Americains*, the liberators, and the war was over.

Three women were lined up, hands bound. One of them was Huguette. No—Claude had to remember her informant name was Hélène. The black-haired woman spit on Hélène's shoes. "Just you wait."

"Wait for what?" Hélène shouted. "I haven't done anything."

She turned and noticed Claude at the same time. Hurt crossed her face. Her eyes said *you betrayed me*. Like the others, she must have thought.

Why had the CID raided the café and taken these women into custody without notifying his branch?

"What's going on?" said Claude to one of the CID officers.

"Orders, sir."

The Americans might have repelled the *Boche* and enjoyed their Champagne, but this was his turf.

"Show me who authorized this."

Beck stepped forward. His deep-set eyes gave no acknowledgment that he knew Claude or that this was a joint operation.

"The commanding general, my superior, authorized my unit to conduct a search. We discovered AWOL American servicemen subject to military law and brought in these females for interrogation. They face charges of aiding and abetting."

"You've got orders to prove this?"

A sheet headlined with SHAEF US Army was thrust at him.

All in military English. He pretended to read it. He couldn't care less what it said.

"We're transferring the soldiers and these women to be processed at SHAEF HQ in Reims."

"Monsieur Beck, that will be impossible. These women are French citizens, subject to French law. Not under the SHAEF."

Beck crossed his arms over his chest. "Read the orders."

"Brief me in your words." Claude gestured him aside and Beck followed him behind a pillar scarred with bullet holes. "What's Hélène Foy doing here?"

"The young one? Why?"

"She's our informer," said Claude. "Working with us on the gangs connected to the GIs. She gave us the café location. Didn't she tell you?"

A brief sheepish look crossed Beck's face. "That's beside the point."

"You didn't believe her, did you? Your duty's to coordinate with us, the local authority." Claude lowered his voice. "Aren't we working together on this?"

"I'm following orders."

"I respect that, but her information's valuable. She's got a lead on those homicides I'm investigating. That angle I told you about."

"That's up for discussion with my boss."

This wasn't going well.

"Let's save all the trouble and paperwork. Just say you're moving her to juvenile detention, I'll take over from there." It had worked once when Huguette had actually been underage; maybe it would work again.

"You don't know the army, Leduc," said Beck. "But I'll see what I can do."

A CID officer gestured toward him. "Beck, telephone call for you."

"Excuse me."

"Give the order now. It's critical. The minute word on the raid gets out, the others will flee."

But he'd left, and with him the two CID officers.

Claude would have to take this in his own hands.

"Stop." Holding the clipboard with the orders, he went to the van. At least he could make out the names. "Juju Seydoux." He looked between the young women. "Who's that?"

The black-haired woman said, "*Moi*."

"And who's this?"

"Albertine Seydoux, my sister. There's a mistake. You have to help us."

No mistake.

"And who's Hélène Foy?"

Huguette didn't even look at him. Her voice was low. "That's me."

He pretended to read something on the clipboard.

"*Excusez-moi*." He tutted and beckoned to the blue uniformed *flic* guarding the van. "This Foy's a juvenile and scheduled for the next convoy. Officer, remove her."

August 1945

Police Prefecture, Outer Courtyard, Île de la Cité

—

Huguette's stomach churned. Rescued from Juju and the GIs, but for how long? The Corsican mafia wouldn't be far behind. According to her father, they paid off the *flics*. Why had she thought she could outwit these people?

At least she had Claude Leduc on her side. For now. He could turn on her, too.

"We don't have much time to get you out of here," he whispered.

"What do you mean?"

He took her arm, steering her away. "You're a protected informant, but there are multiple factors at play here. We'll get you to a safehouse while the rest of the investigation runs its course."

Another *flic* had come over. He ignored her and spoke to Leduc. "Whispering in company. Didn't your mother tell you that's rude?"

"Very funny, Alain." Leduc put his finger to his lips. Together, they hustled her to a back delivery bay. A parked Citroën's motor started, the headlights went on. "I'll meet you there," Leduc said. "Hurry."

Would she be released? Free? Alain bundled her into the back seat and the car took off.

But Leduc hadn't gotten in with them. As they passed under a dim streetlight, she saw the driver's face in the rearview mirror. Beck, the CID interrogator with the German accent.

"You'll take us to the money," said Alain.

He'd been hovering in the background the entire time Leduc had been negotiating with the American police officers, and she hadn't paid attention to him. Mistake.

"What do you mean?"

Lights whizzed by. At a traffic light, Beck ground the gears with a jerk. She tried the door handle. Locked.

"The money's not yours," said Alain.

"Juju and Albertine lied to you."

She wanted to spit on Leduc. Instead of saving her, he'd betrayed her.

"Did they?" Alain eyed her. "The Corsicans told us you were carrying a bagful of cash."

Tino or the Pigalle *mec* with the spider tattoo?

Everything was crumbling around her. They knew too much.

Beck turned around. "You must have stashed the bag somewhere between the alley and where I caught you."

The car pulled out into the boulevard. "Make it easy and we'll let you go. No charges," said Alain.

She'd trusted Leduc, but he was like all the rest. These men were more dangerous, but at least they were honest, in a way. Telling her to her face what they wanted. "How can I believe you?"

"It's not like you have a choice, *n'est-ce pas?*"

The money wasn't hers, wasn't theirs either. These corrupt men sickened her.

Beck got out and opened the door for her. Pigeons clumped

pecking by the trash bins. Huguette looked up and her jaw dropped when she saw the church. "How did you—"

"Of course you hid the bag in the church," said Beck. "It's the only place open and right here."

His hand clamped like iron around her arm. Up the stairs they went and into the church, where a late-night novena was being held after the Mass.

No time to bless herself now.

Flickering candlelight and musk of incense drifted from a side chapel.

"Make it quick."

At the confessional, she moved to scoot behind it.

"What are you doing?"

"It's on top."

"Hold on. Stand on my shoulders."

Suddenly close, he smelled of tobacco laced with shaving cream. He lifted her up in a second. Startled, she swayed and almost lost her balance. He grabbed her feet, steadied her.

She felt like an acrobat in the big ring. The stakes were high and she had to act. Get this over with.

"Hurry up."

The bag was still there. She grabbed its handle, but the top was open—banknotes spilled out, blanketing the confessional roof. She snapped the bag shut, leaving the spilled notes covered by her handkerchief.

"Got it," she hissed to Beck.

She felt her leg braced, a hand guiding her down the church walls. All of a sudden he'd taken her by the waist, lifted her down gently.

"Smart." His hands lingered on her waist. "Any visitors to your hiding place?"

"The mice," she said. "Did you work in the circus?"

He grinned for the first time.

She wished it were Leduc smiling, his hands around her waist.

"You might want to consider it as your next profession."

Beck let go. "I'll keep that in mind." He opened the bag. "That's it? Nothing else?"

What else had he expected? She shrugged. He was the enemy again.

Back at the car parked in the alley, Alain met them. Still no Leduc.

"Where's Leduc?"

"On another case."

Her throat caught. This didn't feel right. Had he been sent off and they'd split the spoils? She had to get out of here.

"I'm done."

"Change of plans." Alain stood smoking on the curb. "You're the errand girl again. Same job, only you're late."

"That's crazy. Do it yourself."

"Cooperate or you'll end back up in prison with your girlfriends."

Her heart went to her mouth. "Don't you understand, it's too late," she said. "They expected me there hours ago. It won't work. They won't believe me."

Alain blew smoke to dismiss her. "Convince them or you're in big trouble."

She was bait on the hook for a double cross.

Her teeth shivered. Leduc and these men had skewered her. She'd been an idiot.

"Get back in the car and we'll tell you the rest of the plan."

Fear flooded her. She swallowed hard. How could this go from bad to worse?

The gang would be suspicious of her showing up late with only half the money inside the bag. The *flics* wouldn't pounce until she gave the bag to Jules, the garage owner, who ran the laundering operation.

The plan was to use the story the conniving Alain had come up with to implicate Jules. Most of it seemed absurd.

He'd told her, "You're young and dumb. He'll believe it. Act the part."

She remembered feeding lines to an actress all afternoon at Louis's house. The actress's dialogue skills amazed her. She inhabited the words and wove a spell like magic. Her laughter at Huguette's admiration: "*It's pretend—playing to the camera and getting inside the character's skin. You can be anyone. Do anything. In life, too. You can be anyone you have to be to survive.*"

August 1945

Garage on Rue Rambuteau, Paris

~

Huguette's breath came in short gasps. Every part of her ached to run away.

If she could manage to fool the Voltaire gang . . . then what? Would Beck or the corrupt *flic* let her go free? Was it worth risking prison to find out? With heaving breaths, she made herself walk.

Ahead, a squealing rat's greasy tail slithered over the cobbles.

She flinched as she knocked three times on the door fronting rue Rambuteau. Then three more times. Code for a delivery arrival.

The door swung open. She nodded to the shadowed guard and proceeded through into the courtyard. She veered left. In a little-used passage, cobwebs on the dark stone brushed her cheeks and sent goosebumps up her arms.

The bag felt heavy from a brick Alain had put under the banknotes. Stupid. This wouldn't fool anyone. He'd insisted she weasel out the Voltaire gang's warehouse location for the gasoline. No doubt he and Beck would raid the garage while pocketing the cash. If it worked, a triple win for them. But why did he think it would? The gang would shoot her or she'd rot in a cell until she was an old woman. She swallowed hard.

The side door hung ajar. A naked hanging bulb illuminated a dank, sparse office with a single desk, on it a black telephone and a Michelin tire manual.

The smudged glass partition revealed an oil-slicked garage floor, corrugated metal ceiling, some tires, and boxes, boxes, boxes. Not a vehicle in sight. She wondered if they ever did any business, or if the garage was purely a front.

She rounded the corner, her breath shallow and her heart knocking in her chest.

A man she'd never seen appeared from behind boxes.

"Where's Jules?" she asked.

"Forget about him. You talk to me now."

This jeopardized the idiot Alain's plan.

A flashlight beam blinded her. Her arm was grabbed so hard it hurt.

"You're late."

Perspiration broke out on her neck. "Of course I'm late. They raided the café. Get your hands off me."

He did and ripped the bag from her hand; he unzipped it, rustling through to examine the banknotes. Tossing the stacks onto the table. She hoped to God he didn't dig out the brick.

"I'm lucky to even be here," she said, talking fast. "I almost didn't make it. It took hours—I had to wait until it was clear. Then I came as fast as I could."

She had to get the information Alain wanted, then get out of here.

"*Alors*, you're supposed to tell me where to go next."

"Wait," he said. The flashlight beam left her face. It took a moment to adjust her eyes to the dim light.

She heard whispers. What sounded like boxes sliding over concrete. Another figure had appeared from the office.

She prayed this *mec*, probably a relay man, bought her story.

"You're short." The one who'd gone through the bag pointed at the stacks of cash.

"I'm tall for my age."

A stinging slap on her cheek. Huguette bit her tongue and felt the warm taste of blood.

"You know that's not what I meant. There's a brick in here, *salope*. Where's the rest of the money?"

"Like I know? Talk to my boss."

She wished she could make herself small, curl up and hide away. She rued believing Leduc would help her.

"But she's in jail, *non*?"

She'd heard that voice before. He'd probably supplied her father in the black market.

Word traveled fast—whether from a lookout or a crooked policeman's tip, the gang knew Juju and the rest were arrested. Huguette wondered if that meant they knew her story was bunk, too.

Stay calm, talk your way out of it.

She shrugged. "She'll be out in no time."

"Very convenient." He tapped the knuckles on each hand together. As if he was controlling himself from hitting her. She tried not to flinch. "Why is there only half the money here?"

"I do what I'm told. And I'm told you're sending me to the next location. Like last time."

"Eh? What do you mean?"

Now she had to give the story concocted by Alain. Make it believable.

"The warehouse, they told me."

"What warehouse?"

"The one you're supposed to send me to, so we can finish the job."

"Wait, you're saying the rest of the money's there?"

Perfect. He'd said it, not her. "You think they tell me? My job's delivering from point A to point B, then picking up at point C."

She averted her eyes. Looked down at the oil-stained concrete. Cracked and veined with dark sludge. Tires piled haphazardly along the walls.

"Like I said, my instructions are to go to the warehouse." She tried to sound matter of fact. "What's the location?"

The first man with the cap approached her. He glanced at a map, then stuffed it in his pocket.

"Oh, no, we'll take you."

Voices ceased. A tense quiet filled the garage.

She backed up against the grease-stained wall. She had to talk her way out of this.

"You remember me, don't you?" She pointed to the *mec* in a blue cap at the table.

"Watch her," the other one said. "I'll get the truck."

Terror-stricken, she realized she'd be found out. She really was an *idiote*. All for a bit of money.

"Wait a minute," he said. "I know you. You're Remy Faure's daughter. Your eyes give you away. So you're following in your old man's footsteps. Surviving like the rest of us."

Her throat caught. Now she remembered where she'd heard the familiar voice. At Libération. It replayed in her nightmares and she'd wake up in a cold sweat, shaking with terror.

"I heard someone got rich with your father out of the way," he said. "Hid his body."

She tried to remember what Leduc had said about his investigation.

"Hid? What do you mean?"

Footsteps. "You're next. You know too much. Maybe I'll collect the reward put on you after Libération."

Reward?

"Ready?" interrupted the first *mec*, the keys jangling in his hand. "Hurry. We go out the back exit. Now. The *flics* and American CID are out the front." He took the bag. Handed the *mec* who'd recognized her a pistol. Slid his own in his pocket. "She brought the law. Shoot her."

As his footsteps pounded out the back, she gave the metal stool near her a sharp kick into the second *mec*, jerking her body away. The floor was slick with oil and she slid, flailing her arms, and fell, bouncing against old tires. Shouts. The loud crack of gunshots filled her ears and echoed in the garage.

Sucking in her breath, she got on her knees.

The dim light revealed blood seeping from a bullet wound in the man's chest. His pistol lay in a puddle of oil by his cap. Who had shot him? His partner?

Pounding came from the door. "Police. Open up."

Acid bile rose in her throat—found with a dead body and a pistol while the gang escaped with the money? Prison was her next stop.

She tried to overcome the rising nausea and with shaking hands she rifled through his pockets. Inside his coat pocket she found papers, the map with names written on the back.

She pulled herself up. Took his Métro tickets and ran out of the back door.

AUGUST 1945

Métro at Notre-Dame-de-Lorette, Paris

—

Huguette ran panting from the last Métro to find the church doors locked. She was stuck here. No Métro went to Boulogne-Billancourt due to the power cuts.

She huddled on the cold church steps, wanting to give up and die right here. On the run, she wouldn't get far without the money in the church. There was the stash hidden in Nathalie's *boulangerie*, but that was Louis's. All her own money was in her wallet forgotten in the café.

Again, she'd gone back to zero. She forced herself to think, rocking back and forth on the church steps.

What did she have to lose? If the *flics* were still at the café and caught her, it was no different than if she'd let them capture her at the garage. At least this way, she had the smallest chance of getting out.

Her raw nerves grated. Tense, with bile roiling in her stomach, she went to the café. Could she actually find her wallet here after the *flics* had searched it? The Corsican with the tattoo could be watching.

But, exhausted, she had nowhere else to go.

She tried to hold her breath as she kept to the alley's shadows. A fat padlock gleamed on the door.

The coal chute shutter's loose lock yielded to her third kick with a terrifying noise so loud it could wake the neighbors. She looked around. No one in the alley, and windows were shuttered or had drawn curtains.

She wedged herself inside the coal chute and somehow slid down. A short drop later, she landed in a straw basket filled with rotted potatoes. It sounded like thunder. She found a matchbox and fumbled around in the dark until she could scratch a match.

Damp.

Then another. The second sparked and she lit a nearby kerosene lantern. The light illuminated a grimy cellar permeated by damp odors of mold and male sweat. There were the timeworn stairs that led up to the café.

She crept up until she reached the empty café, lit by zebra-stripe slants of light from the breaks in the shutters. It should have been eerie, but cafés were home. She'd grown up in one—recognized the smells from wooden wine casks, the shadows of rattan chairs on the floor, the water carafe beaded with moisture. She imagined her mother's smiling face at the cashier station, Luc, the waiter, winking from the coffee machine.

And for a moment they were here with her. She was home in the Café du Soleil, full of laughter at Céline's dog's antics and of the smell of warm frothed milk, the sunset bleeding orange on the Seine outside their door. The ache of missing them almost doubled her over. Tears brimmed and slid silent down her cheeks. Why, Papa, why did you let this happen?

Her wallet was gone from the tiny staff room.

Back at her father's café, they'd kept a nest egg in the wallboards of the bathroom. So in the women's restroom she tried the wallboards and the loose tiles, but the hole she found was empty. No cash now, if it had ever been there.

The upstairs banquet room lay empty, cigarette cartons scattered on the floor. The phone was still connected and she rang the police. After five minutes she got through to Claude's department.

"Leduc's not at his desk. You can leave a message."

She hung up.

Why had she called him? He'd turned on her, hadn't he?

Exhausted, she nestled in the faux leather armchair where the big GI had sat. The building's water pipes hummed and rattled.

She was floating. Weightless. Warm under the duvet in her old bed. And she was cuddling little Hugues. He was eating with a spoon now. Her mother was wiping his mouth.

Then her arm was being shaken. Someone was pulling at her. She didn't want to go. Wanted to stay with her baby.

"What are you doing here?"

MIDNIGHT, AUGUST 1945

Café Central, Ninth Arrondissement, Paris

—

"*Moi?* What are *you*—"

Claude Leduc put a finger to her mouth, took the lantern, then her hand. He whispered and she had to lean close to hear. His scent of damp wool and musky lime vetiver hit her.

"How did you find me?"

"After I was told I got a call, I thought it might have been you. I took the chance you'd be here."

Was it that simple?

He guided her down the stairs to the café's banquettes along the far wall.

"I don't trust you. You used me."

"We need to talk."

Below the aged patinated mirrors were dividers separating the booths. He set down two glasses, uncorked a bottle of wine, and opened some Vittel.

She shook her head. "I won't drink from dirty glasses."

"I washed them twice," said Claude. "How could you stand to work here?"

"After what I've been through, it didn't seem so bad."

He poured them both a bit of wine and added the sparkling water. She had to think of a way to get out of here. Tiredness was making her brain fuzzy.

"Why are you here?" he said. "You were supposed to be at a safehouse."

She had nothing to say but the truth. "Your partner, Alain, and that CID Beck took me to finish my job. Shouldn't you already know? How much was your cut of the money?"

Claude sat up. "My cut?"

"Don't act surprised."

"They insisted the chief needed me to stay at the prefecture." He looked confused, then furious. "They used me, too. What happened?"

His words rang true.

So they'd cut him out.

"They pushed me into a car." She told him: stashing the errand money in the church, how they'd used her as bait, the gang in the garage.

For a moment Claude looked vulnerable. Like a lost boy. Then it vanished.

"They're backstabbing you," she said.

"Alain's greedy, ambitious, and smart. The other one's not my problem. But you are."

"Problem?" She sipped. "My information got you this far."

"Huguette," he said, but paused at the nervous look on her face. "I mean—Hélène—"

"I'll leave before you arrest me."

She stood.

"Wait. There's something more important I have to tell you." He looked her in the eye. "I should have told you more about your father's investigation. I'm so sorry. His was one of my first cases. I believe there's been a cover-up. Now I need your help to prevent more deaths."

She sat back down. Accepted the glass of wine. Tried to keep her hands steady.

"More deaths?"

"Look. Marina Roussel was found wearing the scarf I remember you wore. Her body was found in the same place, in the same way as your father and another victim."

The aching loss of her friend returned.

"But I kept that quiet," he said. "That's not in my report."

She had to tell him.

"Marina was my best friend. My only friend—" The rest of the story tumbled out: Marina's warnings, her visit the night Marina had been killed. "It's all my fault."

He took her hand. "Blame the murderer, not yourself. My chief told me, hands off your father's investigation. Someone involved is connected to de Gaulle. The cover-up runs up to the very top."

"You're a cog in the wheel, the same as others," she said.

"I don't like it either. They're subverting a murder investigation."

Then she told him about the reward on her and someone getting rich on her father's café. "I don't know who's after me. But with the Voltaire gang's money gone, they'll be first in line."

He'd been writing in his notebook. "Voltaire gang? You're sure?"

She nodded again. "Big time. Men with connections to US generals at the Hotel George Cinq. Tino and the others are small fry."

"We'll put the gang under surveillance." He put down his wine glass. Ran his finger around the ring of moisture. "But I need evidence to make it stick."

"More? You want more from me?" she said. "So far it's all one-sided. Nothing in return."

She bit her lip to stop the tears welling up.

He put his jacket over her shoulders. Rubbed her arm.

"Look, you're around these people and know the black market. We all buy on the black market if we can, it's a fact of life. I don't care. But you know something even if you don't think you do."

She'd memorized the map she'd taken from the *mec*'s pocket, the names on the back. She handed it over.

"What's this?"

She hesitated. "I found this at the garage. I didn't want to say this," she said, "but people who we fed during the Occupation denounced us at Libération. Marina said there were rumors accusing my father and me of hiding stolen money, valuables. That Céline who runs the flower shop got tight with the GIs and Gisors, who took over the café. I don't trust her."

Busy writing, he asked her to repeat the names she had mentioned.

"Tell me why you think they're still after you?"

"My father's supposed hidden money?" Sick of the focus, she changed it to her immediate danger. "Those GIs I saw in a jeep with Céline were in the newspaper photo. One of them is her boyfriend. They're part of the gang. No one has fingered him because that gang kills anyone who turns on them."

"When did you see these GIs?"

She took another swig of wine.

"At Libération. You can't imagine what it was like." Her eyes filled with tears. Her throat was thick as she began to sink back into history.

Evening, August 25, 1944 • A Year Earlier, At Libération

The Left Bank, Paris

—

In the small streets of the Latin Quarter, lights shone from open windows—no more blackout curtains. A couple made noisy love in a doorway, a bicycle bumped over the cobbles, a distant celebration at Hotel de Ville throbbed a happy roar. Notre Dame's bells rang loudest.

On the bank of the Seine, the shredded remnants of a flag, the black swastika ripped in two.

It was over.

Except for what grew in her belly.

Since June every step she'd taken had been weighted with the scars of the cruelty of the one-eyed Nazi. With hurt at her papa's betrayal.

You sold me just to save your skin, she'd said.

Our skin, he'd insisted. *There's things you don't know.*

Like what?

He'd refused to say anything else.

Unable to face him, she slept at Marina's. She still worked in the café after school, avoiding him. Her dread and disgust only grew inside her. As her belly started to swell to match, she told no one except Marina—but not who was the father.

All she could do was put one foot in front of the other. Figure out what to do later.

Tonight she'd enjoy a respite from the nightmare. No curfew, no stomping jack boots, no more threat of Siggie.

Crossing the Pont Saint-Michel, her smile faded. Café du Soleil's windows were smashed. Her legs faltered.

The café's glass door was splintered open. Inside, chairs and tables overturned.

She heard someone singing. Drunk.

Old Monsieur Lapont sat on the floor, a bottle in hand, with flower seller Céline's Chihuahua in his lap. Wine stained his mustache.

"What happened here?"

"Eh, your father and Luc told me to help myself, mademoiselle." He whistled an old military marching song from the Great War.

Stinking drunk.

"Where is everyone, Monsieur Lapont?"

"Gone. People took things from the cellar."

Looters.

She tried to take in the scene of chaos: wooden boxes pried open and empty, shelves ransacked, her papa's stock gone. Yvon, the wounded communist, was sitting atop the counter eating a sausage. He was a cousin of someone in Papa's village. His corkscrew brown curls and small frame gave him an elfin look.

"Where's the good stuff, Huguette?"

"You're eating it, Yvon," she said, disappointed in him. "When did the looters come?"

"How would I know? I heard your father's in trouble."

"Why?"

"Eh, he's got to face the music." Yvon chewed, watching her.

Face the music he'd avoided for four years?

She righted a chair. "I mean, why didn't you stop them? Do something?" she said, her throat tight.

"Not for me to stop justice of the people's tribunal."

She stared at him in disbelief. "How can you say that? We fed and hid you, risked the café, everything . . ." She remembered how Yvon's wounded leg had abscessed. "You were hurt, had nowhere to go, Yvon. No one else would help you."

"Give me a violin, Huguette."

How could he be so cold? Ungrateful.

"Five months you've stayed upstairs. Ate our food."

"The Nazis' food."

Strange bedfellows, all right, as Luc often said about Yvon.

"As if he's the only one? You didn't refuse his food, did you?" She wanted to knock him off the counter. Hit him. She tried not to let her shaking fingers show. Stuck them in her pocket. "Show me someone with clean hands, someone who didn't make do as best they could. How can anyone point a finger?" Disgusted, she tried to think. "What does that matter now anyway?"

"There's ledgers in your handwriting, Huguette."

She went still, remembering the books she'd helped cook for her father to hide his profits. She'd always feared the reckoning but would admit nothing to greedy Yvon.

"Prove it."

"We will."

We? Sounded like revenge.

"Where's Papa? Luc?"

"Going to people's court, where they belong."

"People's court?" She snorted. "There's a real court across the street. Le Tribunal. True justice."

"Oh, they'll get justice." Yvon noisily swallowed his final bite of the sausage. "Where's the money, Huguette?"

His greed sickened her.

She spread her arm out over the chaos. "Here and gone."

Yvon watched her. "You've got a tummy bulge. People will wonder who the father is. Céline told me you liked playing mattress for the *Boche*."

Céline, the flower seller next door. A regular. A friend.

"What are you talking about?" she managed. Did she really show? Shame filled her.

"Just a guess." Yvon grinned. "But your face turned all red."

Huguette quivered with alarm and fury. "To think I felt sorry for you," she spat. "Gave the doctor my ration coupons to treat you."

Two men had entered the café; the larger man, who had a silver goatee, in rolled-up shirtsleeves with a linen jacket over his arm, the other in a workman's blue overalls. Both seemed familiar.

"The café's not serving," she said. "We're closed."

"Mademoiselle Faure?" said the one with a goatee. She recognized him from somewhere—but where?

"I might be. Who are you?"

"Honoré Gisors, *notaire*." His official tone chilled her. He speared her with a penetrating look, as if noticing her for the first time, sending a shiver up her neck. Something flickered in his gaze before his calculating eyes roamed and she could almost see computations in his head. "Looters did a lot of damage. Where is your father?"

"Why?" she asked.

"If he's not here I need to speak with the accountant."

Monsieur Peyrach had died six months ago and she'd taken over the accounting. No way would she let this man see a centime. This stank like old fish.

"It's Libération, but you walk in here and want to speak to the accountant. Why?"

"Your father and I have business to settle. We need the accountant's help."

His manner and entitlement raised her hackles.

"You're talking to her."

Gisors snorted. He waved a dismissive hand as if she were an idiot.

Fine, don't believe me.

Gisors turned to the man in the blue overalls, who shrugged. They walked toward the door, their shoes crunching broken glass. Vultures like Yvon.

Just then, her father strode through the café's broken door, surveying the wreckage. She saw the furtive look in his eyes, which were ringed by dark circles.

"Get your things, Huguette. Hurry."

"Not before you settle your debt, Remy," said Gisors.

Debt? Huguette backed away and into Yvon, who'd hopped down off the counter.

"Not so fast," said Yvon.

He blew a whistle, several short shrill cracks like rifle shots. This leech had signaled to his cohorts.

Huguette locked eyes with her father as two men rushed into the café. They wore armbands emblazoned with FFI, Forces françaises de l'intérieur, and the Cross of Lorraine symbol against a blue, white, and red tricolor. De Gaulle's Resistance fighters, late to the party as usual. They grabbed her father by his shirt collar. Three more men poured in, sweat on their faces, red cheeked with rifles over their shoulders.

Her father struggled, striking out until one of the men pulled his arms behind his back.

Behind them appeared a middle-aged man with a people's court armband who consulted a list. "Remy Faure, this the one?"

Yvon nodded. Huguette looked around in terror. But Gisors and his companion had hightailed it out a broken window in the rear.

Cowards.

"I have a Huguette Faure on the list." The man looked at her. "That you?"

"Leave her out of this," her father said.

"Her name's right here."

"What list?" said Huguette. Her hands trembled.

The two men caught her father in a tight grip as he struggled to escape their hold.

"Collaborators. Black marketers," said Yvon.

What a snake. He'd survived thanks to her and her father and returned the favor by denouncing them. Putting them on a list.

"There's a mistake," said her father, panting. "My daughter's seventeen years old. In school. A child."

"The people's court will decide."

Her father struggled with the man who gripped his collar. "*Mon Dieu*, you can't haul her off, she's broken no law."

"How convenient you remember the law now. Not when you were raking in illegal profit."

"Take me but leave her alone." Her father's voice rose. "She's a minor, underage."

"Show me your *carte d'identité*, Huguette," said the man with the list.

"But I don't have one yet, there's no paper to print them on," she said.

"She knows nothing," yelled her father. Blood dripped from his split lip.

Fear and shame cut through her. She cried out. "Let my papa go."

But the red-cheeked men were dragging her papa across the floor. Another one came and kicked him. A crack of bone.

"Please stop!"

Deep down she knew he had this coming. But vigilantes? Huguette ran to her father, lunged, tried to grab his arm.

Yvon pushed her aside and shoved her father into the dimly lit street. An angry crowd was waiting for them, jeering and kicking at her father as he stumbled over the cobblestones.

HUGUETTE'S MIND BLURRED AS SHE followed the surging crowd along the quai's stone wall. She'd lost sight of her father in all the shoving. From the Seine's bank below drifted laughter, the clink of bottles, distant singing. On the bridge, she spotted Céline, singing and drinking Champagne with GIs in a jeep. Euphoria at the end of the gray life under the Occupation. And Huguette was entirely outside of all of it, running in terror and desperation, stained by the Nazi baby she carried. And, in spite of everything, worried for her papa.

Burning candles sputtered on the cobblestones in the people's court in Place Dauphine, the triangular treelined square surrounded by rose brick seventeenth-century buildings. Lantern shadows flickered as screams echoed off the stone. The whole thing breathed witch hunt.

It wasn't supposed to happen this way, was it?

Huguette slipped among the crowd, kept her head low. Felt the palpable hate and menace, thick as wool.

Under the leafy trees, several men stood with their heads down. One sat on a broken stool. She recognized him as the butcher Papa dealt with at les Halles market. Black eye, cuts on his face and a torn shirt.

Where was Papa?

A loud male voice recited a list of indictments: hoarding meat, refusing ration cards, overcharging. She peered over shoulders to see who was talking. She recognized the young red-haired butcher's assistant as his voice rose above the others.

Angry mumblings came from the crowd. Someone shouted, "Enough! We know he's guilty."

Other voices joined in. "His wife sold gasoline coupons and butter. Strutted around in a fur coat."

"You've heard these public accusations. Treasonable offences. The people will decide. Justice by your peers."

"Peers?" said Huguette. Her voice was drowned by shouts.

Someone seized her arm and she turned to see a small rail-thin woman with a stooped back and bad teeth. "Do you want to be next, little mademoiselle?"

Heads turned, watching them. She shook off the woman's grip and slunk back from the crowd.

Her heart ached in understanding. She saw in these candlelit angry faces, hollow cheeked from hunger, that each of them would have done whatever they needed to do to survive.

Like Papa had. Like she had.

"I vote execution," came a voice. "Hanging."

A rope with a noose hung from a tree branch. Scared, she kept to the edge of the angry crowd. Scanning the faces for Papa, Luc.

She found the list of names tacked onto the nearby tree trunk. Names of so many people in the quartier. The wine merchant, the bank teller who lived next door—all with Xs by their names.

And she saw that man, Gisors, marking an X by REMY FAURE. Her Papa.

She tried to breathe. Her papa had been slated for execution by an angry mob. What justice was that?

She heard a moan from the shadows—her father's broken voice.

"Huguette."

There he was, slumped on the ground, one among several people huddled under the trees.

Frightened, she knelt down.

The swollen face, caked with blood, hardly recognizable—*non, non*, it couldn't be.

"Papa?"

A weak pitiful sob rose from his broken body. He'd been beaten. Were they going to hang him, too?

She couldn't let them. With trembling fingers she touched Papa's bruised face, broken nose.

Her eyes, accustomed to the dim light, finally saw he was holding a man's hand. She recognized the bloody face of Luc, their waiter. His limp body slumped against Papa's shoulder. Her chest was wracked with fear.

"What happened?"

". . . must go . . . not safe . . ." Her father's breath was labored.

"I can't leave you. Or Luc."

Shadows flickered. People's shouts rose.

"They knew." Papa's shoulders drooped.

Her gut wrenched.

"Knew? Who did this? This lynch mob?"

"Gisors and the *Boche* with the eye patch—they turned me in. He promised me . . . but now he's escaped . . ."

Siggie, the animal who had raped her and promised to protect her father. A cold fury filled her.

She folded her papa's cold hand in hers.

An undercurrent ran through the crowd as a group of uniforms approached.

"*C'est la police*," someone said.

Huguette realized figures surrounded them, looming over her.

She choked on her tears. "You have no right to take the law into your hands. He needs a doctor."

Arms were pulling her. Dragging her away, kicking and screaming.

"Let me go."

The *flics* blew warning whistles.

"Take down that rope," one of them shouted.

"We want justice!" the crowd yelled back.

As the *flics* battled the people's court, she crawled back over to Papa.

He was semiconscious. Behind his moving lips she saw the broken stubs of bloody teeth.

"I've hurt you, so wrong . . . forgive me. Take my bag . . . papers . . ." Coughing overtook him. "Inside . . . you're next. Go . . . *ma petite*." His blood smeared her hand.

A rattling came from his throat, a small expulsion of air—and he was gone.

She knew no matter how he'd hurt her and what he'd done, she still loved her father. He was the only family she had left. Her insides cracked.

Shuddering, she crossed herself and whispered goodbye.

With her fingers she slid her papa's eyelids closed. Clutched his still-warm body and hugged him one last time.

Got up from her knees and ran into the darkness.

AUGUST 1945 • A YEAR LATER

Café Central, Ninth Arrondissement, Paris

Claude was wiping her eyes with his handkerchief. Huguette had never told anyone this story.

Aching with exhaustion, she took another swig of wine and leaned back.

For a long time they both sat and drank in silence. She wondered if she'd just put herself in more danger by confiding in him.

"FLO," she said at last, and pointed to the map on the table, the names written in the corner. "FLO, that's Whitlaw's code name. There. They launder the money out of here." She touched the map. "According to Albertine, he runs their big supply depot with Pete, the AWOL GI, somewhere near there."

"Thank you," said Claude, his voice soft and serious.

She didn't know what to say. Finished her wine and let her eyes close and fought the memories taking over.

She must have drifted off, because she woke to find herself stretched out on the banquette seat. Napkins under her head for a pillow, Claude's jacket over her. Across the table, she saw Claude watching her.

A shimmer of a smile lit his face.

It felt as if he understood her and what she'd done in a way no one else did. Or had tried to. She leaned over and kissed him hard.

"What are you doing?" But his arm was around her, his hand on her cheek.

She wanted him to keep running his finger over her lips, then kissing them.

Why did she want this? But it was nothing like the last time.

Around dawn, the wine delivery man knocked on the door, but they didn't hear him.

SOME TIME LATER, HUGUETTE CAME to with a pounding in her ears, engulfed in a warm softness. She didn't want to move. But footsteps tramped outside the café's windows.

Claude was gone. His scent of vetiver lingered on her skin.

She pulled on her dress and her cardigan and slipped into her boots.

Where was he?

If a gang escapee had returned, she'd be in big trouble.

The footsteps got louder. Quickly, Huguette hid in the service closet at the back stairs and waited, trying to figure out what to do. She heard the door slam and Claude's voice. Couldn't make out the words. Then another voice, raised. A heated discussion.

"I'm not going to lose my job over this, Claude." She recognized Alain's snotty tone. "There's a warrant out for her arrest. She's complicit."

Shuffling noises. She put her ear to the door to hear more.

"It's all thanks to her I got the gang's map," Claude was saying.

She couldn't hear the rest.

"Look, about the money . . ." said Alain. "We'll work it out, there's plenty. Your wife's—"

Wife?

Her head spun. So Claude was giving Alain the map and splitting the money after all. Betrayer.

What happened to catching the Voltaire gang and the raid on the GIs' black market depot?

Everything told her to get out. Walk away. Never look back.

And once out the rear door to the alley, she didn't.

EARLY DECEMBER 1947 • TWO YEARS LATER
Lumière Film laboratory, Lyon

—

December twilight settled in bands of dusky gray-blue as Huguette entered Lumière's film laboratory, a warren where magic appeared on celluloid. She liked the tang of solvents, the sputtering activity of cutting and splicing in the dim room. Film slapped the air and hit spinning metal film reels as skilled editors painstakingly retouched each frame of close-ups on famous actors—a complex and detailed process to disguise each wrinkle in a bankable star.

Raoul, the head editor, looked up from the images flickering on his editing machine.

"*Bonsoir*, Raoul," Huguette said. "I need a small rush job."

His large teeth glinted in the bluish light.

"Again? I only see you when you want another favor, Lise."

Her funding propped up the lab and paid his salary, but instead of reminding him she held the purse strings, she smiled. She could afford to pay him; she couldn't afford to lose him. Always cautious, she asked him every few months to redo her photo for a new identity card and documents. Keeping another set ready, Louis had warned her, would come in handy for a bank examiner's audit or a quick exit.

She winked. "A much appreciated favor, if you could, please."

Of course he could, he did this all day long. Gruff yet kind, he nodded. "Let's make it quick. We're on deadline, as usual."

She put a small film canister with a roll of negatives into his hand. "There's several shots to work with. Give me a few different looks. You know what works best." Sometimes he'd alter her nose, her eye shape, or give her a pointed chin, fuller cheeks—or merely make her hair a few shades darker.

Raoul set the film in a black developing bag, adjusted his jeweler's loupe, and shooed her out with a professional wave.

"Like usual, I'll have them sent to your office."

FROM HER FIRST DAY IN Lyon two years ago, she'd stressed her connection to Louis and her temporary role here. She insisted she was acting in the interim until Louis came down from Paris to take over the studio and de Jouvenal businesses. But Louis never joined her in Lyon—a final heart attack, just a week after she left, had been too much for him to bear.

After Louis died, she kept a mountain of secrets, and every day, she missed him, wishing he could be here to offer a wise word or a warm smile.

The city grew on her. The rivers dominated the city of hardworking people. The medieval streets in the old section of town were reached by *traboules*, ancient covered passages. When she wasn't working, which was most of the time, she'd steal a break to visit the last remaining silk weavers, the *canuts*, in the Croix-Rousse. Fascinated, she watched them weave whisper-thin silk on looms under high-ceilinged ateliers that housed mulberry moths in the rafters.

It was remarkable how much someone would believe if she sold the story. She'd honed her script according to Louis's instructions on dealing with the traditional, silent Lyonnais with their quiet unexpected humor. Just like he'd told her, they mistrusted outsiders. Most of all, they thought their food was the best in the world. They'd never enjoyed a meal in Paris. How was she going to relate to these people?

But slowly, she'd worked out ways.

Her first day running the office alone, she'd met Louis's proposed pick for manager, Robèrt Delisle. In his forties, according to Louis, he had stone-white hair, a matching mustache, and a curiously young face.

"Louis told me about you, you know," he said, sitting across from her in the pleasantly cramped office.

She wondered what he knew. Louis had warned her to expect she'd have to prove herself.

"Then you know I helped his correspondence. Accounting," she said.

Keep it businesslike. No more, no less.

"There's more to it than that, *non*?"

Her insides churned, but she didn't let it show. "I helped with whatever he needed," she replied simply.

"Down here, you need more help. My kind of help."

Immediately, she understood who he was: another man who liked to take over. She summoned a smile. Hoped he'd prove useful. "What do you mean?"

"We work in places where men don't listen to young women. You'll need help dealing with those kinds of lowlifes."

Buying protection. Louis hadn't mentioned this. But she knew she needed a go-between besides the ones she'd found on the legal side.

"He told me he trusted you," she said. "How do you know Louis?"

Delisle raised his eyebrow in surprise. Had no one ever asked him that? Or did he think her youth precluded a thinking brain?

His tone dropped, sombre. "Louis and I fought in the Verdun trenches in 1916. Without him, I wouldn't be here today. I owe him. He's only asked me for one favor in all these years, and you're it. Even though he's gone, I promised him I'd be here for you."

She hadn't expected that. Touched, she hired him then and there.

Delisle had cleared his throat. "I'd feel better if you'd let me keep an eye on things with you. It's what Louis would want."

"Thank you," she said.

"Lyon counted seventy-six cinemas during the war," he said. "Many went bankrupt after. Different landscape and no subsidies. No wonder the racketeers took over."

She smiled at Delisle. "I'm here now. That'll turn around."

DELISLE INTRODUCED HER WIDELY AS the niece of the iconic Louis de Jouvenal. After that, no questions were asked.

She started by buying two small cinemas in Lyon. Then another. All facilitated by Delisle's intro, a handshake, and black market cash. Louis's Lyon contacts had prevented her from being taken advantage of as a single woman. As "Lise," she managed the cinemas and began by showing first-run films. She laundered Louis's hidden money, invested the shares, and kept investing the returns.

Louis had taught her well. And she hoped her work whitewashed his memory.

Postwar fever for escape hit the cinemas. More films than ever were in production, and with Étoile's distribution connection she showed American films, dubbed with French crowd-favorite actors' voices. Feature films such as *The Lady from Shanghai*, with bombshell Rita Hayworth; *The Big Sleep* with Humphrey Bogart. People flocked to the cinemas for a night out, filling the seats. Business boomed.

Word spread. When the owner of several small cinemas in Grenoble retired, he offered them to her. Diversify, Louis had counseled, so she bought the café next door. A hardware store, several laundries.

She looked over her shoulder every day. Wary the past would catch up with her. And every day she had to prove she could do this. Louis's bible on acting helped her to read people and respond without losing advantage.

She trusted no one completely. She couldn't. But so much needed doing, and she couldn't do it alone. There was no hiring formula except Louis's two rules: *Never leave money out*, and *pick a hard worker*. Her own assistant, Simone, had started as a laundress, but Huguette had seen something in her that was reminiscent of her own fighting spirit. Simone proved enterprising, a quick thinker, hardworking, and loyal. She became Huguette's right hand.

Together, they screened job applicants and hired women from the breadlines eager to work, support their family, and get a roof over their heads. Veterans who struggled to rebuild their life or what was left of it. Injured *résistants*. The destitute with young children or those with family dead or lost. For hard work and discretion she paid well, and Simone helped her negotiate with labor unions to keep everybody happy.

But was Huguette happy?

Would she ever not be afraid?

BONE-TIRED AFTER A LONG DAY, she felt like giving up. A despairing loneliness took her to the river. Moonglow illuminated the nearby former military Montluc prison, once used by the Gestapo as a prison and holding camp for men, women, and children before shipment to concentration camps.

She'd left Paris a fugitive. In another life, she'd have been locked up there herself. Now almost twenty-one, she had more money than she could spend, and a clean record—she couldn't be tied to anything in her past.

As Lise de Jouvenal, Huguette survived.

Louis had told her a business plan driven by fear wasn't a good business plan. But everything drove her to become untouchable.

She contemplated the dark depths of the Rhône's frigid water.

Hollowness filled her.

But even though she felt it, she knew she wasn't alone. Hundreds depended on her—not just Simone and the women she employed, keeping them from the streets or from free-fisted husbands, but the ushers in her cinemas, the waiters in her cafés, even the distributors of the films she made hits. Hadn't Louis trusted her? Said she could do this? She sighed and turned away from the river. Went home.

She didn't notice the footsteps behind her until she reached her street. Her breath caught; she froze. A shadow passed and then it was gone.

"You get around, Mademoiselle de Jouvenal."

The familiar voice behind her sent shivers up her arms. Huguette looked up sharply from her usual spot on the quai overlooking the Rhône. Faint winter sun poked from the clouds speckling the stone.

Mark Beck. Out of his army uniform but still not who she wanted to see.

Claude must have told him. Were they working together behind her back? Again?

He sat down beside her, shifted on the hard stone. The river gurgled below his dangling feet.

"How did you find me?" she said, barely above a whisper.

"We have ways."

Her insides trembled. She'd stayed so careful. Two months had passed since her encounter with Claude asking for her testimony. Yet no word since—had he sacrificed the case for her, put her safety above all else? Or had the case come to nothing?

Buying time to think, she picked up a smooth stone and skipped it in the river. The stone sank. Like all that she'd worked for. Whatever the reason, Beck's sudden appearance meant she'd been discovered.

"What do you want?"

He glanced around. "I'm off to Germany. Frankfurt. I'll be interrogating POWs then translating for the ongoing Nuremberg military trials."

His own people. For the first time, she believed him. But why tell her this? And what was he doing here?

Before she could ask, he said, "I don't know anyone in Lyon apart from the military, and, well . . ."

He spread his palms out. Ridged lines on his fingers.

"You want me to inform again or you'll take me in?"

"Hey, it's not like that. I think in some ways we're alike. We're two people wearing different identities, unable to go back to where we came from."

Rattled, she stared at him. His dark brooding eyes, the cleft in his chin—handsome in a way.

Lonely?

"I don't know who I am anymore," he said. He ran his finger

over the uneven stone. "Now I'm going back to my homeland, but *is* it my homeland? My wife and child . . ." He hesitated. "Well, none of my family survived. My town's rubble—and part of Russia now."

He really couldn't go back to the past. She understood; he was right about their similarities. Paris held bad memories, and fear wouldn't let her return.

"I'm sorry, I know I didn't treat you well," he said. "But of all people, I hoped you would understand. There's no one and no place for me."

He spoke from his heart. She heard it.

But trust him? Never.

"This is my place," she said.

Beck shook his head. "You're not doing a good job of hiding."

He pulled out a folded newspaper and handed it to her, flipping to the financial section, where he tapped an article on the growing Lyon film industry. Alongside it a photo. Her altered features weren't altered enough—she would be easily recognizable to anyone who knew her. Damn. The article mentioned a relative of Louis de Jouvenal's managing the Étoile film distribution. Where did this come from? She'd given no interview, hadn't been consulted. She looked at the date. Yesterday. A Parisian paper, too.

"You didn't know?"

"How did the paper get this?"

Beck shrugged. "You're part of the news cycle. The big papers picked it up."

"I never wanted this."

He took the newspaper from her trembling hands.

"By the way, Juju's out of prison. Her sister, too."

Now the remaining Voltaire gang would track her down. She could have minutes.

Acid fear filled her.

"You mean it's only a question of time, right?"

He looked away at the ripples in the river. "Figured I owed you."

Force of habit made her turn and survey the riverbank. Laughter from a strolling couple on the stone pavers, strains of a Django Reinhardt song drifting from the café where the dairy man loaded empty milk cans on his cart. Nothing unusual.

"Again, why tell me? The goodness of your heart?"

"Look, the info came via Leduc. His advice: Leave Lyon."

Bittersweet feelings rose at his name.

Beck pulled a wallet from his jacket pocket. "Maybe I can help you."

She scoffed at him. "You think I need money? If you read that article, you know I run the business. I don't need anything from you."

Patiently, he held a card out to her. "Don't you?"

She stared. A US military civilian employee card allowing access to restricted zones, commissary and housing privileges, unlimited train travel. The name space left blank.

This was like gold.

"Stick on a new photo. Write in a name. You can work at any base, get lodging, and stay under the wire."

"You'd do this for me?"

"Like I said, I didn't treat you well. I was under pressure and used any means to catch the GIs." He sighed. "But no excuse. I'm sorry."

Something tangled free in her brain.

"Did you read Corinne Lelouche's memoir?"

Beck exhaled through his nose. "I wouldn't touch that garbage with a ten-foot pole. But my colleagues did. They told me all the juiciest stories. Why?"

Seeing the sensational tell-all in the front of all Lyon's bookstores had made Huguette sick for weeks. Finally, she'd steeled herself to read it. She'd stayed up all night. For once, she couldn't make herself go to work in the morning and stayed under the duvet in bed.

What a whiner and bad writer Corinne was. Nauseated, Huguette had watched the actress rationalize her collaboration. Part of her had been expecting it, but reading it still made her furious.

> *People ask me about nightlife during the Occupation, thinking we lived glamorously. Glamorous, my foot. It was work. In the entertainment world it's de rigueur to foster an illusion. We acted in movies and in our lives, played the part—that was the job. The German propaganda minister threatened to fine us if we didn't promote our movies.*

Huguette read the insipid, dishonest prose with dread, looking for the scene Corinne had warned her she was going to write about the treasure hunt. And sure enough, there it was.

> *Famous were the parties thrown by Siggie, very connected in our milieu. An artistic type in the Gestapo, and surprisingly, a Catholic, he invited us actresses weekly to his well-attended parties at the home of a so-called countess. Everyone who was anyone was there. His eye, his only one since he lost his other to buckshot in a hunting accident, picked out the best of the elite. . .*

Huguette couldn't avert her eyes. In a nauseated daze, she read through Corinne's self-absorbed account of that awful night. Reliving every detail of her fear and shame.

As painful as reading that section of the book was, the end of the chapter was salt in the wound.

Not just artistic but an escape artist—Siggie Keller fled Paris at Libération to land in the biggest POW camp near Frankfurt, where, even after being shot, he escaped again.

Siggie was alive and free.

Corinne had lied to her face. Again. Part of Huguette had been expecting it—she knew she couldn't believe a word out of Corinne's mouth. Everything she thought she knew threatened to crumble down.

"I asked you why," said Beck.

Brought back to the quai and Beck sitting beside her, she had to answer.

"Did your colleagues tell you about the—" Her voice quavered, but she tightened her stomach like a fist and braved on. "The treasure hunt?"

A sour expression crossed Beck's face. "You mean that party where Lelouche furnished virgins for that one-eyed Gestapo captain? Disgusting. I know you work in the industry now, but are you really the type for this kind of sensationalism?"

"I . . . was there," Huguette whispered. He'd opened up to her; now it was her turn. She didn't know why she cared what he thought of her, but she didn't want him to see her as an obstinate child anymore. "I . . . I was the virgin. Those memories are what's waiting for me in Paris. Can you blame me for reinventing myself? At least I thought that scum died in a POW camp and I'd never have to think about him again."

An extensive silence. Huguette looked into the roiling water, trying to slough off the memories that threatened to overtake her.

After Claude Leduc's warning, she needed to leave. She hated feeling cornered like a rat.

Beck was offering to help her, and she could use him.

"You came here to warn me to leave, *non*? So I'll travel with you as your assistant."

"You're kidding."

"You said it yourself, I can't stay here."

He blinked. "Do you speak German?"

"Say you're using me as an interpreter for the French witnesses." Once she was out of France with a new identity, no one would look for her, not in a war-torn foreign country.

"You want to track him down, is that it?"

She spit into the river. Watched the water bear it away in a swirl. "I want to know if the Nazi who raped me is alive. Any more questions?"

"Huguette . . . Huguette." Beck was shaking her arm. An intense look in his eyes. "It's a million-to-one chance. What's the point?"

She glared back at him. Beck looked down at his watch.

"We can go now. My jeep's over there."

A US Army jeep like a large green snail, garish and obvious against the cobbles of the city.

"Not a good idea," she said. "Meet me at the southern exit of Gare de la Part-Dieu. Tonight."

USING HER STANDING, SHE CONVINCED the bank manager to hold an emergency late meeting in his office. There, she met Delisle, her lawyer, and Simone, who'd hastily assembled. Nerves jangling, she tried to radiate a concerned calm as she told them a family member's life-threatening illness called her away. Though she still hated lying, it was best to furnish them with a businesslike reply to any curious reporters, or Paris police who could ask about her.

Under the guidance of her lawyer, she added signatory powers for Simone for day-to-day operations, dependent on Delisle's cross-checking. With the paperwork out of the way, Huguette arranged a way to communicate and leave messages. Just like during the war.

"If someone's after you, and I'm not saying they are," said Simone, "they'll learn nothing from me, my family, or the staff. Guaranteed."

Louis had taught her that to keep a business going and growing, you had to delegate.

A quick peck on both Simone's cheeks, a squeeze of her hand, and Huguette was out the door.

Late Evening, December 1947

Gare de la Part-Dieu Station, Lyon

―

Huguette's wood-soled shoes clicked against the cobblestones. She'd dug through her closet, applied the simple makeup techniques she'd learned from Tonette. In her drab utility popover dress—a war staple with its cinched waist, large pockets—she felt invisible among the travelers outside the train station.

Her new US military civilian card read Suzy Dubois—the last touch.

Mark Beck looked at her twice before he recognized her.

"How did you do this?"

"What?"

"You look completely different."

"Guess it worked if you didn't pick me out."

She couldn't read his expression as he put a hand on her elbow to guide her across the street to a taxi. "Let's go."

At the aerodrome on the outskirts of Lyon, they, along with several servicemen, boarded a propeller craft. The servicemen nodded off; Beck called it "catching shut-eye." He conferred with a cohort consulting maps and lists.

She'd never been on a plane. The shaking, noisy metal beast

with no heat and metal seats hit air pockets constantly. She threw up in a "spit" bag. And again.

Beck handed her his handkerchief, then politely ignored her.

Outside Frankfurt, they joined a convoy of jeeps as a blood orange dawn rose over patches of forest. The jeeps passed ravaged villages along the rutted road. Gray, ghostlike figures clustered around a fire burning in an old metal jerrycan.

On and on through a wasteland of a country with gaunt children and rubble women stacking bricks and stones pulled from ruins, until the convoy stopped at another remnant of a village peppered by bullet holes, walls of bombed buildings like jagged teeth, a roofless church spire with its gothic supports like ribs open to the sky.

Her throat choked against the brick and plaster dust swirling in the air. The wind carried another odor: dense, putrid, sickly sweet. All of this under a now-enamel-blue winter sky dotted with cotton-puff clouds.

"What's that smell?" Huguette asked.

"Behind the barbed wire over there." Beck pointed. "That was an extermination camp. The Nazis blew up the crematoriums when they left because they couldn't burn the bodies fast enough." Pain crossed his face.

Horrified, she pinched her nose. Nothing could have prepared her for the smell. Even now, two years after the war, the whiff of the dead lingered.

They entered an enclave of khaki Quonset huts, prefabricated semicylindrical structures of corrugated steel. Flurries of US soldiers escorted ragged men along the dirt paths connecting them. German POWs wearing the unmistakable gray-green fabric of the Wehrmacht—torn, altered, without insignia—stood expressionless in a line.

Beck explained to Huguette in a low murmur as they walked. "Intelligence interviews them here for the continuing denazification process. They write a report and file it with any evidence that could go to trial. Even now, postwar, there's still so many, and it takes time, as you can imagine."

She eyed them: tall, short, young, middle-aged—all different except for their hollow-cheeked faces and gaunt frames.

How easy to hide among them, she thought.

At least she could rule out anyone with two eyes.

"Are their physical characteristics in their files?"

"Of course."

A scuffle had broken out. Raised German voices, grunts, thuds, and crunches as body parts connected.

"What's going on?"

A man was running past them. Beck stuck out his leg, tripping him. He shouted something in German, pulled a pistol out of nowhere, and fired into the air.

Huguette jerked, petrified. The man had fallen by her feet. Beck motioned to an MP who pulled him up and dragged him back to the line of POWs, which had quieted down.

"They create a distraction while one of them tries to escape under the fence. There's hundreds of them here with possibly high-ranking Nazis still hiding among them—they know it'll take a while to get through them all. They're hungry and desperate to leave."

How easily Siggie could hide or escape. She shuddered to shake off her reflexive terror. "Did you have to shoot?"

He looked at her sidelong, disapproving. "For men who served on the front, it's what they understand."

Beck hustled her in the direction of one of the Quonset huts. Away from the line of prisoners.

"What do you do with these Nazis when you find them?"

"Military intelligence takes over. It depends on how useful the prisoners are."

A trio of US military officers marched by. Beck stiffened to attention and saluted. After they'd passed, he motioned her forward.

"Useful?" she asked.

"They barter freedom to former Nazi intelligence who give them information on the Russians." Beck's face hardened. "That's the next war."

Disgusted, she watched the prisoners with their frayed cables used as belts, the linings of their caps all that remained to pass for hats. Wondered which of these ordinary men had decreed unspeakable things.

"When you're taking notes during witness interviews, it's important to write down everything correctly. These notes are what I use in court. Can you do that?"

She could run a whole film distribution company, manage hundreds of employees, own chains of businesses, all while laundering dirty money.

He wanted to know if she could take notes?

Huguette nodded and took out the notebook he'd given her.

The sullen German female guard answered Mark in monosyllables. Her dead eyes and straggling blond hair belied her age, twentysomething. She sat upright, her ankles crossed. Her threadbare Wehrmacht greatcoat had had its insignia stripped out, leaving fraying holes. Beck had told Huguette that in the camps, all wore their old uniforms since the only other clothes were the heaped piles that had once belonged to Jewish victims. In France, most walked around in their patched and mended prewar clothing. Could it be, in spite of everything, these people were proud of what they had done?

After Beck had interrogated the guard—fruitlessly, it seemed—for about half an hour, the French witness was brought in. Right away, she pointed at the guard. Spat.

"This *salope* whipped me. Set her dog on me and laughed."

She pulled up her shirtsleeve to reveal scars near the number inked on her skinny arm.

"Take her to court and I'll testify. But what good will that do? She'll get a short prison sentence and be out in no time."

Beck shook his head. "This interview is a formality. A legal procedure. She'll hang."

"Hanging's too good for her," the French woman said. "Too quick. Set dogs on her so she can suffer the same painful death my cousin did."

Huguette was stunned to see an indifferent look on the guard's face.

Beck nudged Huguette. "Are you writing this down?"

AT THE CANTEEN IN ANOTHER Quonset hut she drank the watered-down American coffee and pushed the ersatz scrambled eggs around her plate with the fork. Her appetite was gone.

"Eat. Keep up your strength or you'll get sick." Beck handed her a pill bottle. "Diphtheria and typhus are rampant, so take two of these each day."

"The French witness said there's a record of escapees. I want to see it."

Beck put down his spoon. "Forget finding him here. He escaped. What's the point? Look, this was a bad idea. I shouldn't have gone along with this. It's not even a needle in a haystack. Soon, the Russians will control this area. Any POW who's still here will get shipped to Stalin's gulags. And we're leaving soon."

After coming all this way? She couldn't let the journey end here.

"Then why did you bring me here? I don't understand."

"It's the army. No one understands." He sighed, took a paper out of his jacket pocket. "My new orders. I'll be interviewing a POW in a relocation camp closer to Frankfurt. After that, I'll go back to the Nuremberg Military Tribunals."

"But I need to find him."

"The survival rate's low for these German POWs. Even if he did manage to escape once, he's likely long dead by now. Again, what's the point? And what makes you think he'd have been here, anyway? These camps are all over the country."

The clatter of silverware and loud American voices echoed through the canteen. Louder than a train station. Frustrated, she crumpled the thin paper napkin. "Even if he wasn't here, you told me the camps share records. I could find something. A date, a name on a list. Someone could know."

Beck was silent for a moment, contemplating. "From 1945? No one's left from then. Military staff rotate every six months."

"Can't I see the records? Then I'll know for sure."

He pushed his empty plate aside. "I'll say it again. This was a bad idea."

"Why?"

"Revenge sucks away your soul."

Her hands twisted the napkin, shredding it. "You're a fine one to talk," she said. "Aren't you getting revenge for your family?"

Leduc had told her.

His face shuttered.

"It's your business if the Americans use you. Just don't act pious with me. You understand or you wouldn't have allowed me to come here."

He drummed his fingertips on the tabletop.

Idiot. Her emotional outburst alienated him. Not only was this unwise for many reasons, but she sensed a good man underneath.

"I'm sorry," she said. Her cheeks flushed. "I . . . I didn't mean to say that."

"Yes, you did." He took a breath. "I do understand. I scoured every Red Cross station, hospital, deportation center, and camp list for my wife and child. Then I found proof they died in the camp. I can't bring them back. After this trial I'm done. Finished."

A deep sadness filled his eyes.

"You'll get through this," he said. "But you should let it go."

Let it go?

"But I have to know."

His eyes changed and she couldn't read what was behind them. He took her hand. Warm, soft, enveloping.

Why did she like how he held her hand? Nobody had touched her since Leduc. Nobody had gotten close enough.

"I'll see what I can do. We leave in two hours. Meet me at the gate."

He stood and joined the army brass clustered by the coffee station.

Now that she was on her own, the hungry stares of the soldiers made her uneasy. She headed to the records office. Closed.

At the barbed wire gate of the nearby displaced persons camp she prepared to show her ID. No one even asked to see it.

This camp, a former Stalag, now housed the human flotsam of war. She heard a baby's cry. Skinny children ran around, a guitar twanged, and a few cooking fires smoldered. A plethora of languages drifted—Yiddish, Romanian, Russian, Polish. What was she doing here? But she didn't know where else to go to get away from the hunted looks of the arrogant German POWs. Or the hungry gazes of the GIs.

"Looking for someone?" asked a thin young Romani girl. She looked twelve, but she could have been Huguette's age.

Huguette scanned the rows of water-stained wooden barrack-like buildings. "I doubt he's here."

"You never know." Her grin revealed jagged teeth. "People always come here looking for someone. I can help you."

Huguette recognized—and respected—a negotiating tone when she heard it.

"I'm Suzy," she said, using her new name. She offered her a cigarette from the pack Beck had given her. The currency here, he'd said.

The girl's hand whipped out to take it before anyone else could see.

"*Merci*," she said. "Call me Gia."

"Gia, anyone still here from 1945?"

Without a second's thought she pointed. "In the old Stalag II. It's the next block over there."

"How's that?"

"People still waiting for papers, visas, hoping their family will sponsor them. It takes a long time. We've got a system."

There were hundreds here. She'd never be able to navigate herself.

"How about this?" Huguette handed Gia a full pack of cigarettes. "In exchange for—"

"I'll need more than that. I spread the word and you give me another pack when I deliver, okay?"

"Deliver?"

Gia saw her hesitation.

"I guarantee to find you people here since 1945. I can circulate a name, a hometown, village, whatever you want. Someone always knows something—from camp to camp, on a march, all the survivors knew someone, heard a name, or saw something. Passed word of mouth. It's what people do."

Huguette knit her hands. What was the harm in giving it a shot? "I'm looking for information on a German officer. I'll give you the cigarettes anyway, but I doubt—"

The girl tutted. "People see everything. You can't hide anything here." She stuck her finger out, indicating the German POW camp. "Or there."

A small hope flickered and she knew she had to try.

"Okay." She gave Gia all the details she knew about Siggie, between her own awful memories and what Corinne Lelouche had claimed in her book about his time in prison camp.

Gia showed her to one of the many prefab huts by the wood barracks. "Wait here."

Inside Huguette noted a wall message board. Scraps of paper covered in names along with the latest Red Cross lists. Muffled German voices floated through the dense air, whispers layered by an undercurrent of desperation. All of a sudden the whooping blast from a noon siren startled her. Her nerves sparked. By the time the siren wound down, the voices had switched to accentless French.

Suspicion and mistrust jarred her.

Germans were hiding here.

Was no one here who they said they were?

Gia motioned to her from the doorway. Huguette saw the couple who'd been speaking German. A young woman and man holding hands as they walked out past her.

Huguette took Gia aside. "Gia, did you know he's a German soldier hiding here? I heard him switching languages."

"Oh, really?" A small uptick of Gia's chin before she gave Huguette's arm a friendly punch. "He's Alsatian. *Malgré-nous.* Men like him got conscripted by the Germans because it used to be their land. Anyway, he's allowed to visit from the POW camp since he's still French and she's pregnant."

"How can you be sure?"

That jagged grin again. "Nazis get a knife in their ribs if we find them. Means they prefer to stay among their own kind."

This she believed.

Huguette followed Gia along the dusty path to the former prisoner building. Inside, the smell of cooking onions, and the sound of more crying—Huguette couldn't tell whether it was a child or an adult. The wood bunks with straw mattresses were piled to the ceiling.

Josette, the woman Gia introduced her to, looked up from her knitting. She had short white hair, wore a man's jacket and Russian soldier's boots laced with string. Josette looked around with keen brown eyes, then leaned forward.

"My sister and I have been here the longest. Since 1945. We keep waiting for papers. So you want to know what I remember?"

Huguette heard a bargaining tone in her voice. Another one like Gia. Had she just stumbled into a ring of scammers, or could these women really help her?

"Josette, I'll help you get a job in Lyon," Huguette said. "Provide for your family, too."

"You can do that?"

"Promise."

"*Alors*, I can't tell you much, but I saw many escapes. Several escapees got caught. Shot."

Gia looked at Huguette as if to say, *See?*

But Huguette didn't get her hopes up. She needed more. "What about a one-eyed Nazi? He was blond."

"They all look the same to me." Josette harrumphed. "The injured were hospitalized and the dead shoved in a pit."

"Would they be on a list? There should be a record."

Josette's gaze flickered. Assessing. Huguette recognized the look.

"Sometimes."

"Where do I find out?"

"In hell." The woman spit at her. "Find your Nazi lover's gold yourself."

"What?"

Gia grabbed Huguette's wrist in a pincer-like grip. "Eh, just cut us in and things will go fine for you."

"You're crazy. I just want to know if this man's dead or alive."

"So you say."

Huguette shook off Gia's hold. She couldn't help but remember Juju and Albertine. But these women were nothing like them. They led a hand-to-mouth existence. Just like her, they'd lost everything and struggled to survive. And they could still help her. She stepped closer and handed Josette a cigarette pack.

"I want to know."

A sardonic laugh. "You'd be better off finding their treasure. They escaped to retrieve the gold."

Gold?

"How do you know?"

"I have ears, don't I? We were billeted by the fence and I heard them talking all the time."

"You speak German?"

"Polish, Czech, too. They talked about the gold, and the next day there was an escape."

"Did you see a one-eyed man?" Huguette asked again.

A nurse from the clinic pushed a cart with medicine into the room. She looked surprised to see Huguette. "You're here with the French and American officers? They're about to leave," she said. "Hurry."

Huguette handed Gia her last box of cigarettes and stared at Josette. "Tell me the truth."

"I told you." She thrust her hand out again.

Now Huguette saw they'd given up all they had. And so had she. Feeling it useless to continue, she turned to go and heard the woman snicker.

She doubted Josette knew anything more. However, it matched some of Corinne Lelouche's secondhand account, and it was better than nothing. She could keep digging at the next camp.

BECK PACED IN FRONT OF the jeep. In a biting chill wind his boots kicked up chalky dust. Dark gray clouds hovered close to the ground. The jeep's driver hit the horn.

"Get in. I'm late."

She climbed inside and grabbed the roof rail bar. Once Beck joined her in the back, the driver tore off.

"Where were you?"

"I found some information."

Beck snorted. "Your Nazi's alive?"

Huguette's cheeks reddened. Something inside her snapped.

"My Nazi? You're calling the man who raped me 'my Nazi'?"

"Huguette—"

"Stop the car." She pounded on the driver's seat. He turned around, shocked. "Let me out."

The clutch ground and the jeep screeched to a halt by the forest. Huguette wrenched the door open.

"Wait!" Beck's hand on her arm. Furious, she tried to pull away. He let go. "I shouldn't have let you come on a fool's errand, I stand by that. But I'm sorry. I didn't mean that."

Of course he did.

"We're all the same to you."

She gathered her bag.

"Look, it came out wrong." His German accent thickened when he got uncomfortable. "I know during the war, it was either rape or a bullet. It made me sick. Forgive me."

He sounded sincere and full of guilt. It was hours to the nearest functioning town and train station. Better the cold bite of the wind than one more minute in this jeep.

"I'm walking." She got out, feet landing heavily on the dirt road. This pointless sad trip left a sour taste in her mouth.

She expected him to say *suit yourself* and drive off. But he'd got out and caught up with her.

"Stop." His breath came in jagged puffs of vapor in the cold air. "Here. I haven't read it."

He thrust into her hands a file stamped CONFIDENTIAL. Inside were wrinkled carbon copies of a typed report dated 1945.

His name stared at her. KELLER, Sigmund. Former rank, sturmbannführer.

Three escape attempts listed. Then nothing else in the file.

"There must be something more. What happened to him?"

"Escapees are made examples of," said Beck. "Then and now the army means business."

Josette had said the escapees were shot, then buried in a mass grave.

"So he's dead?"

Beck didn't say anything. He was watching her with sad eyes.

Why did she feel hollow inside instead of relieved or vindicated?

The sky opened. Fat drops of rain bounced off the paper, splattered her cheek.

Beck motioned to the jeep. "I don't expect a conversation, but please accept a ride."

She didn't like the look of the shafts of lightning, the cracks of thunder, and the dark, dank woods.

"As far as the train station."

AFTER A LONG DAMP RIDE into Frankfurt, she alighted without a word at the station. Beck made no attempts to stop her this time; the jeep sped off in the night.

Inside, there were few people, and the schedule board showed no trains.

"Track repair," said a man in the ticket booth. "Maybe a train tonight. Or tomorrow."

The train station was boarded up except for one exquisite window with a crack in its mullioned glass. In the second-class waiting room people settled down for the night on the benches with shared blankets. The flat surfaces were covered with bread and bits of wurst on brown paper, playing cards.

Huguette watched from a distance, wondering if she would ever belong anywhere again. With the US ID card Mark had given her, she could work at an American base. Start again. Her past didn't matter anymore. Why tie herself up in pain thinking of the scum?

Siggie was dead. Even if somehow he wasn't, she decided, he was as good as dead to her.

Mark Beck, despite his faults, had lost his whole family. His home. He tried to do his best, he and so many damaged men, broken after the terrible things that happened in the war. Wasn't she a criminal herself—a liar, black marketer?

She was tired of running.

Huguette Faure was legally dead, and Lise de Jouvenal existed only on paper.

Huguette had built a good life for herself. One in which she prospered and provided for many other people. Shouldn't she focus on that, on making a good life, giving back to those who deserved it, instead of always operating from fear?

Could she face the music but face it her way?

GIVING UP ON THE TRAIN, she found a bus to the airbase. Prayed this US military ID would hold up while she tried to come up with a convincing enough story to board a flight.

"Sorry, mamselle," said a fresh-faced sentry at the aerodrome. "You need orders to board."

"Last-minute emergency," she said. "I have to get to Lyon. I'm sure there's a flight leaving."

"Can't confirm or deny," he said, smiling and showing buckteeth—which meant there was. "But like I said, you need orders."

"We took this morning's flight here and important files were forgotten. I must go back."

"That may be, but—"

"I'm here as Mark Beck's aide," she said. If he really meant it about wanting her forgiveness, he'd accept her using his name for this. "He should have sent the orders. Look it up. Please, monsieur."

He rubbed the back of his neck, said something into a radio clipped to his belt. She shifted from foot to foot in the damp cold, watching jeeps being unloaded from the cavernous interior of a huge-bellied plane.

"Out of my hands, mamselle," said the sentry. He pointed to a Quonset hut. "Go talk to the sergeant in air control. Over there."

— — —

"**No orders for a Suzy** Dubois here. But there's a truck convoy leaving tonight, arriving in Lyon in two days." The sergeant shrugged and handed back her ID. "Get orders and I'll put you on it. That's all I can wangle."

Two days was too long. "This is urgent, monsieur," she said. "Monsieur Beck needs these papers for the trials in Nuremberg."

"Then why hasn't he issued orders?"

Beck's voice rose over the propeller noise from the runway. "I'll do that right now, sergeant."

Shocked, she looked up as he strode toward the sergeant's desk. He scribbled something on a clipboard then waved her forward.

"Get her on this flight."

A minute later he was walking her out onto the runway.

Guilt worked wonders. She'd read him right.

"Thank you," she said, reluctant but meaning it. "We'll call it 'square'—isn't that how you say it?"

"Gutsy, eh?"

She didn't know what that meant. Squinted against the wind instead of replying, hoping it would make her look tougher than she felt as they approached the plane.

At the stairs, her stomach dropped. Scared to board the beast, she stopped in her tracks and tried to stifle her anxiety.

"I'm sorry," Beck said. "Forgive me?"

She hadn't boarded the plane yet. He could still rescind the order.

She nodded. Blew air out of pursed lips.

The propellers whined and hot gasoline-laced air buffeted her ankles. He gestured her forward—then caught her hand.

He pulled her to him. Enfolded her in his arms.

"You're a fighter. You'll be all right, Huguette. Move on. Think of this as a passport to the future."

Passport to the future. *Her* future. She liked that.

Was it Mark Beck that caused the feeling in the pit of her stomach—fear and longing at the same time? She felt herself letting go.

Kissed him hard.

When she came up for air, he caressed her cheek.

"You and me . . . we could move on together," he said, his voice husky. "Stay."

But she'd pulled free and ran up the stairs onto the cargo plane.

DECEMBER 1947

Lumiére Brothers Film Association Boardroom, Lyon

~

"Poetic realism in cinema is dead. The '30s are long over." The young film director with wild black bushy hair pounded his fist on the mahogany table. "We must fund independent directors' films to reflect the upcoming generation. Go avant-garde and lead the industry in a new direction."

The shareholders' board meeting in the Lumière brothers' mansion ground on in painful detail, and Huguette had to struggle to stay focused. She had spent the long flight battling apprehension, nausea, and maybe a little regret. Again and again, she wondered how smart it was to return here when her cover was possibly blown. She felt as though she'd gone from the frying pan straight into the fire.

Yves, the young director, was here as a representative of his infirm uncle, a shareholder. He carried on in his grating tone. "We can't follow the postwar Italian working-class mentality. Forget Rossellini."

Uneasy, Huguette shifted on the brocade chair. *Le cinéma* to her had been Saturday matinees on the Grands Boulevards—tales of love, adventure, escape, and afterward, sorbet or a *chocolat chaud* with her mother.

Entertainment—that's what you bought with the price of a movie ticket. Admission took you to another world, lifted you out of yourself, maybe taught you something. But what did she know of art or cinema besides what she liked?

Then again: What qualified these men to be here besides their money?

At least Yves's high-pitched voice was cushioned by the plush Turkish rug.

"Where's the money for this?" asked Monsieur Sarthe, stroking his goatee.

The important question.

The four other shareholders, all white-haired men in morning suits, sat mute. Sarthe, it seemed, spoke for them.

"To sponsor the Cannes Festival last year we resorted to public subscriptions," said Sarthe. "Even this effort became a stretch. Before you talk about new French films and artistic direction, where do we find the money to produce them?"

Yves started to speak, but Sarthe raised his hand, silencing him. "I haven't finished," he said. His cigar sent noxious fumes into the air. Commanding attention of all. She didn't like him.

"Of course film is art and opens a window into the human condition..." Sarthe let his words linger. "But rather than focusing on what's going to be the most French, we should focus on what's going to sell the most tickets."

A grim reminder that boardrooms weren't about art. Business was conducted here.

If only Louis could see them now.

"Mademoiselle Director?" asked Sarthe, his tone with a faint sardonic tinge. Patronizing. "Your thoughts?"

Huguette's nerves jangled. No doubt to him, she was here as a figurehead only. A woman could never be anything more.

But if she didn't try, everything would go up in smoke.

She had come prepared with a viable business plan, detailed notes, every number considered. Clearing her throat, she shuffled through her balance sheets and bank documents.

She had to get these fossils on board.

"*Merci*, Monsieur Sarthe," she said. "And *merci*, Yves. Both of your points are valid." Nodded to give herself an extra moment to calm her breath. Speckled winter light reflected from the beveled glass windows onto her wrists. "I'm submitting Étoile's plan to benefit and grow the Cannes Film Festival," she said. "Of course, with the board's approval."

Sarthe blinked.

"Speaking on behalf of Étoile and Lumière, pursuant to the agreement in place after Monsieur de Jouvenal's tragic death, Étoile will underwrite seventy percent of the next Cannes Festival. In so doing, we will initiate a debut director prize, fund a contest for top creative script, and establish an open international contest for best film. We, Étoile, ask you, the board, to work with your contacts at the Ministry of Culture for additional film production funding."

Silence greeted her. Why didn't any of them say something?

But she'd keep going and stick her foot all the way in her mouth.

"Furthermore, I nominate Yves to chair the debut director prize committee," she said. "He will help foster fresh creativity while continuing the traditions of our countrymen who invented modern cinema—in this very building, as we all know."

She paused for a dramatic moment.

Then she smiled.

"Of course, we welcome your suggestions for members of various committees. I am sure our partners in Hollywood will have thoughts, too."

"Hollywood?"

The already minuscule warmth in the room lowered to a chill.

"Hollywood's rich," she said. "And they want class. They need our prestige."

She couldn't read their looks.

"Our name and prestige aren't for sale," said the man sitting across from her.

"Of course," Huguette agreed readily, having anticipated this. "Hollywood would be generous donors without voting power."

The stained glass window's blue beam of light funneled onto the carpet. A foot tapped under the table. The tension nearly choked her, but she couldn't turn back. She needed them on board for her passport to the future.

"*Et alors*, gentlemen, if you have other ideas to meet the nine hundred thousand franc shortfall, please share."

Silence.

"Nine hundred thousand francs?" repeated Sarthe.

Huguette began to pass around copies of the report she'd had printed. "On page eleven, you'll see the numbers. Our balance is to be paid in five weeks. As you can see from the bank statement, we're short nine hundred thousand francs. We have no funds, subscription or otherwise, for Cannes in 1948. Or for any productions."

All the men thumbed through the report.

"How could this happen?"

No way she'd throw blame on the doddering, senile Lumière brother who'd gotten fleeced by an accountant. Or outline how he'd let the film foundation fall into benign neglect over the years. "Now's not the time to point fingers."

Sarthe shook his head. "This can't be possible."

"Numbers don't lie, monsieur."

"But in front of our very eyes?"

You should have opened your eyes, she almost said.

"Messieurs, what's done is done. We need to move forward. Please know I will never sell out the festival to Hollywood, but I'll take their money and regulate their participation."

Louis had wanted to do all these things. She was using the road map he'd left her. Delisle and Simone had helped her unearth his memos, notes, and Hollywood contacts. Louis had produced films by wrapping the Nazis around his finger; in comparison, Hollywood would be easy, he'd boasted.

Had he been too optimistic?

One of the shareholders grinned. "I hear the echo of Louis de Jouvenal's ideas in your thinking, *n'est-ce pas?*"

"*Exactement.*" She looked around the table. Smiled. "Louis taught me well. This was originally his idea—I'm merely helping to carry it out."

An almost audible sigh of relief drifted around the table. Now the plan seemed acceptable since it was sanctioned by the *éminence grise*. Louis knew how to play to those holding the purse strings while fostering young creatives who'd keep the cinema alive. Always the director, he'd all but given her a script to use—and she was finally ready.

"My calculations, all outlined in the report before you, estimate Cannes could grow financially independent within five years while increasing its international stature," Huguette said. She took a deep breath, recalling a long-ago conversation with Louis that felt a whole lifetime away, and let his words flow through her: "Picture Cannes, the turquoise waters of the Côte d'Azur a backdrop to the red carpet. The glitter of diamonds decorating movie stars. Thousands of eager attendees. We merely have to create, then maintain, the illusion. The world will flock to Cannes if we do it right."

Was it wishful thinking, or did Yves look ready to burst into applause?

"Do I have the board's approval?"

"Messieurs, let's vote." Sarthe, now the diplomat, looked around the table while Huguette held her breath.

Unanimous.

"Thank you," she said. "A more detailed plan of required next steps is outlined on page seventeen. Finally, although we can announce the relevant public-facing aspects, I request you keep my name intra muros, since I am only the acting director."

"*Bien sûr*," said Sarthe.

The boring de rigueur business of the shareholders meeting carried on for what seemed like forever. She'd made her point, gotten their agreement and couldn't wait until this wrapped up. The old clock struck twelve and the shareholders closed their reports.

"Please join us for lunch, it's a tradition," said Sarthe.

He looked at her as if she'd be part of the menu.

She cited an appointment with the bank to excuse herself. She'd succeeded—she wouldn't let a slimy shareholder ruin that for her.

Yves caught up with her on the sweeping staircase in front of a long stained glass panel. "Mademoiselle, you're smart. You've got a head for figures."

A patronizing tone. She didn't need him—or any man—telling her she was smart.

"I don't understand you taking a back seat to these old men," he said. "Or do you think no one will take you seriously as a woman?"

Irritating, too.

"As the saying goes, to live well is to live hidden," she said, then turned to pass him on the stairs. "*Excusez-moi*."

"Or maybe you live hidden because you have something to hide?"

Was that a threat? A pang of fear vibrated up her spine.

Did he see through her self-preservation tactics? But what business was it of his?

She gave a small smile. "Maybe you're right." She shrugged. "Maybe I hide to live quietly after losing someone in the war. There's no timeline for grief."

She hoped this shut him up. Didn't he know better than to bite the hand that would feed him?

She didn't wait to find out before she beat a retreat down the stairs.

IN THE OFFICE SIMONE GAVE her a letter addressed to Huguette Faure, care of Lise de Jouvenal.

Her heart jerked.

"Who brought this?"

"No idea. The girls said it was *un Parisien*, but that's all they could tell me. Who's Huguette?"

"Thank you, Simone," Huguette said, and shut her out of the office.

The envelope stayed unopened, burning a hole in her pocket. Unless they'd blown her cover, only Beck and Claude Leduc knew her location. Was this from Claude, about that case he'd wanted her to testify at? Thoughts of him and his dark eyes ran through her mind. She could feel his warm hands enveloping hers. But he was in the past and she'd determined to look ahead.

Or—worse—someone might have recognized her in the newspaper: a former neighbor, an undercover policeman, Juju's henchman, Marina's parents, the Corsican?

She kept telling herself she'd open it later.

Tonight.

Right away, she'd decamped to new rooms in a modest pension atop the corner resto opposite the Lumière brothers' building. With art nouveau wallpaper and a small marble fireplace, it was full of light, with a vantage of three directions from her window. Smells of fresh baked baguettes wafted from the *boulangerie* next door.

Simone had helped transport her few belongings in a horse-drawn cart, and each morning she brought over the daily paperwork. Delisle's visits were kept to a twice-weekly minimum unless for an emergency. No one else knew she was here.

She visited the offices, cinemas, and laundries to keep her face in front of the employees. Joined them for lunch at the canteen. All unannounced. She kept to no schedule.

Now she lived independently, just as she wanted when she left Beck. Free of fear.

Apart from the letter.

By the end of the second week, she still hadn't opened the envelope. So far no one had appeared. No sightings of any Parisians, Corsicans, or anyone else asking after "Huguette" in the office.

She'd prepared for the worst. Even though she was afraid, she had to open the envelope and face it. She didn't want to run away again.

She held it up to the light but couldn't see through.

Could she gather her courage, slit the thick paper envelope with a bread knife?

DECEMBER 1947

Leduc Detective, Paris

—

"*Allo*, Leduc Detective," said Claude Leduc, his voice echoing through his recently rented office, bare apart from his telephone and folders stacked on the floor.

He'd been headed out the door but managed to answer the black rotary dial phone with one hand while reaching for his raincoat with the other. The toy store closed soon and it was his son's birthday.

"I need your help, Claude."

That voice. The one he'd been longing to hear. Huguette.

"They've just scheduled the court case here," he said. "Where are you?"

"Not on the telephone," she said. "Please, can we meet?"

He remembered meeting her on the bench in the tree-lined square in Paris, her light scent mingling in the soft air. Then in the café by Notre-Dame de Lorette church, her glowing warm skin, those strange eyes—one green, the other with topaz glints. The last time, the charming way she sipped coffee as they overlooked the lapping Saône in Lyon. She'd changed so much from the young desperate girl he'd helped stay out of prison. Fragile like a bird with a damaged wing, crying on the *commissariat* kitchen floor.

"Tell me where."

Hopeless. Every bit of him wanted Huguette, or Hélène, or whatever she went by now. But he'd never leave his marriage, because he would never leave his son.

"Beck knew where to find me," she said dryly. "So you must, too. Meet me at the bistro opposite."

So Beck had found her, too. Of course, he'd gone to warn her. Claude tried not to be jealous. He had no right.

"Wednesday."

The day after tomorrow.

How was he going to get to Lyon in time? He'd figure something out. And persuade her to come to Paris.

"I have news for you. The trial—"

But she'd clicked off.

"Would you like the toy gift wrapped, Monsieur Leduc?"

Gift wrapped?

"Isn't paper still rationed?"

"These days wrapping's a ribbon and bow. Blue, red, white?"

"All three, *s'il vous plaît*."

"So he's a little patriot like his papa," said the shopkeeper.

Claude's smile carried on until he knocked on the door of Alain's office. Alain, his first partner who'd betrayed him, was the reason he'd left the force. Or part of the reason. He'd hated the politics, the frauds who'd claimed they'd fought the Nazis. Claude had and knew well who hadn't.

Alain's promotion moved him upstairs to the Renseignements généraux, domestic surveillance, a service he'd formerly denigrated. Here he'd joined the de Gaulle-era slime who'd migrated from the *police judiciaire*. De Gaulle was out, but his influence remained.

However, when Alain needed a PI who went where the RG couldn't go, and when Claude needed info from a file, they scratched each other's back.

And Alain owed him.

Alain looked around the office. No one. Then took out something from his desk drawer. "Bring these files back tonight," said Alain.

"It's my boy's birthday," said Claude.

"I'm little Jean-Claude's godfather. Of course I remembered." Alain thrust him a basket of fruit.

He doubted his son had ever tasted a banana. These days, fruit was like gold, and only available through the black market.

But Claude didn't ask. This relic of their friendship was a bond Claude would milk. He tucked the file into the basket and took his leave.

HIS SEVENTEENTH-CENTURY APARTMENT ON ÎLE Saint-Louis, bought at auction, had two-franc plumbing, if that. It was a jewel in a rundown townhouse—original parquet floors, filigreed crown moldings in high ceilings, brass handles on the stained glass terrace doors—but it had only a wood stove for heating. The floor-length flat had tarnished over the centuries. The fuse box was temperamental and water was still piped from the well, when it cooperated. From its windows, a million-franc view onto the Seine.

The Germans forgot to requisition it and the wealthy Jewish owners had never returned to this *hôtel particulier*, where Baudelaire once smoked hashish and wrote poetry.

He'd bought it as an investment for his son. Once he'd planned to bring his family up from Auvergne. But his wife had refused to leave the farm. Or her lover.

So here he was, living alone in this empty flat, scrimping and saving to furnish it, haunting the auction houses to fill it.

He opened the folder Alain had given him. Remy Faure, the murder case he'd never given up on, even though he'd long since left the force.

If Remy Faure was killed on Libération evening, why had his corpse been discovered so many months later? Where had it been all that time, and why? What about the other two victims who had been discovered in the same riverbed with cobblestones tied around their necks?

He would never be able to stop thinking about this case until he knew the answers.

AT MIDNIGHT HE RETURNED TO Alain's office. In the hallway, a cleaning lady with a cigarette dangling from the side of her mouth mopped the scuffed linoleum. Her wash bucket slopped with watery scummed suds. Down the hall, a sleepy-eyed guard sat at a glass cubicle.

"Everyone's gone, monsieur," he said.

"Then I'm in trouble because I'm supposed to return the files tonight. I promised." Claude looked around, leaned in closer. "Any chance you could let me into the office? I won't be a minute."

"Kind of late to expect someone to be here, *non?*"

"Tell me about it. My son's sick. I tried to do this sooner."

"I'm not supposed to let people in after hours."

Claude held up his doctored *police judiciaire* ID, updated courtesy of a counterfeiter, a *résistant*, in Claude's debt.

"Please, it's a favor between departments. You know we keep that kind of thing quiet."

Finally, he jerked his thumb.

"Make it quick."

Claude slid the files, as promised, back in Alain's desk drawer. He'd taken few notes since they held little new information; the case seemed like it had stalled. Looking both ways, he beelined for the cabinets in the file room, full of stale, musty scents.

No time to lose.

He pulled open drawer after drab green metal drawer, thumbing through looking for specific dates.

Sweat stuck his shirt to his spine.

This was taking too long.

At last he found Faure. Cross-referenced by four dossiers with photos, rap sheets, and an insurance file clipped to it. He slipped it all under his jacket.

Turned to leave and then remembered.

He looked under August 25 at the files on the evening General Leclerc's tanks followed by the Allies rolled into Paris. The night he and his buddy had defended the *mairie* in Batignolles, firing at the retreating Germans. Before midnight they'd discovered the cache of Champagne the Germans had hidden in the cellar. He hadn't come up for air in a day.

The RG kept interdepartmental duplicates on all branches according to Alain. Quickly he looked at the August file.

A notation in the margins disturbed him.

Footsteps came from the outer office. In a flash he'd stuffed this file under his jacket.

"*Désolé.*" He walked out yawning. "*Merci.*"

Hurrying down the wide worn marble stairs of the prefecture, his mind struggled to fit the pieces. Like a big puzzle, an elusive picture. He had a few more pieces fitting together, but a vital piece was missing.

DECEMBER 1947

La Folie, a Bouchon in Lyon

—

Huguette used the rear door into the *bouchon* and entered the dining room. Very traditional—broken tile floors, moleskin leather benches, timeworn chairs, a Guignol puppet hanging on the wall, and pigs embroidered onto the kitchen towels. Christmas wreaths hung in the windows. This family-run *bouchon* served hearty no-frills Lyonnaise cuisine in spite of rationing.

Claude Leduc sat at a window table, a thick white napkin on his lap.

He looked the same: dark hair curling over the collar of his worn prewar corduroy jacket, big dark alert eyes.

Non, he looked better.

She joined him and sat down, avoiding his gaze.

"Did you leave this for me?" she asked.

Her hands trembling, she set the envelope addressed to her on the wine-ringed tablecloth.

"Not me. Why would I? But may I open it?"

She took the envelope back. "Later. Too many prying eyes." She was nearly disappointed the message hadn't come from him.

He looked behind his shoulder then into her eyes. "What do you think this means?"

"It means whoever wrote this has traced me and I'm not safe."

Again.

Claude poured red wine from the pitcher into their glasses.

"Depends. I take it no demand or threat yet, *n'est-ce pas?*"

"So what?"

"Not having read it, I'd think it might be a money-making venture. For example, an offer of information in return for cash."

She hadn't thought of that. Was she too paranoid and running on fear? Again, reacting, not acting?

"You sound familiar with this."

And she wasn't quite sure why she'd trusted him again.

"My detective work involves searching for people lost in the war," he said. He fingered the stem of the wine glass. "Sad to say, but con artists run scams to take advantage of grieving relatives. Even now displaced persons, forced workers, and POWs keep dribbling back. Desperate families pay anything for information."

She'd seen some of those displaced at the camp and the Frankfurt train station.

His hand went to the back of his neck. "Don't you have any idea of who sent this?"

She hesitated. The chef, in a waist-straining apron, was shouting in the kitchen.

"You think it's a scam," she said at last.

He sipped.

"Or you're not telling me something."

Hadn't Yves implied she was hiding something, too? Did her actions behind the scenes and keeping to herself invite scrutiny? She felt tired of having to defend herself.

Over pike quenelles smothered in créme sauce, she told him. Some of it anyway.

"I want to hire you to find out what this means." She didn't have time to hunt down the sender while running several businesses. People depended on her.

Claude looked around.

"Hugu—Hélène—"

"Lise," she corrected.

"Lise." Claude took a breath. "This isn't why I thought you called me. You know I need your help with the trial. It's scheduled for next week and Lyon is dangerous for you—that's what I told Beck. Didn't he come here to help you leave?"

"It's complicated—I returned for business."

Claude swallowed. Looked around. The only other patrons, a couple, sat in front at the window. "I've gotten information you might want to know."

A chord in her heart vibrated.

"Not here," she said. "Finished?"

"*Oui. Magnifique.* I'm full for once. Good thing I don't enforce the law anymore—"

"You'd arrest me?" She thrust out her wrists. "Guilty."

Claude clasped her hand in his large warm ones.

"I don't want to know." His brow furrowed. "All of this is dangerous. Don't be like your father."

Pain lanced her. Always with Claude the past resurfaced.

She'd vowed never again to go hungry, have empty pockets, or let a man control her.

"Survival costs, Claude."

Claude reached to pay with his ration coupons. The waiter looked at her, and she gave a slight nod.

The waiter waved it off.

"Mademoiselle's guest is welcome."

— — —

"**Interesting. You must pay off** a crew," said Claude as she led him through the vapor-clouded kitchen past steaming pots of simmering beef stock, bunches of ruby radishes, hanging strings of glistening sausages. Warm scents of coriander and nutmeg.

She paused on the back kitchen stairs.

"The chef does."

She owned the place but Claude didn't need to know. Living above this *bouchon* felt like growing up over her father's café. Home and safety. What felt like a lifetime ago.

She led him to her rooms. Closed the door.

He peered out the windows. Pursed his lips.

"Nice vantage point if you're expecting an enemy."

"I always am," she said. A bitter sadness filled her.

"May I?"

She nodded.

Claude sat down at the desk and unbuckled the worn leather satchel bag hanging from his shoulder. A child's drawing fell out: a yellow sun, a stick figure, and "for Papa" in large childish letters.

He noticed her gaze.

"It's my son's birthday," he said. "He's turning five."

Three years older than her little Hugues.

"You're lucky," she said, wistful, a catch in her throat.

Claude's gaze took in her pain. "I'm sorry."

"Why?"

Guilt and longing overwhelmed her. She'd wanted to take care of her baby, inhale his milky smell. Hold him once more. Life had dealt her a different card.

A sob welled up. Claude held her and she buried herself in his arms. Claude stroked her cheek.

"Is he why you're making money and building an empire?" Claude asked quietly. "For your son?"

Hugues had depended on her once.

"I used to think so. But I understand it's better he's safe with good parents."

Not a wanted mother on the run.

"You were young and struggling to survive," he said. "It took courage to put his needs first. To let go."

A survival haunted by fear. She'd wanted to move on, as Beck encouraged, but being with Claude brought it all up again. She wiped her cheeks with the back of her hand. Pushed him away. "What did you want to tell me?"

"Since de Gaulle resigned, thirty-one insurance companies are up for trial," said Claude.

"Insurance companies?" she said, perplexed. "What's that to me?"

"The man who took over your father's café is involved. Honoré Gisors."

"*Et alors*, he's a notary," she said. "Fireproof."

"Maybe not anymore. My client hired me to investigate Gisors's dealings for this upcoming court case." He thumbed through a file he'd set on the desk. "He's worked for several of the insurance companies going to trial."

"How does this link to me?"

"Bear with me. I've been fitting the pieces together. I don't have them all yet, but there's a connection to your father's murder."

Stunned, words dried in her mouth.

He showed her a page of German writing.

"Can you make this name out?"

"Barely . . . I don't know much German."

She turned on the desk light against the dim afternoon shadows. Zeroed in on what she could understand. The signature was nearly illegible but she made it out.

"It's Gisors," she said. "The entry's difficult to read, but the *kommandantur* recorded it."

"How about this signature? Does it mean anything to you?"

Huguette stared hard at the cursive. It was clear enough. Sigmund Keller.

She swallowed. "They were working together. Siggie and Gisors."

"And now look at this."

Claude produced another document. This was in French: a notarized deed of sale for Café du Soleil, signed September 1, 1944. Honoré Gisors had purchased the entire property from Remy Faure for a nominal amount. There was her father's signature.

Huguette stared at it. "But—it's fake. In September 1944, Papa was already dead."

Claude was looking at her meaningfully.

"Like I told you, Gisors is a crony of de Gaulle's, but the power's shifted," he said. "With this we might be able to prove that he had your father murdered so he could take over the café."

Huguette's heart was pounding. Could it be true? And if it was, could anything be done to bring about justice?

"Claude Leduc, don't tell me the police just let you have these files."

"Working on my own means I do it my way."

"An outlaw investigator without restrictions?" she said.

"I find reasonable proof for a client. Then it's up to them."

"Did you steal these files?" She couldn't help the catch in her voice.

"Borrowed. I need to return them." He glanced at his watch. "I've got a train soon to Clermont-Ferrand."

Dust motes around him caught the light, flickering like fireflies. What was it about him?

She wished she hadn't pushed him away. Wished he kept holding her.

"Please, read this," she said. "It's why I asked you to come."

Down to business, Claude opened her envelope.

On the first sheet were written six words.

Consider this what I owe you.

Signed: *the Grasshopper.*

With steady hands, she lifted the top sheet to reveal what was beneath. On the page was a list of names and addresses, dated 1943-44, detailing sales of properties in Paris. The paper was stamped with a swastika and *Kommandantur, Place de l'Opéra.*

"Want to explain?" Claude asked. "Who is this 'Grasshopper,' and why does he owe you?"

Huguette pursed her lips.

"Just an old classmate. There was a little fracas at Libération," she said. "Look at this list. You'll promise to find out what this means, right?"

"I promise. Do you recognize any of these names?"

She scanned the names on the list.

"This *Croix* is the Grasshopper's father, Marc Croix. According to this, Croix purchased a building on rue de Rivoli for a hundred francs."

A hundred francs for a building in a block of prime real estate? She caught her breath.

"But why would he incriminate his own father?" She kept

running her finger down the list. "Here's Gisors again. He paid the sum of two hundred francs for buildings on the block of 44 avenue d'Italic, including a building called Pension Richelieu, also recorded at the kommandantur."

Her finger felt dirty.

And then, at the bottom of the page, a signature she now recognized.

Sigmund Keller.

She had to stop her hands from trembling.

What was Rafael trying to tell her? But she knew he hated his father. Revenge?

Still, what had this list of people done for Siggie? She'd had no idea Gisors was *this* involved with the one-eyed Nazi.

"Maybe you should see this," she said. She pulled out her father's old case from under the bed and handed him a bundle of papers. "My father called it his insurance. But I don't know how it connects. Or if it does. Read it later."

Claude nodded.

"Huguette, the night Marina Roussel was murdered, I believe you were the intended target. She was wearing your scarf and either the murderer thought she'd lead him to you or she got mistaken for you."

Her hands went to her neck—a reflex—but of course her mother's soft scarf was gone. Like her mother. Like Marina.

Her throat caught.

Hurting, she turned away.

"I know I'm responsible."

"*Non*, the killer's responsible."

Nothing eased the loss for Marina's parents. All because of her.

Claude tapped his files. "And this could be the proof we need to get justice."

"Collabos pay people off to avoid prosecution. All this proves is they got rich by collaborating with the Nazis."

"This, along with the file I already had, shows that Honoré Gisors is connected to the man who raped you. That he could have had your father killed."

She hated all this being brought up again. "What's the use of bringing up all the painful past when the powers that be get away with whatever they want?"

Claude took her arm. "It's painful, I'm sorry. But I can't let this go." He fingered the button on her sleeve cuff. "Don't you understand? The killer didn't stop. I just learned of a fourth victim who was found in the river. I have to get to the bottom of these murders—your father's, Marina's. And you do, too. Facing this tragedy is hard, but maybe that's how you can get past it. Not let this past haunt you."

Why couldn't this end? She averted her gaze.

"Your life's ahead of you."

And his awaited him in Auvergne. His wife, his son. Her tone hardened.

"You don't want to miss your train."

He picked up the files, some stained with coffee rings, and tucked them in his bag.

"You're right," he said.

He slid his sleeves into a prewar wool raincoat. A look she couldn't decipher passed over his face.

Then he kissed her, cupping his hands around her face, engulfing her in warm wool and his faint vetiver scent, just how she remembered. She kissed him back, didn't want to stop. Pulled him into her and they fell onto the bed's duvet.

He pulled off his shirt. His pants.

"Why are you wearing grandpa underwear?"

He grinned. "I'll have you know it's 1947 and my ration booklet allows me one pair, the first new *artes utilitaires* since 1939."

He pointed to the label with *République française* by the emblematic rooster.

She collapsed into laughter.

And it was like before—like their night in the café.

December 1947

Countryside Outside Clermont-Ferrand

—

"Papa."

Little Jean-Claude ran into Claude's waiting arms as he opened the blue farmhouse door.

He lifted up his button-eyed boy. Kissed him and made a face.

"But you've grown. Weigh a ton. How'd you get so big?"

Jean-Claude laughed and his shining face caught Claude's heart.

"*Maman* makes me eat her cheese. She says growing boys must eat."

Claude hugged him.

"She's right."

Right about many things. And so wrong about others.

His wife, Anne, poked her head out from the kitchen. Smiled, showing her dimple.

"Just in time. I have to go meet the vet to pick up medicine for our goats. But can we talk quickly?"

"Of course," he said.

Jean-Claude pulled at Claude's bag and a small box fell out, spilling a red wood truck tied with tricolor ribbon. His gaze locked on the small black wheels. Then the banana in Claude's hand.

"Happy birthday, my boy."

"*Merci*, Papa." Laughing, Jean-Claude ran to play with his birthday present.

Claude joined Anne in the kitchen. "You're leaving right away?" he said. "What about my father?"

"That's what we need to discuss. I'm sorry, but your father's declining. He says he doesn't want to be a burden, and Mathilde and I have our hands full running the farm . . ." She took off her apron, sighed. "He wants to go live with your sister."

"Because you have your lover here, *c'est-ça*?"

"It's not that, Claude. Please, try to understand. Your father and I have discussed this. He realizes we married young, and then you went away—"

He interrupted. "To war, remember?"

"And then you never came back, Claude," Anne said sharply. "The war has been over for two and a half years."

"So you're ignoring how I support all of you and the farm. The only way I earn money is in Paris, where the work is."

"And you're good at what you do. I understand. But you have someone else too, *non*?"

Did he?

"You do. Your eyes say it. You're happier. So am I." She took a deep breath. "You know we've both changed. I keep my life private, you'll never need to worry about what people say. Let's work out what is best for Jean-Claude."

He picked up a ladle from the counter. Felt the smooth wood. On the counter, runny cheese spilled onto a blue plate. Like the runny threads of his life.

"Look, we can do this our way," said Anne. She sounded calm, like she'd given this plenty of thought. "We grew up here. We've known each other all our lives. Nothing changes that. We're better as friends—I think you know that. Let's make this work and be good friends for Jean-Claude. I love this farm, I ran it for years while you were gone. My life's here—I won't leave it. It doesn't just make me happy, but it's also the best place for our son."

Maybe she was right. He'd try to ignore the dent to his pride.

Maybe someday his son would come to Paris for school.

"I'll go see my father," he said. "But I have an upcoming court case. I leave tomorrow."

With that, he mounted the stairs, his steps heavy, and opened the door to his father's room.

DECEMBER 1947

Étoile Office, Lyon

—

Winter moonlight shimmered on the river. A part of her had wanted to follow Claude to Clermont-Ferrand. *Mais non*, not now, not ever. Could she see him again, knowing his child would suffer?

What would the priest at confession say? She knew the answer: Cut it off.

But she needed Claude's help.

Conflicted, she did the only thing she knew: immersed herself in work. At the office, she ran calculations, tallied the wages and expenses, made calls to follow through on the plan she'd just passed with the Lumière shareholders.

TO HER SURPRISE, CLAUDE CALLED the next morning. They met again on a bench overlooking the lapping Saône. Before them in the distance lay the seventeenth-century Hôtel-Dieu de Lyon hospital, its limestone walls spreckled with bullet holes.

"So what's this about?"

She hoped that didn't sound cold.

The smile he'd been wearing faded. He checked his watch.

"My train's delayed, so I've got to find another one or I'm in big trouble."

He rubbed his brow. Rings under his eyes—he was exhausted.

He pulled a flask from his pocket. Poured a thimbleful of brandy into the wide cap and offered it to her.

"*Non, merci.*"

He drank. Exhaled a light sigh. A long barge glided past fanning silver ripples in the river.

"Things are complicated at the farm." He poured himself another thimbleful. Drank. Put the flask back in his pocket.

"You mean your wife doesn't like you fooling around on your son's birthday. I wouldn't either, Claude."

"What?"

"It's over. You're married."

She hadn't meant to say that. Or get angry. She had no right to be jealous.

Or feel anything for him.

He raised his hands palms out as if to halt an oncoming car.

"My wife's nursing my dying father. It's doubly hard for her, running the farm and raising my son."

The wood bench felt hard under her. As hard as expressing sympathy.

"I'm so sorry about your father."

Claude shrugged.

What else could she say?

Uncomfortable, she watched the pigeons strutting on the lichen-spotted stone bank.

"My father's never complained over his backbreaking work on the farm. Or the sacrifices he made. It's hard saying goodbye to him."

Again all she could say was a mumbled "I'm sorry."

"Me, too."

"You're dealing with so much right now."

"And you're my ray of light, Huguette. It's your smile I came for. I promised myself to be truthful with you. I have been, mostly."

"You never hid having a wife and child. Still, it's not right."

"*Alors*, it's not like you think."

Didn't men say that when they had an affair?

"My wife took a lover during the war. A common story. I came home to find the two of them running my family's farm. I wanted to take my son away, but my father asked me if it was worth it to rip our family apart. Now we have an agreement for living our separate lives. I work in Paris and she's on the farm. I visit."

She couldn't help but feel Claude's pain.

Still, too complicated for her.

"In a small village, people talk, right? Her lover living right there with her in your house?"

Claude helped himself to another hit from his flask.

"My wife's lover is my cousin Mathilde."

She chewed her lip. That *was* complicated.

"That's your business," she said finally.

Was being his mistress enough for her? Could she continue seeing him knowing he had a family, whatever form it took?

She needed time to think.

"You promised to help me, Claude. Or have you changed your mind?"

"A promise is a promise. When you come to Paris, I'll have answers."

Then he was hurrying away down the quai, swallowed up by the bare-branched linden trees. She'd never felt more alone.

JANUARY 1948

Leduc Detective, Paris

―

All of his notes in front of him, with an orange crate for a desk, Claude sat cross-legged on his bare office's herringboned floor, a blanket under him, and got to work.

Claude had duplicated the RG files for himself and returned the folders, Alain none the wiser.

He'd wanted to protect Huguette since the first day he'd found her on the *commissariat* kitchen floor, racked with sobs. Now, instead, he'd saddled her with more worries by pulling her into his investigation.

Fortified by what passed for coffee these days, now that his black market connections were gone—a chicory blend tasting like sludge—he worked through his notes. He was piecing it all together.

Remy Faure's death, which had been made to look like the work of random vengeance by vigilantes, had been premeditated murder.

For months now Claude had pursued the linked cases of what were now four corpses pulled from the same spot of the Seine at Saint-Cloud: Remy Faure, forty-six years old, café proprietor, of 15 boulevard du Palais, and the now-identified Maurice Brion, twenty-seven years old, street cleaner, of Pension Richelieu, 44 avenue d'Italie, both discovered together in May 1945; Marina Roussel, eighteen, student, of 5 rue Galande, recovered at the same location two months later, July 1945; finally, the fourth victim, Elena Pouget, fifty-two years old, a concierge at the Pension Richelieu at 44 avenue d'Italie, also recovered at the same location in August 1945. Now he saw two of the victims had the same address. An undeniable connection.

The first had been killed by blunt force trauma, the second and third by a single gunshot to the head, the fourth by strangulation. But all four river victims bore post-mortem ligature marks around their necks from a rope tied to a cobblestone to weigh them down.

But now, after months of searching, Claude had found the missing piece that might crack his case. Alain had shown him an addendum to the file of the fourth murder victim, Pouget. Concierge at Pension Richelieu, part-time cleaner at Institut Dentaire, 11 rue George Eastman. The addendum stated Elena had been universally disliked by the Institut Dentaire staff, who said she took gossip to a new level and paraded a gold watch, too expensive for a cleaner's part-time salary.

Two of the victims, Brion and Pouget, had lived at the same address. Pension Richelieu at 44 Avenue d'Italie. Two of the victims, Faure and Roussel, had had close ties to Huguette, who might have been the intended target.

There were no coincidences in an investigation, he'd learned at the police academy. Connections, not coincidences.

It felt as if the killer had been tying up loose ends.

Connections, not coincidences.

He pulled out the bill of sale for the Café du Soleil dated in September after Remy Faure was dead, and the German list sent to Huguette by the Grasshopper.

Along with yet another demonstration of Honoré Gisors's

connection to the Nazi Keller, this showed Gisors had bought, in a ridiculously cheap purchase recorded at the *kommandantur*, the block of buildings that included the Pension Richelieu, where two of these victims lived.

The connection.

He kicked off his shoes, warmed his toes near the sputtering radiator and loosened his collar. Winter sunlight spread like vanilla cream over the carved boiserie framing the high ceiling. He'd gotten a sweet deal on this office from an old POW camp buddy. He could have done much worse.

He reread the file on Georges Tison, the milkman arrested for disposing of Roussel's body in the river. Tison had made a plea deal. Served six months, then disappeared; no further follow-up after that. Sloppy police work.

Or intentional?

Tison's interrogation report read:

Pascal Dolent, a real lowlife and bully, threatened to beat me up if I didn't take a package to the river for him.
Why?
I did things like this during the war on my milk deliveries.
Paid?
Yes, he'd pay me. The package was waiting where he'd said it would be.
Where?
Same place, off avenue d'Italie in the bushes.
Where exactly?
Where it hits rue des Deux-Avenues, near the Institut Dentaire.
Why there?
Easier, I guess, since Pascal works at the Institut Dentaire. I'm talking because he said he'd pay but he never did.

And he never would. A note in the margin cited traffic report #578; Pascal Dolent had been hit by a bus and pronounced dead on arrival at the hospital.

But Claude knew the area and this place. The Institut Dentaire, built by the American millionaire philanthropist George Eastman, provided dental care for poor children. Pouget, the murdered Pension Richelieu concierge, cleaned there part-time.

Another connection?

He continued thumbing through his notes. Found the short addendum about the Pension Richelieu, cheap housing that was traditionally favored by dental and notary students.

What if Gisors had roomed at the Pension Richelieu when he was a notary student? Thanks to the Grasshopper, Claude had proof he'd purchased the property later during the war. In either case, the pension connected Gisors to two of the victims; his purchase of Café du Soleil connected him to the other two, given Huguette and Roussel's close friendship.

He'd been so tired when he got home from Lyon that he hadn't yet read the papers Huguette said her father called his "insurance."

Drinking another cup of sludge coffee, he did.

The link.

In police work, he'd learned it was all about collecting the details: a name, a place, a small thread to tease out and unravel. The breakthrough in a case was not dramatic, like the cinema; it was the result of tedious slogging follow-up.

Time to do a quick record search at the archives. He grabbed his coat.

LATER THAT AFTERNOON, THE MOVERS knocked on the office's open door.

"Delivery from Drouot."

About time.

Eighteenth-century chairs, a *directoire*-era mahogany desk, and baroque recamier from the auction house he'd gotten for a song.

"Please put the desk by the window," he said. "I'll do the rest."

Claude lifted his black melamine phone from the floor as it rang. He paid extra for a single line instead of a party line. He set the recently connected phone in pride of place onto his new desk and answered.

It was his contact at the records office; her thin, reedy voice was instantly recognizable.

"Sorry, it took me a while after I saw you."

"You found something?"

"That's the problem. There's two. They got crossed and it took more digging."

"How's that possible?"

"Blame the British embassy."

After a five-minute conversation, he grabbed his hat and locked the freshly painted Leduc Detective office door. Ran to send a telegram. Huguette had to testify in court. No matter what.

JANUARY 1948

The Palais de Justice, Paris

—

Huguette's knees wobbled as she stood on the witness stand. She felt dwarfed by the Palais de Justice's high-ceilinged courtroom. Around her, the murmuring crowd made it difficult to focus. Her nose was running, and she'd forgotten her handkerchief.

She prayed her testimony, well rehearsed with Claude Leduc, would be over soon. But neither rehearsal nor prayer stopped her knees from shaking.

Claude had taken her to his newly furnished office for the coaching. Impressive. They kept to business; he promised he'd tell her about the Grasshopper's information once she was through the trial. Now she had to focus and remember to keep her testimony short and simple. He'd asked her one odd question: Where had she gone to the dentist as a child? Nodded at her answer.

"Remember, it's your corroborating testimony which validates the evidence."

"But what if those allegations against me for collaborating with Papa come up?"

Claude took her arm. Warmth generated from his touch. She wanted him to fold her in his arms, make this go away.

"No one reported you to the police," he said, "and anyone who said they did lied to scare you. You're nervous, I understand. But your testimony's important."

Her mind spun trying to digest this.

"Why didn't I know?"

Claude squeezed her hand.

"You do know Louis de Jouvenal adopted you and your name was changed legally. You'll testify under your legal name."

Fear fizzed in her veins that this would all unravel.

Could she trust Claude?

Too late, now.

Dusty chandeliers emitted feeble light in the crowded courtroom. Reporters and curious onlookers gawked from wood benches, reminding her of the lynch mob that had killed her father. In the crowd she noticed Rafael, the Grasshopper, wearing new glasses, his gaze intent. Was he for or against her? But he'd sent the list of names and must expect an outcome.

A red-robed judge on a dais watched her impassively as she put her hand on the cracked leather cover of a Bible and swore she would tell the truth.

"State your name for the court," said Gisors's defense attorney.

She took a breath. "Lise de Jouvenal."

"For the court, please state your real name."

Boucher, the prosecution lawyer whom Claude had introduced her to, objected. "The witness is providing her legal name."

"I'm referring to the witness's birth name."

"How is this relevant? For the purposes of her testimony, *monsieur le juge*, her birth name has no bearing on this case. Privacy laws are clear in this regard."

The reporters leaned forward like crows ready to pick at

something shiny and tear it apart. Nervous, she searched for Claude, but she didn't see him in the courtroom.

"*Au contraire.* Her birth name is essential to establish her credibility," said Gisors's defense attorney.

A hyena ready to pounce.

Her pulse sped. Her dirty laundry was about to come out.

"I'll allow it. Mademoiselle de Jouvenal, please state your birth name," said the judge.

She felt naked. Exposed. Vulnerable.

But Claude had cautioned her to stay perfectly calm on the stand. She took another breath. "*Oui, monsieur le juge,*" she said. "In consideration of my privacy, I wish to do so without the press and public."

The courtroom buzzed. She kept her gaze on Boucher, who'd gone to the bench to confer with the judge and the defense attorney.

They spoke for what felt like a lifetime. Her palms prickled with sweat.

She kept standing, wishing her knees didn't knock so much.

The judge decided in her favor and the courtroom began to empty. Relief ebbed through her and she felt stronger. Maybe she could do this and get it over.

Once the room was empty of anyone except those immediately associated with the trial, Gisors's attorney resumed his place, clearing his throat. "Again, please state your birth name, mademoiselle."

"Huguette Faure."

"Mademoiselle Faure, do you know the defendant, Honoré Gisors?"

She'd seen Gisors twice, but those occasions had burned into her memory. Wearing a tailored suit, he sat expressionless, his gaze on documents in front of him. A man she never wanted to see again.

"I was acquainted with him, more like."

His middle-aged attorney adjusted his ermine collar. "Where was this? Please describe the events of your acquaintance."

She took a breath. "At Libération. August 25, 1944. At the Café du Soleil, where I worked. Looters had trashed the café, leaving nothing, and he appeared, saying he was the owner's partner and insisting on seeing the accounting books."

"By 'he,' you mean the defendant, Honoré Gisors?"

"Yes."

Gisors looked bored.

She kept to the script.

"At this time, a band of vigilantes burst in. One of them claimed Remy Faure, the café owner, was a collaborator. The group dragged him away to a so-called people's court and killed him."

"Remy Faure, your father?"

"Yes. The vigilantes tried to take me, too. My father protested that I was just a juvenile, and in the end they left me."

"Weren't you also a collaborator, mademoiselle?"

Boucher objected. "This witness isn't on trial. The defendant is."

"Of course," the defense attorney said, smug. "That's all, mademoiselle. No further questions."

That was it? The lawyer had planted a bad taste in the judge's mouth. Disgusting. She couldn't let this go.

"But I did see Gisors again," she said. A bitter char of dust settled in the back of her throat. She made herself continue. "That night at this 'people's court,' they weren't celebrating the Libération but demanding vengeance. It was a lynch mob in Place Dauphine. I'd seen my father dragged from the cafe and beaten. Gisors was there. It was Gisors who made an X by my father's name so he would be executed."

"But mademoiselle, you said it was night. Wasn't it dark, and how among the crowd, as you say, could you identify him? Do you expect the court to believe this allegation?"

"There were lanterns, candles. I recognized him." She took a breath. Tried to steady her beating heart. "My father died in my arms."

Her spine felt damp against her blouse. The expressionless face of the judge kept her wondering. Did he believe her?

"It was much later I saw the bill of sale of our café to Gisors signed by my father in September 1944, but how could that be? He was already dead."

Gisors's attorney shot up. "Judge, I move to strike this testimony as inadmissible. We're in civil proceedings, not a criminal case. This has no bearing on the case at hand."

So this was all for nothing?

"We'll recess and examine the implications of this testimony pertaining to the fraud case in these proceedings. Dismissed."

CLAUDE MET HER IN THE colonnade outside the courtroom. He ushered her to a narrow side corridor in the medieval section with leaded glass windows throwing bands of blue light on the parquet.

"Boucher said you did a good job."

All for nothing.

"What does it matter, Claude?"

The grimy statues of the champions of law and justice in the niches above looked worn and weary, like she felt.

"This isn't a murder case, and even if it was, you never found any evidence," she said. "Did you?"

Before Claude could answer, Honoré Gisors rushed by them, his manner distracted.

"Monsieur Gisors, I'd like to ask you some questions," said Claude.

Gisors looked up, irritated. Paused.

"Questions? Who are you?"

Claude fobbed a card. "Leduc Detective."

"Not now." Gisors waved his hand as if shooing a fly.

"We need to talk, Monsieur Gisors."

"Make an appointment."

"In private," said Claude. "Here and now."

Huguette felt Gisors's glare on her. Boring into her. Cold shivers rippled her neck.

"And your accusations will go nowhere, mademoiselle," Gisors said. "Spouting nonsense. You're deluded."

Claude stepped forward. "The *juge d'instruction* will be in possession of certain documents proving you collaborated. That means your statements are tainted. We'll let the judge decide."

Gisors's jaw hardened. "How convenient. Forgeries, no doubt. It's all hearsay, anyway."

"You've hunted me," she said.

"And you've got *proof* of that?" he said with a snort.

Claude pulled out a file from his bag. "This contains copies of the documents proving you collaborated extensively with the Nazis. You notarized documents for the German office requisitioning apartments, businesses. Took kickbacks and deeded yourself stolen property for a ridiculous price. You can keep this—I've made copies."

Gisors expelled air, shrugged. But no denial, though his expression was strange, tense. He tossed the file on the floor. Papers scattered like fat confetti. "All this *merde* again? You mean about the dead Jews' property? No one cares. They're not coming back for it."

He sickened her.

"You're accountable, Gisors," Claude insisted.

An incredulous look passed his deep eyes.

"You're crazy. I'm a *notaire*, no judge will even consider these papers. Find one who wasn't on the Krauts' payroll, eh? No one wants this brought up again. It's over."

It wasn't over for her.

"You're responsible for my father's murder."

"Did you forget, you yourself said a band of vigilantes murdered your father." A mocking tone.

From his battered leather bag, Claude pulled another document with an embossed seal. "That's not technically true, is it, Gisors?" he said. "And vigilantes didn't engineer her father's death, did they?"

Wary, Gisors balled his fist.

"Remy Faure, husband of Jane Roth Faure, a British citizen, isn't the father of Huguette Faure. According to this birth certificate, you are."

"What?"

Huguette's insides dropped.

"I don't understand," she said.

Claude held a statement of a birth recorded at the British embassy stamped 1928. He looked at her, his eyes thoughtful.

"Your mother, Jane, kept and registered documentation to protect you. So did Remy Faure."

The light burned her eyes. Or were those hot tears?

Claude had gathered the papers from the floor. "Monsieur Gisors, you and Jane made an arrangement, according to her statement accompanying this birth document. Remy Faure acknowledged your baby's paternity, married Jane, in return for your gifting the Café du Soleil to the couple. Legally, the deed to the property is still registered in Remy Faure's name. Jane agreed to keep her silence and the secret from your wife, *la comtesse*."

Her mouth dropped open.

Claude continued. "You never gave up on Jane, did you? Always trying to convince her to run away with you. You'd meet her once a year at her daughter's dental visits to the Institut Dentaire, near your Pension Richelieu. Their logs show that you paid for those appointments. Receipts show you paid for Jane's stay in the tubercular sanatorium and later for her funeral. Meanwhile, your wife's gambling losses and the debts of her bankrupt noble family spiraled out of control, and you'd been making up the losses wherever you could."

Gisors's eyes were riveted to the birth certificate in Claude's hand. "Jane hedged her bets, didn't she?" he said, his voice a whisper.

"She protected her child, your daughter. You're bankrupt, lost the château, are being tried here for insurance fraud among other ongoing investigations. At Libération, you paid Yvon Morel to denounce Remy Faure because he wouldn't give you back the café you decided you owned after all those years. After Remy was murdered, you blackmailed a streetcleaner you knew from your student days at Pension Richelieu to recover his body from Place Dauphine and hide it so you could forge his signature on a bill of sale before he was declared dead. Then you killed that man, because you couldn't have any witnesses. You were trying to hunt down your daughter because you thought she knew this, *n'est-ce pas?*"

Disparate pieces floated in front of her, pieces she'd never looked at closely. Quivering as the past's cold hand gripped her, she took a step back.

And then she saw the pistol Gisors pulled out of his pocket, a German Luger. Pointed at her, his aim steady.

"Put down the gun," said Claude, his calm voice layered with menace. "Now."

Her fear suddenly gone, she stared Gisors down. "So you want to shoot me here in the Palais de Justice and toss me in the river, too? Your own flesh and blood?"

Noises echoed off the marble tiles: pounding footsteps, muffled conversations.

At that moment, Claude knocked Gisors's gun away onto the floor, kicked it aside. The Luger's metal handle clanged against the old stone wall.

Alain was running down the corridor toward them, followed by an RG team and blue uniformed police.

"Honoré Gisors," said Alain, panting. "I'm arresting you for conspiracy to the murders of Elena Pouget, Maurice Brion, Marina Roussel, and Remy Faure."

"I never killed anybody."

"Witnesses have come forward—"

"Witnesses?" Gisors waved his hand in annoyance. "Impossible."

"Because none are left, *c'est-ça?* Why not admit you had their bodies dumped in the river to shield the truth?"

"Lies, it's all lies," Gisors hissed.

"*Au contraire*, witnesses will testify to your coercion and full involvement in these homicides. We're in possession of statements from the staff you blackmailed and forced to collude into storing the corpses in the limestone tunnels underneath the Institut Dentaire. And now you're caught possessing an illegal firearm."

Alain snapped his fingers at the policemen.

"Take him into custody."

"Custody? Impossible." Gisors grabbed at Huguette's arm. "I provided for you and Jane. She was the love of my life. Don't you understand?"

Not only was the man deluded, but warped in his sick conviction. It would be almost pitiful if he weren't a murderer.

"I understand you used my mother," said Huguette. Tried to wrench her arm away. "She never trusted you."

"But I'm your father," he begged. "You can't let them take me in."

She shook him off, sickened.

"My father? He's dead. You killed him."

March 1948

Café du Soleil, Boulevard du Palais, Île de la Cité, Paris

―

Huguette inserted the long-handled key into the lock, opened the door, and stood in the bare Café du Soleil. Torn curtains hung from the smudged windows. She tore down the FORCED LIQUIDATION SALE sign in the window.

Her stomach tightened. Here in this café, once her home, she could see her mother's face looking up from the cash register, Luc grinning at the counter, her father winking at her as he stacked the wine crates.

She stared at the mess, imagining their horrified looks.

But this past only floated in her memories. Work, like always, healed. Filled with purpose, she searched for a broom.

By mid-afternoon, she'd swept, scrubbed most of the floor, cleaned out the drawers, wiped down the counter and bar shelves, oiled the cash register, and restocked a crate of liquor.

Someone knocked on the window. She looked up and saw Claude; smiling, she beckoned him inside.

"Just in time for an apéro," she said.

He set down an armful of birch firewood by the wood stove. Took off his gloves and rubbed his hands together. Grinned. "My best offer today. But first there's something you need to see."

Claude handed her an envelope, worn at the edges and sealed.

"What's this?"

"Remy's 'insurance.' It's addressed to you."

She recognized her mother's distinctive cursive.

Heart thumping, she put down a cleaning rag, opened the envelope, and raised the butterfly stationery to smell the scent of her mother's perfume.

My dearest Huguette,

Know that I love you, my smart, sweet girl. Now if you're reading this I've gone. Remy knows everything. He has kept this letter and promised to give it to you. His heart ached but he feels it's right.

There are things I have kept from you that you should know. People often look back on their lives and wish they had done things differently. I have things I wish I'd done differently, but you aren't one of them.

As I've often told you, I grew up in London, a slum in Lambeth. My parents died so I left school when I was fourteen and followed my dream of dancing. I survived working in small dance halls. By hard work and luck I landed a job in a revue in Paris and never looked back. You know all this, but what you don't know is that before I met your father, I met Honoré.

Honoré was at the time a poor student, just scraping by. Still, he would wait for me with flowers at the stage door. He said he was in love and, well, I was alone here.

I learned more about Honoré over the months of our dalliance. His mother was the cook on a count's estate where he grew up. He had been raised like part of that noble family. Honoré was brilliant in math and you know how I like puzzles and numbers. We had a lot in common. But I always knew he'd move on and do well, since the count financed his studies and he was on his way to becoming a respected notary. Only after we had been seeing each other for months did it come out that he was already engaged to be married to the count's daughter. Turns out the count was close to bankruptcy. He'd paid for Honoré's studies so that Honoré could prosper and save the family from ruin.

I'd met Remy working in a café by the music hall and, well, he was the man for me. Coup de foudre, love at first sight. This has never changed. One door closes and another one opens, as I always say. But I found out I was pregnant by Honoré the day he came to say goodbye. He had just graduated and secured a prestigious, high-paying job. I knew he cared for me, almost too much. He tried to give me money for you. By then I was tired of the grueling dance hall life, and wanted to raise you with Remy, make a real home. Simple cash wasn't enough. I knew the owner of a run-down café on the Seine was retiring; I thought if he offered it to us cheap we could fix it up, run it, and live upstairs. Remy's a hard worker, I could do the accounts and be with you while you were growing up, dear one. Finally Honoré agreed to buy the café in Remy's name, out of guilt I guess, if we agreed to keep silent about your parentage. We have. Until now.

We married, you were born, and we moved into the upstairs of the café a week after I came from the hospital with you. The café is truly your home. Later Honoré begged to see you. Do you remember the man who would come to meet us when I took you to the dentist? He's a brilliant man, but he's not a father, in reality he could care less about you. He hates children. Your father is Remy.

Your birth certificate with Honoré Gisors's name listed as father is on file with the British consulate if you ever need it. But you are Huguette Faure, the love and light of my life.

Please try to understand, and forgive me.
I hope you're reading this as brave and happy as I knew you.
With all the love in my heart,

Maman

Huguette touched the letter to her lips, then to her heart. Held it for a long time, inhaling the faint whiff of her mother's scent.

Claude watched her concerned. "Sad news? Are you all right?"

Brought back to the café, she took a breath, giving herself time to think and stare at the Seine glittering outside the window. "Nothing I didn't already know. But I miss *maman* so much." She gathered herself and nodded. "Definitely time for that apéro."

She pulled out freshly washed Champagne coupes and set them on the shining zinc counter. Popped a cork and poured.

"And more to come, I hope," said Claude.

They toasted and he enfolded her in his arms. "How does it feel to be free?"

"I don't know." *Was this freedom?* "There's so much to do."

"Maybe it takes getting used to, *non?*" Claude ran his warm finger along her cheekbone. "Shall I take the wood and make a fire *chez moi* on Île Saint-Louis? I'll keep you warm."

She raised her coupe to his and clinked again.

"You're in my place, so my rules. Upstairs you can help me change the sheets before I move back in."

Epilogue

May 1958 • Ten Years Later

Cannes Film Festival

~

Spotlight beams swept over the Croisette amid the swaying palm trees, illuminating glittering movie stars on the red carpet. The warm breeze from the bay sent a frisson across Huguette's shoulders, bare in a black velvet Balenciaga cocktail dress. That shivering excitement. Film was a business, and it was her business.

And Cannes was just like Louis had imagined it would be.

Tonight, she, as the representative of Étoile, was sponsoring the honorary award for foreign director, the Prix d'excellence, and this see-and-be-seen premiere party. It was stunning and fabulous already. Yet every pop of a Champagne cork would tabulate on the adding machine in her head.

She had checked everything down to the last detail, each napkin crease. Her mother always told her to check and recheck or she'd pay the difference. As the bartender set the frosted bottles in ice buckets, Huguette could finally exhale—and smile at him, saying, *"Parfait."*

Ten minutes later, she kissed Claude and left him in the audience so that she could join the prize award presenter backstage.

This year the prize would go to an acclaimed director in the struggling Hungarian postwar film industry.

Paul, the backstage director, motioned to her as she arrived in the wings. "One minute to go," he said. "Where's Brigitte Bardot?"

Huguette looked around. "She should be here, *non*?"

She'd worked hard to wangle this appearance from the blond sex kitten star of *And God Created Woman* to present this award.

"She left in a hurry for another premiere."

The music started up.

"Impossible. I'll find her."

Cymbals crashed. The orchestra conductor, waving his baton, shot a glance at the stage manager.

"No chance. The awardee's ready. Everything's set to go."

A disaster. What could she do? Think.

Show business—always a last-minute snag.

"I'll find another presenter. Delay the award."

Paul thrust the pointed bronze statuette she'd helped design into her hands.

"You know what a tight schedule we're on. You're the sponsor—just present the award yourself."

"*Moi?*"

A tuxedoed announcer who stood at the podium was beckoning to her. She wanted to slink behind the red velvet curtain. Melt into the background.

"Go."

The horn section rose. Perspiration beaded her upper lip.

"Stage fright? You're beautiful and this will only last seconds. Anyway, who pays attention to the studio representative?"

Then he was taking her arm and leading her from the side curtains to the stage. Huguette felt the glare of stage lights and the choking scent of Chanel No. 5 wafting from the front row. Her heels wobbled and she clutched the statuette, panic filling her.

The announcer was saying, "Studio Étoile will present the Prix d'excellence to Viktor Holasch." Applause mounted.

Yves had pushed for this Hungarian director. Due to a last-minute scheduling conflict, she'd been unable to meet him prior to the ceremony, like she always did with awardees. Unprofessional, but the director fit the criteria and his film had been lauded as a critical success.

Breathe.

She told herself no one knew she was an imposter, a fugitive who'd laundered money. Or how many studio bankruptcies she'd prevented.

Somewhere in the audience, a dark sea of faces, sat Claude. Her rock. He'd want her to smile, act gracious, give the award and bow out—simple.

And she would have if this director wasn't an even bigger imposter than she was.

Flashbulbs popped as the man who called himself Viktor Holasch strode expectantly across the stage. She recognized him in a second.

Time fell away.

Despite his dyed black hair and expensive glass eye, nothing disguised his hawklike watchfulness. The radiating awareness of a hunter.

The Nazi who'd raped her and stolen her childhood wasn't dead.

The applause, the fading music, the incessant flash of the *Paris Match* cameraman paralyzed her. Onstage before hundreds and the newsreels of the world, she was a schoolgirl again. Her feet rooted to the spot and her smile froze. The old descending fear knotted her insides.

He'd leaned in, given her the customary air kisses on her cheeks. She flinched and words came out before she could think.

"Don't touch me, Siggie."

His shoulders stiffened. Alarm crossed his smooth face. Swift as a rat, he'd turned away the microphone on the podium. The applause continued; no one had caught her words.

"You mistake me for someone else." His low voice exuded confidence.

"Never."

He stared, swayed closer. An awareness crept into his gaze and he sucked in his breath.

"So, old friend, we meet again." A sickening grin as if they shared a secret joke.

Did he think she'd smile and go along with him?

"Those special eyes. I never forgot you."

The applause rose. Paul gestured her from the wings, miming to hurry up and give him the award.

"Where's my son?"

He knew.

"You have no son."

He gripped her wrist. His other hand took the award. With a self-deprecating smile, he spoke into the microphone. "I'm honored to accept this award from Étoile," he said, his accent Hungarian. "Words escape me except for 'thank you.'"

Thunderous applause echoed. He bowed, one hand clutching the award, the other hers, as if they were dear friends.

A showman who'd reinvented himself after the war. As had she. But she had reinvented herself to survive—not to cover up crimes of war.

She felt a knot in her chest as the conductor raised his baton to start the orchestra. Every nerve in her body tingled. *Non*, he couldn't escape and get away with it again.

Not this time.

She struggled and broke free, grabbed the microphone.

"Étoile wished to award this honor to a worthy artist we felt deserves recognition," she said, her voice quavering. "But not this man."

Her words sliced the air.

"Not a man who I now recognize for who he is: Sigmund Keller, a wanted German war criminal."

The applause faded. A shocked silence settled. The conductor's baton hovered in midair.

"He's a Gestapo sturmbannführer who escaped Paris in 1944." Her breath caught but she forced herself to continue. "A fugitive. A murderer."

The palpable hush grew. Someone shouted, "Get that crazy woman off the stage."

"I'm not crazy. I witnessed his crimes." She steadied her voice as she turned to him.

Murmurs rose. Boos.

Rattled, he tried to cover up. "Mademoiselle, there's some misunderstanding." He turned to the crowd, his expression pained, as if to elicit sympathy for dealing with a hysteric. "Tragic, but I have no idea what you mean. You have mistaken me for—"

She cut him off. "I have proof. Call security."

"Gestapo?" A man stood up in the front row, hissed. "Those rats tortured my sister."

Siggie looked around, hesitating like a cornered snake as she beckoned to ushers in the aisles.

"Secure the stage and exits," she said. "Sigmund Keller is a fugitive war criminal."

"This is absurd," Siggie scoffed. "I won't stand here and listen to this." But she could see a bead of sweat at his temple, and his gaze was darting as if he was ready to run.

"Lock the doors. Now."

He would have gotten away if she hadn't stretched her leg out behind the podium. He tripped and landed on the statuette.

Shocked gasps and cries from the audience. She heard a moan and pulled her leg back quickly.

The house lights went on, almost blinding her, but she saw blood gushing from his thigh. The statuette's sharp edge must have pierced his femoral artery.

She raised her voice. "Is there a doctor? Call an ambulance!"

Leaning down, she used the ruffles of her Balenciaga dress to staunch the blood, ignoring his yelps of pain. Whispered in his ear by his good eye. "Dying's too good for you, Siggie. Forget escaping again. It's time for justice."

A THOUSAND PEOPLE HAD WATCHED and witnessed, according to Claude. "Quite the actress, eh?"

She'd learned from the best.

Once he was identified as Sigmund Keller, the war crimes court in a hastily convened hearing put in motions to prosecute him. But it would take time to convict a man in a coma.

Reporters swarmed.

"No comment," she always replied.

She would wait. Bear witness when the time came.

Maybe then she'd talk with *Paris Match*, who begged for an exclusive. Or not.

A week later at Cap d'Antibes, she and Claude stood on the

terrace of the Hotel du Cap-Eden-Roc, overlooking the turquoise Mediterranean. Seagulls swooped over the rocky limestone cliffs. Soft warm wind brushed her cheeks.

She felt thankful for her life. For so many reasons. One of them was standing next to her.

"I've been letting go of the past, Claude," she said.

Her gaze caught on a blue butterfly's fluttering wings—stuck in the wild brush clinging to a rocky crevasse. Just then warm licks of wind gusted and the butterfly broke free. Flew away.

"Now it's time to let all of it go."

"Then it must be time for a toast, *non*?" said Claude.

She clinked her coupe of Champagne to his.

"To the future."

Author's Note

In 1895 in Lyon the Lumière brothers released the very first motion picture, *Workers Leaving the Lumière Factory*, much to the wide-eyed wonder of the crowds.

More than a hundred years ago, the Institut Lumière, in a Lumiere brother's Art Nouveau home—is now a museum in Lyon's 8th district of Monplaisir—promoting and preserving anything and everything to do with cinema.

Cannes Film Festival
The Cannes Film Festival was revived after the war, red carpet and all—but not without a struggle. While I've visited Cannes I've never been on the red carpet nor at the 1958 film festival opening but found a glimpse of pics here: https://www.gettyimages.com/photos/1958-cannes#

The first female director was French. Meet Alice Guy-Blanché: https://hundredheroines.org/featured/alice-guy-blache/

The Chateau Rothschild's history is layered—built in 1855 by banker James Mayer de Rothschild in Boulogne-Billancourt. For years the chateau hosted gala parties and receptions with society's elite. The chateau passed through the family until WWII when the Kriegsmarine, the German navy, requisitioned it and the contents. At Libération, the US Army took it over in a deteriorated condition and troops camped in the formal garden. Left to ruin over the years, it was only visited by an urban explorer group, which I joined. The crumbling staircases, walls defaced by graffiti and sagging roof open to the sky inspired me to think about what it once had been like. And the history it could tell.

Film industry in Boulogne-Billancourt
Since 1922, the area of Boulogne-Billancourt has housed several cinema studios home to iconic actors, directors and technicians of French cinema, think Gabin, Belmondo, Delon, Signoret, De Funès and films directed by Marcel Carné. The films were all shot in the two great studios, which were the emblems of French cinema.

One of them, Billancourt Studios, operated between 1922–1992 and was a leading French studio founded in the silent era. During the Second World War the studio was used by Continental Films, a company financed by the German occupiers. Note: They are also known as the Paris-Studio-Cinéma, not be confused with the nearby Boulogne Studios.

Bertrand Tavernier, writer, director and knower of all things in the French cinema directed the film *Laissez-Passe* set during the Continental Films occupation of the Boulogne-Billancourt studios. Search for his talks on YouTube about this era.

The book *Ainsi finissent les salauds* by Jean-Marc Berlière and Franck Liaigre opened my eyes to the settling of scores after Libération.

Acknowledgments

~

This story has been a journey stemming from a 1944 street scene photo of the Paris Libération, spurred by questions raised while I wrote the Aimée Leduc series: Who is this side character, Aimée's grandfather's mistress, who exerted influence and whom we never saw? Along the way came a futile hunt through the Père Lachaise Cemetery columbarium for the ashes of the "real" Huguette.

I owe deep thanks to the many people who contributed to this story. Above and beyond to Françoise Poisson for the many walks, her enthusiasm, wit and help delving into the history of Boulogne-Billancourt where she lives and much more. Inga Hackl for accompanying me to a controversial TV show in the original studio. Gilles Thomas as well as Françoise's and my favorite café in Billancourt. Carla Bach, who miraculously got me an appointment with her dentist to replace a lost filling in Boulogne-Billancourt, somehow inspiring a plot line and much more. The staff at the Institut Dentaire in Paris, the *flics* who invited me to hang at the *real* Café du Soleil—priceless, Anne-Françoise and Cathy *toujours*.

In Lyon, Julie McDonald, for connecting me to her friends who made the story richer, and Jean-Michel Rubio Nevado.

Denise Hamilton for the sparks, for the longtime friendship of Denise Schwartzbach—she is missed—and her memories of her friend, Huguette. Libby Fischer Hellmann, Melba Beals, Susanna Solomon, JT Morrow, James N. Frey. As always Dr. Terri Haddix offered her incredible medical expertise. Jean Satzer, cat *maman* extraordinaire, who's been in my corner from the beginning.

Katherine Fausset, my agent has helped so much. Soho Press has been behind this endeavor all the way with encouragement, support, incredible patience and ideas, especially my editors Juliet Grames and Taz Urnov, *merci*! Deep bows to Rachel Kowal, Steven Tran, Erica Loberg, Paul Oliver, Lily DeTaeye, Johnny Nguyen, Emma Levy, Alex Willcox, dear Rudy Martinez—you do an amazing job. Especially to Bronwen Hruska, who took the helm from her mother, Laura Hruska, cofounder of Soho Press and my first editor, for keeping us independent and family run. Since my first book, twenty-three books ago, I've been lucky to call them family.